THE BEETLE IN THE ANTHILL

THE
BEETLE
IN THE
ANTHILL

ARKADY & BORIS STRUGATSKY

A NEW TRANSLATION BY
OLENA BORMASHENKO

CHICAGO
REVIEW
PRESS

Published by Chicago Review Press Incorporated
814 North Franklin Street
Chicago, IL 60610
ISBN 978-1-64160-678-3

Library of Congress Control Number: 2023931062

Cover photo and design: Jonathan Hahn

Typesetting: Nord Compo

Printed in the United States of America

The animals stood
By the door,
People shot them,
They fell dead to the floor.
(A poem by a very young boy.)

JUNE 1, '78

MAXIM KAMMERER, COMCON-2 EMPLOYEE

Excellentz sent for me at 1:17 PM. He didn't look up at me, so I found myself staring at his bald pate, speckled with pale liver spots. This indicated a high degree of preoccupation and displeasure. Not with my work, however.

"Have a seat."

I sat down.

"We need to find a person," he said, then suddenly stopped. Paused for a long time. Frowned, accordioning his forehead into angry pleats. Snorted. It was as if he hadn't liked his own words. Excellentz has a passion for absolutely precise formulations.

"Who?" I asked, to rescue him from his philological dilemma.

"Lev Vyacheslavovich Abalkin. A progressor. He left the Saraksh Polar Station the day before yesterday, heading to Earth. He hasn't registered himself on Earth. He must be found."

He stopped again, then he finally looked up at me, fixing his round, unnaturally green eyes on me. He was clearly in a quandary, and I realized that this must be serious.

While a progressor that hasn't bothered to register himself upon his arrival on Earth is, strictly speaking, breaking the rules, he can't possibly be of interest to our Commission, never mind Excellentz himself. And yet Excellentz was in such an obvious quandary that I got the impression he was about to lean back in his chair, breathe a sigh of something strangely like relief, and grumble, *Forget it. Sorry. I'll deal with it myself.* This had happened before. Rarely.

"There is reason to believe," said Excellentz, "that Abalkin is in hiding."

Fifteen years ago, I would have eagerly asked, *From whom?* However, that had been a decade and a half ago, and I've long since outgrown eager questions.

"You will find him and let me know," continued Excellentz. "Don't make him interact with you. In fact, don't interact with him at all. Find him, place him under surveillance, and let me know. No more and no less."

I tried to make do with a solemn nod to telegraph that I had understood, but he was staring at me so intently that I felt compelled to restate my assignment in a deliberately measured and thoughtful manner. "I must find him, place him under surveillance, and let you know. Under no circumstances should I try to detain him, allow myself to be observed, or, most important, interact with him."

"Correct," said Excellentz. "Now for the next thing."

He reached into a side drawer of his desk—the one that every normal employee uses to store a reference crystallofile—and from its depths extracted a bulky object whose name I could at first recall only in Hontian: *zakkurapiya*, which literally translates to "document receptacle." And it was only when he had hoisted this receptacle onto the desk in front of him and interlaced his long, knobby fingers on top of it that the word came to me, and I burst out with "A folder!"

"Stay focused," Excellentz said sternly. "Listen carefully. No one in the Commission knows that I'm interested in this person.

And under no circumstances must they know it. Therefore, you will have to work alone. No assistants. You will reassign your entire team to Claudius, and you will report only to me. There will be no exceptions."

I have to admit I was flabbergasted. Nothing like this had ever happened before. I had never come across this level of secrecy on Earth. To be honest, I wouldn't have thought it possible. This is why I allowed myself one rather silly question: "What do you mean, no exceptions?"

"No exceptions in this case means no exceptions. There are a few other people who are aware of this case, but since you will never come across them, we will effectively be the only ones who know about it. You will of course have to interact with many people during the course of your search. This will require you to use a cover story. Please be so good as to come up with this story yourself. You will only speak without the cover of the story to me."

"Yes, Excellentz," I said meekly.

"Moving on," he continued. "It looks like you'll have to start with his connections. All that we know about them is in here." He tapped the folder with a finger. "It's not much, but it's a start. Take it."

I took the folder. This was another thing I had never seen on Earth. Its matte plastic covers were held together by a metal clasp, and the front was embossed with the words LEV VYACHESLAVOVICH ABALKIN in red. And for some reason, the digits 07 were embossed below the words.

"Listen, Excellentz," I asked, "why are they in this format?"

"Because they don't exist in any other format," he answered coldly. "By the way, you are not allowed to crystallocopy these. Any more questions?"

This was of course not an offer to answer more questions. It was simply a bit of venom. At this stage, there were many questions, and it made no sense to ask them without a preliminary examination of the folder. However, I did allow myself two questions.

"How long do I have?"

"Five days. No more." That's not enough, I thought.

"Can I be certain that he's on Earth?"

"Yes."

I got up to leave, but he wasn't done with me. He was staring up at me with intent green eyes, his pupils narrowing and dilating like a cat's. He could of course tell that I was displeased with the mission, that to me the mission seemed not only strange but, to put it mildly, ridiculous. However, for some reason he couldn't tell me any more than he had already.

And yet he didn't want to let me go without saying something. "Do you remember," he said, "how on a planet called Saraksh, a bright kid named Mak led a certain Sikorsky, alias Wanderer, on a merry chase?"

I remembered.

"As you well know," said Excellentz, "Sikorsky wasn't quick enough. But you and I must be quick enough. Because this time, the planet is Earth, not Saraksh. And Lev Abalkin is not a kid."

"Speaking in riddles, boss?" I said, to hide the anxiety that was now gripping me.

"Get to work," he said.

JUNE 1, '78

A FEW THINGS ABOUT
LEV ABALKIN, PROGRESSOR

Andrei and Sandro were still waiting for me and were dumb-founded when they were reassigned to Claudius. They even began to fuss, but I was still gripped by anxiety, so I snapped at them and they left, grumbling resentfully, glancing at the folder with wary concern. These glances awakened a new and entirely unexpected worry: Where in the world should I keep this monstrous "document receptacle"?

I sat down at my desk, put the folder down in front of me, and, as was my habit, glanced at my registrator. Seven messages in the quarter of an hour I'd spent with Excellentz. I have to admit that I got some satisfaction out of redirecting all of my professional communication to Claudius. Then I got started on the folder.

As I had expected, the folder contained nothing but paper. Two hundred seventy-three numbered sheets in a variety of colors, grades, formats, and degrees of preservation. It had been a good two decades since I had dealt with paper, and my first impulse was to shove the whole pile into the translator, but, naturally, I remembered not to in time. If I had to work with paper, so be it. Paper it is.

All the sheets were very inconveniently but firmly held together with an ingenious magnetic mechanism, and I didn't immediately notice the completely ordinary radiocard tucked underneath the top clasp. Excellentz had received this radiogram today, sixteen minutes before he sent for me. It read as follows:

06/01, 1:01 PM. ELEPHANT TO WANDERER
RE: YOUR INQUIRY ABOUT TRISTAN FROM 06/01, 7:11 AM.
REPORTING: 05/31, 7:34 PM. RECEIVED INFORMATION
FROM COMMANDER OF SARAKSH-2 BASE. QUOTE: THE
UNMASKING OF HURON (ABALKIN, CIPHER OFFICER
OF THE HEADQUARTERS OF FLEET GROUP C OF THE
ISLAND EMPIRE). 05/28. TRISTAN (LOFFENFELD, TRAV-
ELING DOCTOR OF BASE) LEFT FOR HURON'S ROUTINE
MEDICAL EXAM. TODAY 05/29, 5:13 PM. HURON ARRIVED
ON BASE IN HIS PERSONAL CRAFT. ACCORDING TO HIM,
TRISTAN WAS CAPTURED AND KILLED BY COUNTERIN-
TELLIGENCE OFFICERS OF HEADQUARTERS C UNDER
UNKNOWN CIRCUMSTANCES. AS HE WAS TRYING TO
RECOVER TRISTAN'S BODY TO BRING IT TO THE BASE,
HURON WAS FORCED TO REVEAL HIMSELF. HE WAS
UNABLE TO RECOVER THE BODY. HURON WAS NOT
PHYSICALLY HARMED IN THE COURSE OF THE TRAG-
EDY, BUT HE IS ON THE VERGE OF A PSYCHOLOGICAL
SPASM. AT HIS URGENT REQUEST, HE'S RETURNING TO
EARTH ON FLIGHT 611. END QUOTE.
    NOTE: 611 ARRIVED ON EARTH 10:32 PM, 05/30.
ABALKIN HAS NOT CONTACTED COMCON AND AS
OF CURRENT TIME 12:53 PM IS NOT REGISTERED ON
EARTH. HE IS ALSO CURRENTLY NOT REGISTERED AT
ANY OF THE STOPS (PANDORA, RESORT) ALONG THE
ROUTE OF 611.
ELEPHANT

Ah, yes. Progressors. To be perfectly honest, I don't like progressors, even though I had probably been one of the first progressors back when this concept only appeared in theoretical calculations. Of course, it has to be said that my attitude toward progressors is far from original. That's no surprise—after all, the vast majority of people on Earth are inherently unable to grasp that there exist situations which do not allow for compromise. It's us versus them, and there's no time to figure out who's right. To a normal earthling, this sounds absurd, and I understand why—after all, I had felt this way myself before I found myself on Saraksh. I can vividly recall having a worldview in which every living being endowed with reason was, a priori, morally equivalent to myself, regardless of whether they shared my ethics and values; back then, the question *Are they better or worse than myself?* simply seemed poorly posed . . .

And it isn't enough to be theoretically prepared, nor will simulated conditioning do—you must walk through the moral shadows yourself, see a few things with your own eyes, feel the fire on your own hide, and accumulate a few dozen of your own nauseating memories. Then you can finally understand—and not only understand but fuse into your worldview—this most trivial of ideas: regardless of what you're like, there exist bearers of reason who are much, much worse than you . . . And only then do you gain the ability to divide the world into friends and foes, learn to make instantaneous decisions in acute situations, and gain the courage to act first and sort things out later.

I think this is at the very core of the progressor: the ability to unapologetically divide people into friends and foes. This is the ability that gets them treated with cautious admiration—or admiring caution—when they are at home and earns them a certain squeamish wariness everywhere else. And that's just how it is. They have to put up with it, and so do we. Because either we have progressors, or Earth has no business meddling in extraterrestrial affairs . . . However, here at COMCON-2, we're lucky enough to rarely have to deal with progressors.

I read the radiogram and then carefully reread it. Strange. It turns out that Excellentz is mostly interested in a certain Tristan, also known as Loffenfeld. And in order to find out about this Tristan, he not only got up at the crack of dawn himself but also didn't hesitate to rouse our Elephant—and everyone knows that Elephant goes to bed when the roosters crow.

And here's another strange thing: you'd almost think that he had known what the answer would be in advance. It only took him a quarter of an hour to decide to search for Abalkin and to get the folder ready for me. You might think he had already had it handy.

And here's the strangest thing of all: Abalkin was, of course, the last person to see Tristan (or at least his body), but if Excellentz only needs Abalkin as a witness in the Tristan case, then why the sinister parable about the kid and Wanderer?

Oh, of course, I had my theories. Dozens of them. For instance, they included the following gem: Huron/Abalkin has been converted by imperial intelligence; he killed Tristan/Loffenfeld and has gone into hiding on Earth, with the goal of inserting himself into the World Council . . .

I reread the radiogram again and put it aside. All right. Sheet 1. Lev Vyacheslavovich Abalkin. Code number such and such. Genetic code such and such. Born on October 6, '38. Early education: Boarding School 241, Syktyvkar. Teacher: Sergei Pavlovich Fedoseyev. Further education: Progressor School 3 (Europe). Adviser: Ernst Julius Horn. Professional predilections: zoopsychology, theater, ethnolinguistics. Professional aptitudes: zoopsychology, theoretical xenology. Work history: February '58 to September '58, graduate residency, Saraksh, an attempt to establish contact with bigheads in their natural habitat—

Here I paused. My goodness! I think I remember him! That's right, this was in '58. They had all shown up in one big clump: Komov, Rawlinson, Martha . . . and this rather gloomy trainee. Excellentz (in those days, Wanderer) ordered me to drop everything and ferry them across the Blue Serpent into the Fortress,

disguised as an expedition from the Department of Science . . .
Yes, a kid with strangely prominent bones, a very pale face, and
the long, straight black hair of a Native American. Right! They
all called him (except for Komov, naturally) Lev the Crier—not
because he was quick to cry, of course, but because he had a full,
deep voice that boomed out like the roar of a tahorg . . . Small
world! All right, let's see what he did with himself after that.

March '60–April '60, Saraksh, mastermind-executor of Operation Man and the Bigheads; July '62–June '63, Pandora, mastermind-
executor of Operation Bigheads in Space. June '63–September '63,
Planet Hope, participant in Operation Dead World with bighead
Puppen. September '63–August '64, Pandora, retraining course.
August '64–November '66, Giganda, first time being indepen-
dently embedded—served as junior accountant in a hunting dog
breeding operation, then as huntsman in the kennels of Marshal
Nagon-Gig, and then as Master of the Hunt for the Duke of Alai
(see sheet 66) . . .

I took a look at sheet 66. This turned out to be a carelessly
torn-out scrap of paper, flattened out but retaining the impressions of earlier creases. In a sprawling handwriting, it said, "Rudy!
Writing so you don't worry. By the will of God, two of our twins
met on Giganda. A complete accident, I assure you, and without
repercussions. If you don't believe me, check 07 and 11. Measures
have already been taken." An illegible, ornate signature. The word
"complete" was underlined three times. There was Arabic text
printed on the back of the paper.

I caught myself scratching the back of my head and came
back to sheet 1.

November '66–September '67, Pandora, retraining course.
September '67–December '70, Saraksh, Republic of Hontia—
embedded as underground unionist responsible for establishing
contact with agents of the Island Empire (first stage of Operation
Headquarters). December '70, Saraksh, Island Empire—prisoner in
concentration camp (no communication until March '71), translator for concentration camp headquarters, soldier on construction

crew, senior soldier in Coast Guard, translator for Coast Guard headquarters, translator/cipher officer of lead submarine of Fleet Group C's Second Fleet, cipher officer of Fleet Group C Headquarters. Attending physician: from '38 to '53—Yadviga Mikhailovna Lekanova; from '53 to '60—Romuald Crăsescu; from '60 onward—Kurt Loffenfeld.

That was it. Sheet 1 didn't contain anything else. However, there was something on the other side: a large symbol composed of blurry brown stripes (like it was painted in watercolors) that took up the entire back of the page and resembled a stylized Cyrillic letter Ж.

Well, Lev Abalkin, Lev the Crier, I now know a few things about you. I can now start looking for you. I know who your teacher was. I know who your adviser was. I know who your attending physicians was . . . However, there's still something I don't know, and that's who this sheet 1 is for and what its purpose is. After all, if a person needed to find out who Lev Abalkin was, he could have loaded the informatorium (I loaded the GWI), typed in his name or code number (I typed in his code number), and after . . . one, two, three . . . four seconds would have had access to all the information that a person is entitled to know about another person who is a stranger to them.

Here we go: Lev Abalkin, and so on: code number, genetic code, born on such and such a day, parents (by the way, why aren't his parents included on sheet 1?) Stella Vladimirovna Abalkina and Borisovich Tsiurupa, Syktyvkar boarding school, teacher, progressor school, adviser . . . Everything matches. All right. A progressor, working on Saraksh since '60. Hmm. Not much. Only the official data. It looks like he didn't bother to report new data to the GWI from that point on . . . And what's this? "Earth address: not registered."

I entered a new query: What addresses was code number so and so registered under on Earth? Two seconds later, I received the following reply: "Abalkin's last address on Earth was Progressor School 3 (Europe)." That's another curious thing. Either

Abalkin hasn't been on Earth once in the last eighteen years, or he's an extremely reclusive man who never registers himself and has no desire to submit any data about himself. Either possibility is conceivable, of course, but this does look rather odd . . .

As everyone knows, the GWI only contains the information that a person wishes to share with others. And what does sheet 1 contain? I see absolutely nothing on here that Abalkin might wish to conceal. It's true that it goes into much more detail—but, then, nobody would ever use the GWI for this data. You would contact COMCON-1, and you'd learn it all. And the things that COMCON doesn't know, you could easily pick up on Pandora by hanging around other progressors—either as they undergo reconditioning, or as they loll about on Diamond Beach at the feet of the vastest sand dunes in the inhabited universe . . .

All right, forget sheet 1. Noting in parentheses, however, that we still have no idea what it's for, especially given its level of detail . . . And if it's so detailed, then why doesn't it say a thing about his parents?

Enough. This probably has nothing to do with the case. But why didn't he register with COMCON after returning to Earth? This can be explained: a psychological spasm. An aversion to his career. A progressor on the brink of a psychological spasm returns to his home planet, which he hasn't visited in at least eighteen years. Where does he go? In my opinion, going home to Mommy in this state is embarrassing. Abalkin doesn't seem like that kind of namby-pamby—or rather, he oughtn't seem like it. His teacher? Or his adviser? That's possible. That's quite likely. So he could have a shoulder to cry on. And the teacher is more likely than the adviser. Because, after all, an adviser is a colleague of sorts, and the issue is an aversion to his career . . . Enough. Enough already! What's gotten into me? I looked at the clock. It had taken me thirty-four minutes to look through two documents. And I hadn't even studied them closely—I only acquainted myself with them.

I forced myself to concentrate and suddenly understood that I was in trouble. I suddenly realized that I wasn't at all interested in *how* to find Abalkin. I was much more interested in figuring out *why* I so urgently needed to find him. Of course, I immediately got angry at Excellentz, even though simple logic suggested to me that if this information would have been helpful in my search, my boss would certainly have given it to me. And the fact that he didn't explain to me *why* we had to search for and find Abalkin meant that this *why* has nothing to do with *how*.

And I simultaneously realized something else. Or intuited it rather than realized it. Or even more precisely, began to suspect it. This whole bulky folder, this vast collection of documents, all these yellowed scribbled-on pieces of paper—they wouldn't give me a thing except for perhaps a few names and a huge number of new questions, which again would have nothing to do with *how*.

JUNE 1, '78

A BRIEF NOTE ABOUT THE CONTENTS OF THE FOLDER

By 2:23 PM, I had finished an inventory of the contents.

As far as I could tell, most of the papers consisted of documents written by Abalkin himself.

First of all, there was his account of Operation Dead World on Planet Hope—seventy-six pages in his large, clear handwriting, almost entirely unblotted. I skimmed these pages. Abalkin wrote about how he and the bighead Puppen had crossed the abandoned city in search of a certain object (I couldn't figure out precisely what object) and were some of the first people to establish contact with the remnants of the wretched native population.

A decade and a half ago, Hope and its terrible fate had become proverbial on Earth, and frankly, it has remained proverbial—both as an ominous warning to all inhabited planets in the universe and as evidence of the Wanderers' most recent and most ambitious intervention in the fate of another civilization. It is now considered established fact that during the last century of their civilization, the inhabitants of Hope lost control over their technological development and made essentially irreversible changes to their ecological equilibrium. Nature had been destroyed. Crazy, desperate experiments attempting to remedy the situation produced industrial waste that polluted the planet so badly that the local population, stricken by a constellation of genetic diseases, was doomed to a complete collapse of their civilization and inevitable extinction. Genetic structures on Hope had gone berserk. Actually, as far as I know, no one has yet figured out the exact mechanism of their malfunctioning. At any rate, none of our biologists have managed to simulate this process. From the outside, it looked as if the development of any organism with the slightest bit of complexity would be rapidly and nonlinearly accelerated with respect to time. For humans, this meant that until age twelve, they developed relatively normally, then they started maturing quickly, and aging at an even faster rate. At sixteen, they looked thirty-five, and at nineteen, they would typically die of old age.

Of course, such a civilization had no historical perspective, but then the Wanderers got involved. As far as we know, this was the first time that they had actively interfered in the affairs of an alien planet. It is now accepted that they succeeded in leading the vast majority of the population of Hope through interdimensional tunnels, seemingly in order to rescue them. (Where they've taken these millions of sick, desperate people, what happened to them there, and where they are now—these are all questions we don't know the answers to, nor are we likely to find those answers any time soon.)

Abalkin only took part in the very beginning of Operation Dead World, and his part in it was rather modest. Then again, looking at it from a theoretical perspective, he was the first (and so far, the only) Earth progressor who had gotten to work alongside a representative of an intelligent nonhumanoid race.

Looking through this report, I discovered that Abalkin had mentioned a large number of names, but I came away with the impression that I only needed to take note of Puppen. I knew that an entire delegation of bigheads currently resided on Earth, and it probably made sense to figure out whether this Puppen was among them. Abalkin wrote about him with such warmth that I couldn't rule out the possibility of him meeting with an old friend. By this time, I had already noticed that Abalkin had a special fondness toward "all creatures great and small": he spent several years of his life working with bigheads, he was a kennel-man on Giganda, and so on and so forth.

And there was one more report from Abalkin in the folder, about the operation he participated in on Giganda. However, this operation was, in my opinion, insignificant: The Master of the Hunt of His Highness, the Duke of Alai, was fixing up his poor cousin with a job as a courier in a bank. The Master of the Hunt was Lev Abalkin, while the poor cousin was a certain Korney Jasmaa. This material seemed completely useless. As far as I could tell from scanning it quickly, it didn't contain a single Earth name other than "Korney Jasmaa." Instead, it was full of Zoggs, Nagon-Gigs, equestrians, excellencies, masters of armor, conference directors, ladies of the court . . . I noted down Korney's name, although it was clear I was unlikely to need him. In total, the second report contained twenty-four pages, and the folder turned out not to contain any more of Lev Abalkin's reports. This seemed strange, and I decided that at some later point, I ought to ponder the following: Why is it that out of the many reports of a professional progressor, only two made it into folder 07, and why specifically these two?

Both reports were written in the "lab assistant" style and, in my opinion, strongly resembled school compositions of the "What I Did Last Summer" variety. These reports are a pure pleasure to write but are, as a rule, a sheer torment to read. Psychologists (who are now a fixture at headquarters) demand that, instead of mostly containing objective data about events and circumstances, these reports largely consist of purely subjective feelings, personal impressions, and the author's stream of consciousness. The author does not select the style of the report ("lab assistant," "officer," "artist")—it is chosen for him, guided by some mysterious psychological considerations. Truly there are lies, shameless lies, and statistics, but let's not forget about psychology, my friends.

I'm no psychologist, at least not a professional one, but I thought that maybe I, too, could extract something useful about Lev Abalkin's personality from these reports.

Looking through the contents of the folder, I kept finding similar—I might even say identical—documents, which I couldn't understand at all. They were on heavy bluish paper with green edging and contained a monogram of either a Chinese dragon or a pterodactyl in the top right corner. "Tristan 777" was written on each sheet in the already familiar sprawling handwriting— sometimes in stylus, sometimes in marker, and a few times for some reason in a laboratory electrode pencil. They were dated and signed with the usual elaborate signature. As far as I could tell from the dates, these sheets began to be added to the folder in '60, and as they were added approximately every three months, they took up about a quarter of the folder.

Twenty-two more pages were dedicated to Abalkin's correspondence with his higher-ups. This correspondence gave me some food for thought.

In October '63, Abalkin writes to COMCON-1, expressing as of yet mild bewilderment about the fact that Operation Bigheads in Space had been canceled without consulting him, even though it was progressing well and had wonderful potential.

I don't know what answer Abalkin got to this, but in November of the same year, he writes an utterly desperate letter to Komov, requesting him to restart Operation Bigheads in Space, and he also writes a very sharply worded letter to COMCON protesting the fact that he, Abalkin, was being required to take a retraining course. (We note that for some reason he does all this in writing, and not in the usual way.)

As is clear from subsequent events, this exchange has no effect, and Abalkin begins working on Giganda. Three years later, in

November '66, he again writes to COMCON from Pandora and asks to be sent to Saraksh to continue working with bigheads. This time, his request is granted, but only partially: he's sent to Saraksh, but not to the Blue Serpent—instead, he's sent to Hontia as an underground unionist.

In February and August '67, as he's taking another retraining course, he writes to COMCON two more times (first to Bader, and then to Gorbovsky himself), pointing out the impracticality of using him, an expert in bigheads, as a resident agent. The tone of his letters gets harsher and harsher; for instance, the letter to Gorbovsky can only be described as offensive. I'm very curious how Leonid Andreievich, that sweetheart, had replied to this outburst of rage and contemptuous indignation.

And in October '67, by which time he was already a resident agent in Hontia, Abalkin sends Komov his last letter: a detailed plan for promoting our relationship with the bigheads, including exchanging permanent delegations, enlisting bigheads in zoopsychological work being carried out on Earth, and so on and so forth. I have never intentionally followed work in this area, but I had the impression that this plan had been adopted and was being implemented. And if that's so, then the situation is paradoxical: the plan is being implemented, but its originator is stranded in either Hontia or the Island Empire.

Anyway, this correspondence left a certain painful impression on me. OK, maybe I'm not an authority on bigheads, I can't judge, it's quite possible that Abalkin's plan is entirely trivial and that there's no reason to use fine words like *originator*. But it's not only that or mainly that! It looks like the kid is a zoopsychologist by nature. "Professional predilections: zoopsychology, theater, ethnolinguistics . . . Professional aptitudes: zoopsychology, theoretical xenology . . ." And yet they turned him into a progressor. True, there's a whole class of progressors for whom zoopsychology is their bread and butter. For instance, the ones who work with the Leonidans or with the aforementioned bigheads. But no, the kid is forced to work with humanoids, to work as a resident agent, as a soldier, even though for five years, he's been shouting from the rooftops: *What are you doing to me?* And then they are surprised that he has a mental spasm!

Of course, by the nature of his job, a progressor is absolutely required to have strict, I might even say military, discipline. A progressor constantly needs to do not what he wants to but what COMCON orders him to do. That's why he's a progressor. And resident agent Abalkin was probably much more valuable to COMCON than zoopsychologist Abalkin. But this story still stinks of a breach of norms, and it wouldn't be a bad idea to discuss this with Gorbovsky or Komov . . . And whatever mischief Abalkin has been up to (and he has clearly been up to some mischief), I swear to God, I'm on his side . . .

However, this all seemed to be unrelated to my problem.

I also noticed that there were three pages missing after Abalkin's first report, two pages missing after his second report, and two more missing after Abalkin's last letter to Komov. I decided not to worry about it.

JUNE 1, '78

ALMOST EVERYTHING ABOUT
LEV ABALKIN'S POSSIBLE CONNECTIONS

I made a preliminary list of Abalkin's possible connections on Earth, which turned out to contain only eighteen names. Practically speaking, only six of them were of interest to me, and I put the list in order of whom (in my opinion, of course) Lev Abalkin was most likely to visit. The list looked like this:

Teacher Sergei Pavlovich Fedoseyev
Mother Stella Vladimirovna Abalkina
Father Vyacheslav Borisovich Tsiurupa
Adviser Ernst Julius Horn
Progressor school attending physician Romuald Crăsescu
Boarding school attending physician Yadviga Mikhailovna Lekanova

There were a few others remaining in reserve—namely, Korney Jasmaa, the bighead Puppen, and Jacob Vanderhuze, as well as another five people, most of whom were progressors. I had also put down such luminaries as Gorbovsky, Bader, and Komov, but mostly as a matter of form. I could never speak to them—on the one hand, they would never be taken in by a cover story, and on the other, I was not authorized to speak openly about the case to them, even if they contacted me themselves.

In the course of ten minutes, the informatorium provided me with the following dispiriting data.

Lev Abalkin's parents didn't exist, at least not in the usual sense of this word. It's possible they didn't exist at all. You see, more than forty years ago, Stella Vladimirovna and Vyacheslav Borisovich were among the Yormala group on the one-of-a-kind starship *Darkness*, which was being submerged into Black Hole EN 200056. There hadn't been any communication with them—nor, according to current scientific theories, could there have been. It turned out that Lev Abalkin was their posthumous child. Of course, the word "posthumous" wasn't entirely accurate in this context: it was entirely possible that his parents were still alive and that they would continue to live for millions of years according to our calendar, but from the point of view of an earthling, they may as well be dead. They hadn't had any children, and when leaving our universe for all eternity, they, like many married couples in similar circumstances, left a mother's egg fertilized by a father's sperm in the Institute of Life. When it became clear that the submersion was successful and they would never return, the egg was allowed to develop, and this was how Lev Abalkin came into this world—a posthumous child of living parents. At least I now understood why sheet 1 had never mentioned Abalkin's parents.

Ernst Julius Horn, Abalkin's adviser at the progressor school, was no longer living. He had died while scaling Strogov's Peak on Venus in '72.

Physician Romuald Crăsescu resided on a planet called Lu, which, as far as I could tell, was impossibly remote. I had never even heard of such a planet, but the fact that Crăsescu was a progressor suggested that the planet was inhabited. It was interesting to see, however, that the old man (116 years old!) had entered his most recent home address into the GWI, along with the following characteristic message: "My granddaughter and her husband will be delighted to welcome any of my charges at this address." The charges were presumably fond of the old man and visited him often. I should keep this fact in mind.

I got lucky with the other two.

Sergei Pavlovich Fedoseyev, Abalkin's teacher, was living and thriving on the shores of Lake Ayat in a villa alarmingly named the Midges. He was also over a hundred, and he was apparently either extremely modest or extremely reserved, because he hadn't provided any information about himself other than his address. The remaining facts were a matter of public record: educated at so and so, archaeologist, teacher. That's it. As they say, the apple doesn't fall far from the tree—this was very reminiscent of his student, Lev Abalkin. And yet when I sent the relevant request for additional information to the GWI, it turned out the Sergei Pavlovich was the author of more than thirty articles on archaeology and had participated in eight archaeological expeditions (in Northwest Asia) as well as in three Eurasian teachers' conferences. He also maintained a private museum of the Paleolithic period of the northern Ural Mountains at his residence at the Midges, and this museum was of regional significance. A character. I decided to contact him as soon as possible.

Yadviga Mikhailovna Lekanova, on the other hand, had a surprise in store for me. Pediatricians rarely change their professions, and I had already visualized a sweet granny of an old lady bent beneath an astonishing load of very specialized knowledge—the most valuable knowledge in the world!—still briskly scurrying through the hallways of the Syktyvkar school. Yeah, right—scurrying! She really had spent a while working as a pediatrician, and it really had been in Syktyvkar, but she then retrained as an ethnologist, and what's more, worked successively in the following fields: xenology, pathoxenology, comparative psychology, and levelometry. And she had clearly excelled in all these rather loosely related sciences, judging by the number of papers she had published and the importance of the posts she had held. Over the past quarter century, she had worked for six different organizations and universities, and she was now working for the seventh—the mobile Institute of Earth Ethnology in the Amazon Basin. She didn't have an address, and interested parties were invited to get in touch with her through the institute's permanent outpost in Manaus. Well, we must be thankful for small mercies, although of course I was skeptical whether my client, given his current state, would drag himself to visit her in that still-primitive jungle.

It was completely obvious that I should start with his teacher. I put the folder under my arm, got into my glider, and flew to Lake Ayat.

JUNE 1, '78

LEV ABALKIN'S TEACHER

Despite my misgivings, the villa called the Midges stood on a high, windswept cliff right over the water, and there were no biting insects in sight. The owner greeted me fairly amiably and without surprise. We made ourselves comfortable on the porch, taking seats in wicker chairs arranged around an antique oval table containing a bowl of fresh raspberries, a jug of milk, and a number of glasses.

I again apologized for the intrusion, and my apology was again acknowledged with a silent nod. He was looking at me with calm expectation and seeming indifference—in fact, his face was generally immobile, as is indeed often the case with these old men who retain complete clarity of thought and full bodily strength after more than a century of life. It was an angular, very tanned face, almost free of wrinkles, and his thick, bushy eyebrows stuck out from it like a visor. Amusingly, his right eyebrow was jet black, while the left eyebrow was entirely white—not gray but bright white.

I introduced myself in more detail and related my cover story. I was a journalist, a zoopsychologist by profession, and I was currently collecting material for a book about the relationship between mankind and the bigheads . . . You must know, I said, that your student Lev Vyacheslavovich Abalkin was instrumental to the development of this relationship. I once knew him myself, but that was a long time ago, and I've since lost touch with the relevant people. I just tried to find him, but COMCON told me that Lev Vyacheslavovich wasn't on Earth and they had no idea when he'd be back. In the meantime, I wanted to learn everything I could about his childhood, how he had gotten started on this path, why everything had happened the way it did—I was primarily interested in the psychology of the researcher. Unfortunately, his adviser was no longer with us and I didn't know his friends, but I was lucky to have this opportunity to speak to you, his teacher. I am personally convinced that all our propensities have their roots not just in childhood but in early childhood . . .

I have to admit, I kept holding out hope that right at the beginning of my litany of lies, I'd be interrupted by a cry of "Wait, wait! Lev was literally here yesterday!" Alas, I was not interrupted, and I was forced to finish my speech, to try to look intelligent as I stated all of my glib judgments about how a creative personality is certain to have been shaped in childhood—childhood and not adolescence and certainly not adulthood—and furthermore, that it must have been shaped and that it couldn't have simply been, say, an innate proclivity that was nurtured or encouraged . . . What's more, when I finally ran out of steam, the old man stayed silent for a whole minute, then he suddenly asked me what a bighead was.

I expressed my completely sincere astonishment. Apparently, Lev Abalkin had never bragged about his accomplishments to his teacher! You know, only an extremely unsociable and reserved person doesn't brag about his accomplishments to his teacher . . .

I readily explained that the bigheads were an intelligent canid species that had appeared on planet Saraksh as a result of radiation-induced mutations.

"Canid? Dogs?"

"Yes. Intelligent doglike creatures. They have giant heads, hence the name."

"So Lyova works with doglike creatures . . . Got his way . . ."

I objected that I had no idea what Lyova was doing now, but that twenty years ago he was indeed working with bigheads, and very successfully so.

"He always loved animals," said Sergei Pavlovich. "I was convinced that he should become a zoopsychologist. When the Appointments Board decided to send him to the progressor school, I did my best to protest the decision, but they wouldn't listen . . . On the other hand, it was all very complicated, and if I hadn't even tried, maybe . . ."

He fell silent and poured me some milk. A very, very undemonstrative man. No interjections, none of the usual "Lyova! Of course! He was such a great kid!" Of course, it's entirely possible that Lyova hadn't been a great kid . . .

"What exactly would you like to find out from me?" asked Sergei Pavlovich.

"Everything!" I answered quickly. "What he was like. What his hobbies were. Who he was friends with. His reputation at school. Everything you remember."

"All right," said Sergei Pavlovich without any enthusiasm. "I'll try."

Lev Abalkin had been a reserved boy. From the earliest of ages. This was the first thing you noticed when meeting him. But he was not reserved due to a sense of inferiority, or feelings of inadequacy or self-doubt. It was rather the introversion of the constantly busy. As if he hadn't wanted to waste time on those around him, as if he was always deeply engaged with his own world. Roughly speaking, this world seemed to consist of himself and all living beings besides humans. This isn't so rare among children, it's just that he had a *talent* for it, but that wasn't the surprising thing about him; the surprising thing was that despite his obvious introversion he eagerly, nay, joyfully, participated in a variety of competitions and also in drama—especially in drama. Of course, he always gave solo performances. He categorically refused to participate in plays. He usually recited something, sometimes he even sang, with real feeling, with an unusual gleam in his eye—he seemed to open up onstage, and then on his way back to the stalls he'd become himself again: evasive, silent, unapproachable. And he was like this not only with his teacher but also with the other kids, and Sergei Pavlovich never did figure out what the issue had been. He could only assume that his talent for communicating with nature so dominated the other promptings of his soul that the kids—and, indeed, all human beings—around him were simply uninteresting to him. In actual fact, everything must have of course been more complicated—his introversion and immersion in his own world must have been the result of a thousand microevents that had happened outside the teacher's field of vision. He recalled the following scene: Lev was walking along the park paths after a downpour, picking up the earthworms and throwing them back into the grass. The kids thought this was funny, and there were those among them that knew not only how to laugh but how to cruelly ridicule. The teacher, without saying a word, joined Lev and began to gather the earthworms with him.

"But I'm afraid that he didn't believe me. I doubt that I managed to convince him that the fate of the worms really interested me. And he had another notable quality: absolute honesty. I can't recall a single instance of him lying. Even when he was at the age when children tell eager, pointless lies purely for the fun of it. But he didn't lie. And what's more, he despised those who did. Even if they were telling silly lies for fun. I suspect that there must have been an incident in his life when he first realized, with horror and disgust, that people are capable of telling untruths. I had missed that moment, too . . . However, this is unlikely to be what you need. After all, you're far more interested in the blossoming of the future zoopsychologist . . ."

And Sergei Pavlovich began to tell me about the blossoming of the future zoopsychologist.

In for a penny, in for a pound. I listened with a fascinated expression, inserting "Oh, yes?" at appropriate times, and even cursing once, exclaiming, "Damn, that's exactly what I need!" Sometimes I really don't like my job.

Then I asked him, "So then he didn't have many friends?"

"He had no friends at all," said Sergei Pavlovich. "I haven't seen him since he graduated, but the other kids from his class tell me that they never see him, either. They felt awkward telling me that, but, as far as I can tell, he simply declines invitations."

And then suddenly it burst out of him: "Why did it have to be Lev? I've launched one hundred and seventy-two kids into the world. Why did you have to be interested in Lev? You have to understand, I don't think of him as my student! I have no right! He's my failure! My one and only failure! From the very first day I met him, and for the next ten years, I tried to establish a connection with him, to extend any, even the most tenuous of threads between us. I thought about him ten times more than I thought about any of my other students. I turned myself inside out, but everything, literally everything I tried, only backfired and made things worse."

"Sergei Pavlovich!" I said. "What do you mean? Abalkin is an excellent researcher, a first-class scientist, I've met him myself."

"And how did you find him?"

"I thought he was a great kid, a true enthusiast . . . This was back during the first bighead expedition. Everyone there thought the world of him. Komov himself had such high hopes for him . . . And he justified those hopes, mind you!"

"Please have some raspberries," he said. "I have excellent raspberries. The earliest raspberries in the region . . ."

I broke off and took the proffered dish of raspberries.

"Bigheads . . ." he said bitterly. "Perhaps, perhaps. But you see, I've always known that he was talented. It's just that I can't take any credit for it . . ."

For a while, we silently ate raspberries and drank milk. I sensed that, any minute now, he was going to turn the conversation to me. He clearly didn't intend to talk about Lev Abalkin any longer, and simple politeness demanded that we now talk about me.

I quickly said, "Thank you very much, Sergei Pavlovich. You've given me a lot of interesting material. The only thing I regret is that he had no friends. I was really counting on finding some of his friends."

"I can tell you the names of his classmates, if you like . . ." He fell silent and then suddenly said, "I'll tell you what. Try to find Maya Glumova."

The expression on his face amazed me. It was completely impossible to imagine what he was remembering or what his associations with this name were, but you could be sure they were most unpleasant. He even broke out in dark red patches.

"His girlfriend from school?" I asked, trying to cover up the awkwardness.

"No," he said. "I mean, she did go to our school, of course. Maya Glumova. I believe that she later became a historian."

JUNE 1, '78

A LITTLE INCIDENT INVOLVING
YADVIGA MIKHAILOVNA

At 7:23 PM, I came home and started looking for Maya Glumova, historian. Within five minutes, I had the information at my fingertips.

Maya Toivovna Glumova was three years younger than Lev Abalkin. After graduating from school, she took the COMCON-1 training course for support personnel, immediately got involved with the infamous Operation Ark, then applied to the History Department at the Sorbonne. She initially specialized in the early years of the scientific-technological revolution, then she became interested in the history of early space research. She had a son, Toivo Glumov, who was eleven years of age, and she didn't report anything about a husband. Currently—oh wonder of wonders!—she was an employee of a special collection of the Museum of Extraterrestrial Cultures, which was located three blocks from here, on Star Square. And she lived very nearby—on Canadian Pine Avenue.

I called her immediately. A serious-faced blond individual with a peeling upturned nose surrounded by an abundant scattering of freckles appeared on the screen. This was doubtlessly Toivo Glumov the younger. Looking at me with transparent Nordic eyes, he explained that his mother wasn't at home, that she had planned to come home, but she had then called and told him that she wouldn't be back until tomorrow, and that she'd go straight to work. Did I want to leave a message? I told him that I didn't and said good-bye.

I see. I'll have to wait until the morning, and in the morning she'll spend a long time trying to remember who this Lev Abalkin was, then when she finally figures it out, she'll sigh and tell me that she's seen neither hide nor hair of him for twenty-five years.

All right. There still remained one person on my list of the likeliest people, but I didn't dare pin much hope on her. When all is said and done, after a quarter century of separation, people eagerly reunite with their parents, they often visit their teachers, they frequently meet with their school friends, but it is only in very specific, I might say peculiar, circumstances, that their memory brings them back to their school pediatrician. Especially considering the fact that this school pediatrician is currently on a research expedition in the jungle on the other side of the planet, and that, according to the weather report, null connectivity has been glitchy for the last two days due to fluctuations in the neutrino field.

But there was simply nothing else left for me to do. It was now daytime in Manaus, and if I was going to call at all, this was the time.

I got lucky. Yadviga Mikhailovna Lekanova was at the communications center that very moment, and I was able to speak to her immediately—an outcome I hadn't in any way expected. Yadviga Mikhailovna had a round face so tan it shone, apple-red cheeks with coquettish dimples, sparkling blue eyes, and an impressive cap of completely silver hair. She had a mild but very appealing speech defect and a deep, velvety voice that induced completely inappropriate thoughts about how it hadn't been long since this dame was able to sweep anyone she liked off their feet. And had obviously done so.

I apologized, introduced myself, and related my cover story. She narrowed her eyes, trying to remember, knitting her sable brows.

"Lev Abalkin? Lev Abalkin . . . Excuse me, what's your name?"

"Maxim Kammerer."

"Excuse me, Maxim, I'm not quite following. Are you acting on your own or are you the representative of some organization?"

"Well . . . I have a deal with an interested publisher . . ."

"But what about you, personally? Are you a freelancer or do you work somewhere? What does 'journalist' mean?"

I gave a deferential giggle, frantically trying to figure out what to say. "You see, Yadviga Mikhailovna, it's a bit hard to explain . . . I'm primarily . . . w-well, I'd probably have to say that I'm a pro-gressor . . . although when I started out, that job didn't exist yet. In the recent past, I was a COMCON employee . . . and in a certain sense, I'm still affiliated with them . . ."

"Struck out on your own, huh?" said Yadviga Mikhailovna.

She kept smiling, but now her smile was missing something very important. And at the same time, something very, very ordinary.

"You know, Maxim," she said, "I would be happy to talk to you about Lev Abalkin, but if you don't mind, not right now. Let me call you back in an hour or two."

She was still smiling, and I finally figured out what was miss-ing from her smile—it was simple goodwill.

"Of course," I said. "Whatever works for you."

"I apologize."

"No, I should be the one apologizing . . ."

She wrote down the number of my channel, and we parted ways. That had turned out to be a rather strange conversation. It was as if she had somehow figured out that I was lying. I felt my ears. They were red hot. Damn my job . . . *There is no hunt-ing like the hunting of man . . .* O tempora, o mores! How often they were wrong, after all, those classics . . . Well, I'll wait. And it seems like I'll probably have to fly to this Manaus. I loaded the weather report. Null connectivity was still glitchy. Then I ordered a stratoplane, opened the folder, and began to read Lev Abalkin's report on Operation Dead World.

I only managed to read about five pages. There was a knock on the door and Excellentz stepped over the threshold. I stood up.

We rarely have the chance to see Excellentz except behind his desk, and we always somehow manage to forget what a bony giant he is. An immaculately white pair of linen pants hung on him as if on a hanger, and something about him reminded me of a man on stilts, even though his movements weren't at all awkward.

"Sit down," he said, folding himself in half and lowering his body into the chair in front of me.

I hastily followed suit.

"Report," he commanded. I did so.

"Is that all?" he said with an unpleasant expression on his face.

"For now."

"That's not good," he said.

"It's not that bad, Excellentz," I said.

"That's not good! His adviser's dead. And what about his school friends? I see they aren't even on your list! And what about his classmates at the progressor school?"

"Unfortunately, Excellentz, it seems like he had no friends. At least not at the boarding school, and as for progressors—"

"Spare me your logical deductions. Check everything. And stay focused. Why are you bothering with his pediatrician, for example?"

"I'm trying to check everything," I said, starting to get angry.

"You don't have the time to zoom around on stratoplanes. Files, not flights."

"I'm using the files. I'm even planning to see that bighead. Puppen. But I had a specific order in mind . . . I don't think his pediatrician is a waste of time—"

"Be quiet," he said. "Give me your list."

He took the list and studied it for a long time, occasionally wiggling his bony nose. I'd have bet my life that he spent the whole time staring at one line without taking his eyes off of it. Then he gave me back the paper and said, "Puppen—that's not bad. And I like your cover story. But all the rest is no good. You believed that he had no friends. That's not true. Tristan was his friend, even though you won't find anything about that in the folder. Keep looking. And this . . . Glumova . . . that's a good idea, too. If they had a love affair, that's a chance. But leave Lekanova be. You don't need her."

"But she's going to call me back!"

"She won't call you back," he said.

I looked at him. The round green eyes weren't blinking, and I realized that no, Lekanova wouldn't call me back.

"Listen, Excellentz," I said. "Don't you think that I'd do a much better job if I knew what was going on?"

I was sure that he's snap out a curt *No*. It was a purely rhetorical question. I simply wanted to show him that I was aware of the aura of mystery surrounding Lev Abalkin, and that it was getting in my way.

But he didn't say that. "I don't know. I'd guess not. I can't tell you anything right now, anyway. And I don't want to."

"A secret of identity?" I asked.

"Yes," he said. "A secret of identity."

FROM LEV ABALKIN'S REPORT

By ten o'clock, we've established a protocol for moving forward. We're walking in the middle of the road: Puppen is walking in front of me, keeping to the painted center line, and I'm walking behind him and to the left. Our usual protocol—hugging the walls—had to be abandoned, because the sidewalks are cluttered with fallen plaster, brick rubble, shards of window glass, and rusty roof tiles, and we've already had two incidents in which fragments of ornamental moldings fell down for no obvious reason and almost hit us on the head.

The weather is not changing—the sky is still cloudy, and there are gusts of a warm, humid wind driving unidentifiable garbage along the broken pavement, rippling the fetid water in the stagnant black puddles. Hordes of mosquitoes swoop down on us, scatter, and swoop down again. Assault teams of mosquitoes. Entire tornadoes of mosquitoes. There are a lot of rats—rustling in the garbage heaps, scurrying from doorway to doorway in ginger-haired packs, standing on their hind legs in the glassless windows. Their beady eyes sparkle warily. I'm not sure what they manage to feed on in this stone desert. Maybe snakes. There are also a lot of snakes, especially near the manholes leading to the sewers, where they gather in tangled, wriggling balls. I'm not sure what the snakes eat, either. Maybe rats. Then again, the snakes are rather lethargic and not all aggressive—although they aren't fearful, either. They are minding their own business, not paying attention to anyone or anything else.

The city has certainly long since been abandoned. The man we met outside the city was, of course, insane and must have wandered this way by accident.

A message from Rem Zheltukhin's team. He still hasn't met a single person. He's delighted with his garbage dump and swears that he will shortly approximate the index of development of the local civilization to an accuracy of 0.01. I try to imagine his garbage dump—vast, with no end in sight, covering half this planet. This spoils my mood and I stop thinking about it.

The mimicrite suit isn't functioning properly. The protective images emulating the environment appear on the mimicrite with a lag of five minutes and sometimes not at all, and in their place, there appear monochromatic splotches in astonishingly pure, beautiful, and bright spectral colors. There must be something in the local atmosphere that disrupts the carefully calibrated chemical activity of this substance. The experts of the Committee on Camouflage Technology have given up trying to debug the suit remotely. They give me suggestions about how to fix it in the field. I follow these suggestions, and as a result, my suit stops working entirely.

A message from Espada's team. Apparently they miscalculated by a few kilometers when landing in the fog: they can see neither the cultivated fields nor the settlements that they had observed from orbit. Instead, they see the ocean and the coast, which are covered by a black crust more than half a mile wide—probably solidified fuel oil. This spoils my mood again.

The experts strongly object to Espada's plan of turning the camouflage off entirely. A small but noisy fight erupts over the radio waves.

Puppen grumbles: "Your fabled human technology! It's funny . . ." He isn't wearing a suit, nor is he wearing a heavy helmet with converters, even though some were made especially for him. As usual, he refused them all without explaining why.

He's running along the faded center line of the avenue, waddling slightly, his hind legs drifting slightly off to one side, just like Earth dogs sometimes do. He's fat and shaggy, and he has a giant bulbous head, which is as usual turned to the left, so that his right eye is looking straight ahead while his left eye seems to be glancing sideways at me. He pays no attention to the snakes, nor to the mosquitoes; the rats, on the other hand, do interest him, but only from the gastronomical point of view. However, he's currently full.

I get the feeling that he has already reached certain conclusions about the city and possibly about the planet itself. He coolly declined to look around the mansion in District 7—a wonderfully preserved structure, its neatness and elegance grotesquely out of place among the timeworn, creeper-covered, windowless buildings. He barely bothered to squeamishly sniff the two-meter-tall wheels of the armored vehicle half-buried beneath the ruins of a collapsed wall, despite the sharp strong stink of gasoline. And he wasn't the least bit curious earlier today, when the unfortunate native jumped out at us to perform his frenzied dance—jingling his bells, making faces, his colorful rags or possibly ribbons fluttering in the wind. Puppen has been taking all these oddities in stride—for some reason, he doesn't want to consider them separately from the catastrophe looming in the background, even though to begin with, for the first few miles of the journey, he was clearly agitated—searching for something, constantly violating our protocol for moving forward, sniffing things then snorting and spitting in disgust, mumbling indistinctly in his language . . .

"Here's something new," I say.

It looks like an ion shower stall—a seven-foot-tall cylinder three feet in diameter, made out of a translucent amber-like material. The floor-to-ceiling oval door is open. It looks like it was once upright, and then someone set off an explosive underneath one side—and now it's really tilted, with part of the bottom face up in the air, having pulled up the attached layer of asphalt and clay along with it. It's otherwise undamaged, although there's nothing in it that could be damaged, anyway—on the inside, it's as empty as an empty glass.

"A glass," says Vanderhuze. "But with a door."

"An ion shower," I say. "But without equipment. Or maybe a controller's booth. I've seen very similar ones on Saraksh, except those were made out of glass and tin. By the way, that's really what they are called in the local idiom: 'glasses.'"

"What do they control?" asks Vanderhuze curiously.

"Traffic at intersections," I say.

"It's a bit far from an intersection, don't you think?" says Vanderhuze.

"So then it's an ion shower," I say.

I dictate a report to him. After he takes it down, he asks, "Do you have any questions to record?"

"I can think of two. Why did they put this thing here, and who was it bothering? Note that it doesn't have any cables or wires. Puppen, do you have any questions?"

Puppen is more than indifferent—he's scratching himself, his rear end to the booth. "My people don't know these objects," he informs us arrogantly. "This doesn't interest my people." And he again begins to scratch himself with an air of open defiance.

"I'm done," I tell Vanderhuze, and Puppen immediately gets up and starts walking forward.

Oh, so this doesn't interest his people, I think as I walk behind and to the left of him. I want to smile, but I shouldn't smile on any account. Puppen can't stand that kind of smile; he's amazingly sensitive to the slightest nuances of human facial expressions. It's strange—how did bigheads get so sensitive? After all, their faces are almost devoid of expression, at least to the human eye. An ordinary Earth mutt has a much more expressive mug. And yet Puppen is extremely well versed in human smiles. Bigheads generally understand people a hundred times better than people understand bigheads. And I know why. It's because we have our scruples. Bigheads are intelligent creatures, and we feel awkward studying them. But they feel no such compunction. Back when we were living with them in the Fortress—when they were hiding, feeding, and protecting us—I lost track of the number of times that I suddenly discovered that I had been the subject of yet another experiment! And Martha also complained to Komov about this, and so did Rawlingson; only Komov never complained, and I think that was only because he was too proud. And the Tarasconian eventually simply ran away. He left for Pandora, where he now works with his abominable tahorgs and is as happy as a clam . . . Why was Puppen so interested in Pandora? He was trying to delay our departure by hook or by crook. I'll have to check later whether it's true that the bighead group has requested transportation for relocating to Pandora.

"Puppen," I say, "would you like to live on Pandora?"

"No, I need to be with you."

He needs to be. The problem is that their language only has one modality. There's no difference between "need," "should," "want," and "can." And when Puppen speaks Russian, it feels like he's choosing a word at random. You can never be sure what he means. Maybe he was trying to say that he loves me, that he'd be sad without me, that he's only happy when he's with me. And maybe he means that it's his duty to be with me, that he's been given this responsibility, and that he intends to nobly fulfill his duty, even though what he wants more than anything in the world is to be making his way through the orange jungle, eagerly listening for every rustle and relishing every one of Pandora's myriad smells . . .

A layer of plaster detaches itself from a dirty white balcony on the third floor of a building up ahead on the right and crashes down onto the sidewalk. The rats squeak indignantly. A column of mosquitoes erupts from a pile of trash and whirls around in the air. Across the street, a giant patterned metallic ribbon of a snake slithers toward Puppen, coils itself into a spiral in front of him, and threateningly raises its rhombic head. Puppen doesn't even stop—he casually swings a front paw and keeps trotting ahead as the rhombic head flies to the pavement, leaving the tangled, wriggling headless body behind.

Those oddballs were afraid to let me go alone with Puppen! A first-rate fighter, a quick thinker, with an unbelievable instinct for danger, absolutely fearless—fearless in a way that no human ever could be . . . But. Of course, there's always a *but*. If it came down to it, I'd fight for Puppen like I would for another earthling, like I'd fight for myself. And Puppen? I don't know. On Saraksh, they had fought for me, of course, fought and killed and died hiding me, but for some reason, it always felt like they weren't fighting for me, their friend, but for a certain very dear to them and yet abstract principle . . . I've been friends with Puppen for five years. When we first met, he hadn't yet lost the webbing between his toes, and I taught him how to speak our language and use the Supply Line. I stayed by his side when he got sick with the strange illnesses that the Earth doctors never did understand, I tolerated his bad manners, put up with his blunt remarks, forgave him things that I don't forgive anyone else. And I still don't know what I mean to him . . .

There's a message from the ship. Vanderhuze reports that Rem Zheltukhin found a rifle in his garbage dump. This is a trivial update. It's just that Vanderhuze doesn't want me to stay silent. He gets very worried, kind soul, when there are long silences. We make small talk.

While we make small talk, Puppen dives into an entryway. I hear rustling, squeaking, crunching, and chomping coming from that direction. Then Puppen reappears in the doorway. He's vigorously chewing and cleaning rat tails off his snout.

Every time I'm in contact with the ship, Puppen starts behaving like a dog—either hunting, or eating, or scratching himself. He knows perfectly well that I don't like this and does it ostentatiously, as if to get back at me for getting distracted from our shared solitude.

He makes his apologies, citing the tastiness of the treat and his inability to help himself. I reply coldly.

It's beginning to drizzle. The avenue up ahead becomes obscured by gray haze. We leave District 17 behind (the cross street is cobblestoned), pass a rusty van with flat tires and walk by a relatively well-preserved building faced with granite, with ornate bars on the first-floor windows. And then we see a park on the left side of the street, separated from the avenue by a low stone wall.

Right as we're passing the sagging arches of the entrance gates, a ridiculous, colorful, lanky man noisily jumps out of the wet, wildly overgrown bushes and hops onto the stone wall, his bells jingling.

He's as thin as a skeleton, his face is yellow, his cheeks are sunken in, and his eyes are glazed over. His messy, wet red hair sticks out in every direction, his floppy and seemingly multijointed arms are flailing, and his long legs are twitching and dancing in place, spraying fallen leaves and soggy crumbling cement from beneath his enormous feet.

He is covered from head to toe in some type of red, yellow, blue, and green checked leotard; the bells sown haphazardly onto his sleeves and pants jingle incessantly, and his knobby fingers are loudly snapping out a fast, intricate rhythm. A clown. A harlequin. His antics would probably be funny if they weren't so horrible in this dead city, beneath the gray drizzle, in front of the wild, overgrown park that is now a forest. He is certainly crazy. Yet another crazy man.

For a brief instant, I think that this is the same man we saw in the outskirts. But that one was festooned with colorful ribbons, and he wore a silly cap with a bell, and he was much shorter, and he didn't look as emaciated. It's just that they are both colorful and both insane, and it seems wildly improbable that the first two natives we'd meet on this planet would be crazy clowns.

"This isn't dangerous," says Puppen.

"We must help him," I say.

"Do as you like. He'll get in our way."

I know that he'll get in our way myself, but there's nothing I can do about it; I start to creep closer to the dancing clown, getting a tranquilizer suction cup ready in my glove.

"Danger behind us!" says Puppen suddenly.

I turn around sharply. But there's nothing unusual on the other side of the street—only a two-story house with decorative columns, covered in remnants of bright purple paint, all of its windows broken and a gaping black hole one and a half stories tall in place of a door. It's just a house, yet this is precisely what Puppen is staring at so intently. He is crouching on spring-loaded paws, lowering his head, and flattening his small triangular ears. A chill runs down my back; this pose is rare for Puppen, and he hasn't assumed it once yet on this route. Bells jingle frenziedly behind my back, then it's suddenly silent. There's only the pitter-patter of rain.

"Which window?" I ask.

"I don't know." Puppen slowly shakes his head from right to left. "It's not in a window. Do you want to see? But there's already less of it . . ." He slowly lifts his heavy head. "It's gone. Everything is back to normal."

"What?"

"It's like before."

"Is it dangerous?"

"It was dangerous before. A little dangerous. Then it was very dangerous. And now it's like before."

"People? An animal?"

"A very big anger. I don't understand."

I look back at the park. The crazy clown is gone, and I can't see anything in the dense, wet greenery.

Vanderhuze is terribly worried. I dictate a report. Vanderhuze is afraid that this was an ambush and that the clown was supposed to distract me. He can't seem to get it through his head that if this had been the case, the ambush would have worked—the clown had been so successful at distracting me that I couldn't see or hear anything but him. Vanderhuze offers to send us some backup, but I decline. This is an unimportant mission, and we'll probably soon be reassigned to be backup ourselves, quite possibly for none other than Espada.

Message from Espada's team: they've been shot at. With tracer bullets. Probably warning shots. Espada keeps going. So do we. Vanderhuze is extremely alarmed, and his voice now sounds utterly plaintive.

We probably got unlucky with our captain. Espada's captain is a progressor. Zheltukhin's captain is a progressor. And who do we have? Vanderhuze. This isn't without reason, of course: Espada's team is in charge of contact, and Rem is our main source of information, while Puppen and I are simply unmounted scouts in an empty, relatively safe region. A secondary team. But when something happens—and something always does happen—then we can only count on ourselves. After all, dear old Vanderhuze is nothing more than a starship pilot, an extremely seasoned space dog. He has Instruction 06/3 in the marrow of his bones, which tells him that "if signs of intelligent life are discovered, you must leave the planet *immediately*, destroying all possible traces of your stay . . ." Whereas we've encountered warning shots and a completely obvious unwillingness to make contact, and not only is no one planning to leave the planet, but they are continuing onward and generally looking for trouble . . .

The rain stops. Frogs are hopping on the wet pavement. It becomes clear what the snakes eat. And what do the frogs eat? Probably mosquitoes. The houses keep growing in height and splendor. Peeling, mildewy splendor. Then we come across a very long convoy of mismatched trucks parked along the left side of the road. It looks like they had left-handed traffic. Many of the trucks are open on top, and there are household goods piled in the back. It seems to point to a mass evacuation, except in that case, I don't understand why there were driving toward the city center. Maybe to the port?

Puppen suddenly stops and pokes his triangular ears out of the thick fur on top of his head. We're very close to the intersection, the intersection is empty, and the avenue past the intersection is also empty, as far as we can make out through the gray haze.

"It stinks," says Puppen. And after a short pause, "Of animals." And after another pause, "Lots of animals. Coming here. From the left."

Now I can also smell something, but it's just the smell of the wet rust from the trucks. Then suddenly, I hear the stamping of thousands of feet and the clatter of bony bodies, along with yelping, muffled growling, snorting, and sniffing. Thousands of feet. Thousands of throats. A pack. I look around, trying to find a suitable doorway in which to weather the storm.

"Damn," says Puppen. "Wild dogs."

And at that very instant, they pour out of the alley to the left. Dogs. Hundreds of them. A dense gray and yellow and black stream that stamps, snorts, and stinks strongly of wet dog. The front of the stream has already been sucked into the alley to the right, but the stream keeps pouring, except for a few beasts that separate from the pack and turn sharply toward us—large, mangy animals, very thin and covered in tufts of matted fur. Their cloudy eyes are darting around, and their yellow fangs are covered in saliva. They trot toward us, emitting high-pitched yelps that almost sound plaintive; they aren't approaching in a straight line but rather following a complicated trajectory of their own, arching their lumpy bodies and tucking their quivering tails beneath their torsos.

"Get in the house!" shrieks Vanderhuze. "Don't just stand there, get in the house!"

I ask him to stop making so much noise. I stick a hand beneath one of the flaps of my suit and grab the handle of my scorcher. Then Puppen says: "No need. I'll do this myself."

He slowly ambles toward the dogs. He isn't assuming a fighting stance. He's simply walking.

"Puppen," I say. "Let's not get involved."

"All right," says Puppen without slowing down.

I don't understand what he's doing, so I walk alongside the parked trucks, my arm at my side and the scorcher pointing down. I need to widen my field of fire in case the entire dirty yellow stream turns toward us. Puppen keeps walking, but the dogs stop. They are backing away, arching their bodies even more and hiding their entire tails between their legs—then, when they are about a dozen feet away, they suddenly flee with panicked squeals and instantly merge back into the pack.

And Puppen keeps walking. He's walking right along the center line of the road, ambling slowly along, as if the intersection in front of him were completely empty. I grit my teeth, hold my scorcher at the ready, and move to the center of the road, behind Puppen. The dirty yellow stream is right in front of us. The intolerable stench (or is it the fear?) is turning me inside out. I try to stare straight ahead and think: one shot to the left, then a quick shot to the right, two shots to the left, then a shot to the right . . .

Then suddenly the entire intersection is full of panicked squealing. The pack disperses, clearing the way. The dogs climb, crush, bite, and trample each other in their hurry to get away, yelping, howling, and growling. In a few seconds, there isn't a single dog remaining in the alley on the right, while the alley on the left is packed tight with a wriggling mass of furry bodies, tensed legs, and bared teeth. A white pillar of malodorous steam is rising above this mass, and a thousand-voiced howl of despair clogs my ears like wads of cotton.

We cross the intersection, now strewn with tufts of dirty fur, leaving the screeching pandemonium behind us, then I make myself stop and look behind me. The middle of the intersection is still empty. The pack has changed course. The dogs are now heading away from us along the avenue, engulfing the parked trucks. The yelps and howls gradually subside, and a minute later everything is back to normal, except that we can still hear the stamping of thousands of paws, the clatter of bony bodies, and the snorts and sniffs.

Vanderhuze chews us out. We get reprimanded. Both of us. For arrogance and juvenility. Puppen is usually extremely sensitive to reprimands, but for some reason, this time he doesn't react. He only grumbles, "Tell him there was no risk." And he adds, "Almost." I dictate the incident report. I don't understand what happened at the intersection, and Vanderhuze naturally understands even less than I do. I deflect his questions. I keep emphasizing the key point that the pack is now moving toward the ship.

"If they get close to you, scare them away with fire," I conclude.

Vanderhuze again expresses his displeasure with us, then allows us to continue. I can see him as well as if he were before me: after expressing his displeasure, he gives his left sideburn his habitual flick to fluff it up, adjusts his right sideburn, then again begins apprehensively watching the monitors, in resigned anticipation of the inevitable next problem.

When we reach the end of District 22, I notice that all the living things have disappeared from the streets—there isn't a single rat or snake or even frog to be seen. They must be hiding from the dogs, I think hesitantly. I know that this isn't true. It's because of Puppen.

In the fourth year of our acquaintance, I suddenly discovered that Puppen speaks decent English. At about the same time, I found out that Puppen composes music—not symphonies, of course, but little songs, simple melodies, very charming and perfectly agreeable to the human ear. This must be another thing.

He gives me a sidelong glance at me with one of his yellow eyes. "How did you guess about the fire?" he asks.

I prick up my ears. It turns out that I guessed about the fire! When did I manage to do that? "It depends on what fire you mean," I hazard.

"You don't understand what I'm talking about? Or you don't want to say?"

Fire, fire, I think hurriedly. This feels like an opportunity to learn something important. If I don't rush. If I choose my words carefully. When did I mention fire? Aha! *Scare them away with fire.*

"Even children know that animals are afraid of fire," I say. "That's how I guessed. Was it really that difficult?"

"I think it was difficult," grumbles Puppen. "You hadn't guessed before."

He goes silent and stops giving me sidelong glances. The conversation is done. He really is quick. He has realized that either I hadn't figured it out, or I don't want to talk about it in front of strangers . . . In either case, it's best to end the conversation . . . Let's take stock. I guessed about the fire. As a matter of fact, I hadn't guessed a thing. I simply told Vanderhuze to *scare them away with fire.* And then Puppen concluded that I guessed something. Fire, fire . . . Puppen had no fire, of course . . . Except he must have! I didn't see it, but the dogs did. My God, that's just what we need. Damn, Puppen!

"You burned them, too?" I ask blandly.

"Fire burns," Puppen responds dryly.

"And any bighead can do this?"

"Only earthlings call us bigheads. The geeks from the South call us fiends. Those from the mouth of the Blue Serpent call us nightmares. And in the Archipelago they call us *tsehu* . . . There's no such word in Russian. It means 'an underground dweller able to conquer and kill with the power of his will.'"

"I see," I say.

It only took me five years to discover that one of my closest friends, from whom I have never hidden anything, has the ability to conquer and kill with the power of his will. Hopefully only dogs, but who knows . . . A mere five years of friendship. Why the hell does it bother me so much, anyway?

Puppen instantly hears the bitterness in my voice, but he interprets it in his own way. "Don't be jealous," he says. "You have many things that we don't and never will. Your machines and your science."

We come out into a square and immediately stop, because we see a cannon. It's around the corner to the left—squat and low, as if pressing itself to the ground, with a barrel that has a heavy muzzle brake at the front; a low, wide gun shield covered in camouflage zigzags; wideset tubular trails; and thick wheels with rubber treads . . . Many a shot has been fired from this position, but it was a long time ago, a very long time ago. The scattered shell casings are oxidized red and green all the way through, the recoil spades have split the asphalt down to the ground and are now drowning in deep grass, and there's even a small tree growing by the left spade. The rusty gunlock is pushed back, the sight is missing, and there are rotten, half-decayed ammunition crates lying around at the rear of the position, every single one empty. They kept fighting here until they ran out of ammo.

I look over the top of the gun shield and see what they were aiming at. To be more precise, I first see the giant, ivy-covered holes in the wall of the house across the street, and only then does a certain architectural incongruity catch my eye. There's a small single-storied, flat-roofed pavilion standing at the foot of the damaged house, dull yellow in color and looking completely out of place—and it's now obvious that this is what they were aiming at. They had been shooting it at close range, firing directly at it, almost point blank, from about 150 feet away, and the gaping holes in the wall above it must be from the times they missed, even though it's hard to imagine missing at this distance. Then again, they didn't miss all that many times, and you have to marvel at how sturdy this nondescript yellow structure must be—it was fired at so many times, and yet it's still standing.

The pavilion is in a bizarre location, and at first I get the odd impression that the terrible blows from the cannon must have shifted it out of place, throwing it backward, driving it up onto the sidewalk, and almost jabbing its corner into the wall of the house. But of course that's not possible. The shells did punch round holes with melted, charred edges into the yellow facade, and then they must have exploded inside, blasting the wide entrance doors—now hanging askew from invisible threads—out onto the street. There must have been a fire, and everything inside it must have burned to a crisp, and the tongues of flame must have licked those black marks over the entrance and some of the shell holes. However, the pavilion is obviously standing exactly where it was originally erected by some eccentric architect: completely blocking the sidewalk and taking up part of the road, which must have obstructed traffic.

Everything that happened here took place a long time ago, many years in the past, and the odors of fire and shooting have long since evaporated, but the atmosphere of virulent hate and frenzied rage that drove the unknown artillerymen had in some strange way been preserved, and it's weighing heavily on me.

I begin to dictate yet another report, while Puppen, sitting a good distance away, grimacing in disgust, mutters in an ostentatiously loud voice, shooting me sidelong glances with his yellow eye: "Humans . . . They must have been humans . . . No doubt about it . . . Fire, steel, and destruction, it's always the same . . ." Apparently, he can also sense the atmosphere—in fact, he probably feels it even more than I do. After all, on top of everything else, this must remind him of his homeland—of the forests filled with murderous technology, and of the expanses burned to cinders in which the charred radioactive tree trunks stick out lifelessly from the ground and the soil itself is imbued with hatred, fear, and death.

There's nothing left for us to do at this square. Except maybe to form hypotheses and visualize scenarios, each more terrible than the last. We move on, and I think about how in this era of global catastrophes, civilizations keep spewing out all the scum they've accumulated in their collective DNA onto the surface. This scum can take on extremely varied forms, and these forms can be used to judge how dysfunctional the given society was at the time of the cataclysm, but they tell you very little about nature of the cataclysm, because the scum erupting to the surface is always the same: whether there was pandemic, a world war, or even a geological catastrophe, we see the same hatred, primitive egoism, and cruelty—the cruelty that seemed justifiable but in fact had no justification . . .

Message from Espada: he has succeeded in establishing contact. Komov orders all the teams to prepare their language processors to receive linguistic information. I reach behind my back, feel for the switch of my portable translator, and flip it on . . .

JUNE 2, '78

MAYA GLUMOVA, LEV ABALKIN'S GIRLFRIEND

I decided not to warn Maya Toivovna about my visit and instead headed to Star Square at 9:00 AM sharp.

It had drizzled at dawn, and the museum—a huge cube of rough marble—glistened wetly in the sunlight. Even from a distance, I could see a small, colorful crowd in front of the main entrance, and when I came closer, I heard disgruntled and disappointed exclamations. It turned out that the museum had been closed since yesterday in order to get some new exhibition ready. The crowd mainly consisted of tourists, but the ones sounding most indignant were the scientists, who had chosen this particular morning to work with the exhibits. They didn't care in the least about the new exhibition. There ought to be advance warning about these kinds of administrative stunts. And now, look, they had wasted their whole day . . . The chaos was exacerbated by the cybernetic cleaners—someone had forgotten to reprogram them, and they were now wandering aimlessly through the crowd, getting in everyone's way, scurrying away from the irritated kicks, and constantly causing explosions of malicious laughter due to their pointless attempts to walk through closed doors.

Having assessed the situation, I didn't linger here. I had visited this museum more than once and knew where the service entrance was. I walked around the corner of the building and followed a shady path to a wide, low door barely visible behind a solid wall of some kind of climbing plant. This was a plastic door disguised as stained oak, and it was also locked. There was another cybercleaner hanging around near this entrance. It looked hopelessly dejected: the poor thing had clearly lost a lot of charge overnight, and now that it was here in the shade, it had little chance of accumulating energy.

I pushed it aside with my foot and gave an annoyed knock. A sepulchral voice responded with: "The Museum of Extraterrestrial Cultures is temporarily closed while we reconfigure the central rooms for a new exhibition. We apologize. Please come visit us again in a week."

"Massaraksh!" I said out loud, looking around in some bewilderment.

Naturally, there was no one around—only the robot anxiously whirring by my feet. It seemed to be interested in my shoes.

I shoved it away again and again banged my fist on the door.

"The Museum of Extraterrestrial Cultures—" the sepulchral voice began to drone again, then suddenly it went silent.

The door opened. "That's more like it," I said, and entered. The robot remained outside. "Well?" I told it. "Come in."

But it backed away, as if hesitating, and at the same moment, the door slammed shut again.

There was a noticeable smell in the hallway—not particularly strong but quite specific. I've long since observed that every museum has its own odor. In my experience, zoological museums smell the strongest, but this museum also had a distinct aroma. I suppose it was the smell of extraterrestrial cultures.

I looked into the first room I came across and discovered two very young women holding molecular soldering irons, tinkering with the interior of a structure that most resembled a giant ball of barbed wire. I asked where I could find Maya Toivovna, got detailed instructions, and began roaming the passageways and halls of the Special Department for Artifacts of Unknown Purpose. I didn't come across anyone else. It looked like the rank and file were in the central rooms, busy with the new exhibition, leaving nothing here but the artifacts of unknown purpose. But I certainly did see my fill of these, and in the course of my wanderings, I became convinced that the purpose of all of these artifacts, now unknown, would remain so forever and ever, amen.

I found Maya Toivovna in her combined office/workshop. When I came in, she looked up at me—a pretty and, what's more, a charming woman, with lovely chestnut hair, large gray eyes, a slightly upturned nose, bare, muscular arms with long-fingered hands, and a loose blue blouse decorated with vertical black-and-white stripes. An enchanting woman. There was a small black mole above her right eyebrow.

She was looking at me vacantly, and not even at me but through me—she was gazing at me silently. Her desk was empty except for her two hands, which looked as if she had put them there and then had forgotten about them.

"Excuse me," I said. "My name is Maxim Kammerer."

"Yes. I'm listening."

Her voice also sounded vacant, and her statement wasn't true: she wasn't listening. She didn't see or hear me. She was obviously in no state to deal with me. In this situation, any decent person would have apologized and quietly gone away. But I couldn't allow myself to be a decent person. I was a COMCON-2 employee doing his job. Therefore, I didn't even apologize, never mind go away, but simply sat down in the nearest chair and, arranging my features in an expression of simpleminded amiability, asked, "What's going on at the museum today? They aren't letting anyone in."

She seemed a little surprised. "They aren't letting people in? Really?"

"That's what I just said! I barely got in using the service entrance."

"Right, right . . . Excuse me, who are you? Do you need something from me?"

I repeated that I was Maxim Kammerer and began to relate my cover story.

And then a surprising thing happened. As soon as I spoke Lev Abalkin's name, she seemed to wake up. The vacant expression disappeared from her face—she blazed up and eagerly fixed her gray eyes on me. But she didn't say a word and heard me out to the end. She only slowly lifted her powerless arms from her desk, steepling her long fingers and resting her chin on them. "Did you know him personally?" she asked.

I explained about the expedition to the mouth of the Blue Serpent.

"And you'll write about all that?"

"Of course," I said. "But it's not enough."

"Enough for what?" she asked. A strange expression appeared on her face—it was as if she was barely holding back her laughter. Even her eyes began to sparkle.

"You see," I began again, "I want to show how Lev Abalkin became a leading specialist in his field. He was working at the intersection of zoopsychology and sociopsychology, and—"

"But he didn't become a specialist in his field," she said. "They turned him into a progressor. They turned him into . . . They . . ."

No, it wasn't laughter she was holding back but tears. And now she stopped holding them back. Dropped her face into hands and burst into sobs. Good Lord! I always find women's tears hard to bear, and this time, on top of that, I had no idea what was happening. She was crying her heart out, unselfconsciously, like a child, her whole body shaking with sobs, while I sat there like an ass and had no idea what to do. In these situations, you're supposed to offer a glass of water, but her office / workshop didn't have a glass or water or any possible substitutes—only shelves filled with artifacts of unknown purpose.

And she was still crying. Tears were trickling down between her fingers and dripping onto the desk, she was sobbing and taking deep, shuddering breaths, and she was still covering her face—and then she suddenly began to speak, but it was as if she was thinking out loud, without any order or purpose, disjointedly, interrupting herself . . .

He'd thrash her—and how! He'd let her have it whenever she defied him. He didn't care that she was a girl and three years younger than him—she belonged to him, period. She was his thing, his very own thing. She became his thing immediately, almost the very first time he saw her. She had been five and he had been eight. He had been running around in circles, shouting out a counting rhyme he had made up himself: "The animals stood by the door, people shot them, they fell dead to the floor!" Ten times, then twenty times in a row. She thought it was funny, and that had been the first time he thrashed her . . .

It was wonderful to be his thing, because he loved her. He never loved anyone else. Only her. He didn't care about the others. They didn't understand anything and didn't know how to understand. But he would go onstage, sing songs, and recite poetry—all for her. That's exactly what he'd tell her: "That was for you. Did you like it?" And he'd compete in the high jump for her. And he'd do deep dives for her. And he'd write poetry at night for her. He really valued her, his very own thing, and he was constantly striving to be worthy of such a precious possession. And no one knew a thing about it. He always knew how to make sure that no one learned about it. Until the very last year, when his teacher found out . . .

He owned lots of other things, too. The whole forest near the school was his—a very large possession of his. He owned every bird, and every squirrel, and every frog in every ditch in it. He was the ruler of the snakes, he started and ended wars between anthills, he knew how to treat the sick deer, and they were all his, except for an old moose named Rex, whom he recognized as his equal, until they had a fight and he had driven Rex out of the forest . . .

She'd been a fool, a damn fool! Everything had been so good, and then she had grown up and gotten it into her head to break free. She told him plainly that she didn't want to be his thing anymore. He thrashed her, but she was stubborn; she insisted, the damn idiot. Then he thrashed her again, mercilessly, remorselessly, like he used to thrash the disobedient wolves. But she wasn't a wolf—she was more stubborn than all of his wolves put together. And then he whipped out a knife from his belt, the knife he had himself carved from a bone he found in the forest, and, smiling wildly, cut his arm open from the wrist to the elbow, slowly and terribly. He stood there in front of her, the wild smile on his face and the blood gushing from his arm like water from a faucet, and he asked, "How about now?" And even before he collapsed, she realized he had been right. He had always been right, from the very beginning. But she never did want to admit it, the damn fool . . .

And then in his senior year, when she came back from summer vacation, it was all over. Something had happened. They probably already had him under control. Or maybe those idiots had found everything out, and were horrified, of course. Damn rational morons. He had looked right through her and turned away. She had ceased to exist for him, just like the others. He had lost his thing and had come to terms with his loss. And by the time he remembered about her, everything was different. Life could never again be a mysterious forest in which he was the ruler and she his most valuable possession. They had already begun to change him, he was already almost a progressor, he was already halfway to a different world in which people betray and torture each other. And it was clear that he had gained a firm foothold on this path, that he had turned out to be a diligent and talented student. He wrote to her—she didn't answer. He called to her—she didn't respond. But he should have stopped writing and calling—he should have come in person and thrashed her like in the old days, and then maybe everything would have returned to the way it was. But he was no longer a ruler. He was now merely a man like any other, and he had stopped writing to her . . .

His last letter, handwritten as usual—he believed only in handwritten letters, he never used crystals or magnetic records—his last letter had come from over there, from beyond the Blue Serpent. "The animals stood by the door," he had written, "people shot them, they fell dead to the floor." And there was nothing else in this last letter of his . . .

She was feverishly pouring her heart out, sniffling and blowing her nose into crumpled laboratory tissues, when I suddenly realized something, and a second later, she said so herself—she saw him yesterday. Right when I was dialing her number and speaking to the freckled Toivo, right when I was trying to reach Yadviga, and when I was talking to Excellentz, and when I was lying around at home, reading the report on Operation Dead World—she had spent that entire time with him, looking at him and listening to him, and something had happened between the two of them that was making her cry on a complete stranger's shoulder.

JUNE 2, '78

MAYA GLUMOVA AND JOURNALIST KAMMERER

She fell silent, as if she had come to her senses. I had also come to my senses, just a few seconds earlier. After all, I was doing my job. I had to do my job. Duty. The call of duty. Everyone needs to do his or her duty. These are musty, lumpy words. After the things I'd heard. The hell with my duty; maybe I should do everything I can to pull this wretched woman out of the morass of her incomprehensible despair. Maybe that's my real duty?

But I knew that this wasn't the case. For a plethora of reasons. For one thing, because I don't know how to pull people out of morasses of despair. I have no idea how it's done. I don't even know where to begin. And therefore, what I most wanted to do right now was to get up, apologize, and leave. But I wasn't going to do that, of course, because I absolutely had to find out where they had met and where he was right now—

She suddenly asked again, "Who are you?" She asked this in a cracked, cold voice, and her eyes were now dry—they were glistening, very sick eyes.

Before I came, she had been sitting here alone, despite the fact that she was surrounded by colleagues and probably even friends. She was all alone, and even though people may have approached her and tried to talk to her, she was still alone, because no one here knew anything or could know anything about the person who had filled her soul with this terrible despair, with this burning, enervating disillusionment, and with all the other feelings that had accumulated inside her during the night, and were fighting to break free, and couldn't find a way out. And then I had appeared and spoken Lev Abalkin's name, as if slashing a scalpel across an intolerable pus-filled wound, and it had all burst out of her, and for a time she felt immense relief—she had managed to scream and cry herself out and to free herself from the pain. And this set her reason free, and then I ceased to be a healer and became who I really was—a random, unfamiliar stranger. And it was now becoming clear to her that I couldn't merely be a random stranger, because coincidences like this didn't happen. It wasn't possible that she'd part with her beloved twenty years ago and not hear a word about him—not even his name—for twenty years, and that twenty years later, she'd see him again and spend a night with him, a terrible and bitter night, more terrible and bitter than any separation, and that the very next morning, for the first time in twenty years, she'd hear his name from a random, unfamiliar stranger . . .

"Who are you?" she asked in the same cracked, cold voice.

"My name is Maxim Kammerer," I answered for the third time, expressing complete bewilderment in every possible way. "I'm a sort of journalist . . . But for God's sake . . . It looks like I came at a bad time . . . You see, I'm collecting material for a book about Lev Abalkin . . ."

"What's he doing here?"

She didn't believe me. Perhaps she could sense that it wasn't material about Lev Abalkin I was looking for, but Lev Abalkin himself. I needed to adapt. The sooner the better. And of course, I adapted.

"What do you mean?" asked journalist Kammerer, looking confused and rather anxious.

"Is he here on a mission?"

Journalist Kammerer was dumbfounded. "M-Mission? I-I don't quite understand . . ." Journalist Kammerer was pathetic. There was no doubt that he had not been prepared for such a meeting. He had inadvertently found himself in an awkward situation and had no idea how to get out of it. More than anything, journalist Kammerer wanted to run away. "Maya Toivovna, you see, I . . . My goodness, don't think that . . . Just pretend I didn't hear anything . . . I've forgotten it all already! . . . I was never even here! . . . But if I can help you in any way . . ."

Journalist Kammerer was babbling incoherently and was crimson from embarrassment. He was no longer sitting down. He was hanging over the desk in a solicitous and extremely uncomfortable position, and he was constantly trying to reassuringly take Maya Toivovna by the elbow. He was probably rather repulsive to look at, but he was certainly completely harmless and a bit foolish.

"This is how I like to work, you see," he was babbling in a pathetic attempt to justify himself. "It's probably controversial, I don't know, but it has always worked before . . . I begin at the periphery: friends, coworkers . . . Teachers, naturally . . . And advisers . . . And then—when I'm fully armed, so to speak—I tackle the primary object of my investigation . . . I asked COMCON, and they told me that Abalkin was about to come back to Earth . . . I've already talked to his teacher . . . and his pediatrician . . . I thought I'd see you next . . . But I came at a bad time . . . I'm sorry, I'm so sorry. I'm not blind, you know, I can see that there must be some sort of extremely unpleasant coincidence . . ."

And he managed to soothe her after all, the awkward and foolish journalist Kammerer. She leaned back in her chair and covered her face with one hand. Her suspicions evaporated, awakening shame and a crushing fatigue. "Yes," she said. "It must be a coincidence."

At this point, journalist Kammerer ought to have turned around and tiptoed away. But that wasn't the kind of man he was, this journalist. He couldn't simply leave a depressed, overwrought woman all by herself—she clearly needed his help and support.

"Just a coincidence, nothing more, of course . . ." he babbled. "We'll forget this ever happened, and anyway, nothing did happen . . . And at some point later, when it's convenient . . . when it works for you . . . I would of course be enormously grateful . . . Naturally, this won't be the first time in the course of my work that I've had to speak to my primary object first, and only then . . . Maya Toivovna, maybe I should call someone? It'd only take a moment . . ."

She was silent.

"Right, right, of course, no need . . . What for? I'll just stay here a bit . . . just in case . . ."

She finally took her hand away from her eyes. "You don't need to stay with me," she said wearily. "You'd better go find your primary object."

"No, no, no!" protested journalist Kammerer. "I have time. Primary object or no primary object, I don't want to leave you alone . . ." He glanced at his watch with a certain anxiety. "And my object won't get away from me now! . . . Just you wait! . . . And chances are, he's not even at home. I know what progressors on vacation are like . . . probably roaming the city, indulging in sentimental memories . . ."

"He's not in the city," said Maya Toivovna, still holding herself back. "He's a two-hour flight away."

"A two-hour flight?" Journalist Kammerer was unpleasantly surprised. "Wait, wait, I had the distinct impression—"

"He's in Valdai! At the Osinushka Resort! On Lake Velyo! And just so you know, null-T isn't working!"

"Hmmm!" said journalist Kammerer very loudly. He had clearly not allotted time for two hours of air travel in today's schedule. One might even suspect that he was generally opposed to air travel.

"Two hours," he babbled. "Right, right, right . . . I have to admit, that isn't turning out at all like I imagined . . . I beg your pardon, Maya Toivovna, but is there a way to get in touch with him from here?"

"There probably is," said Maya Toivovna in a voice that was now completely faded. "I don't know his number . . . Listen, Kammerer, leave me be. I'm no good to you right now, anyway."

And only then did journalist Kammerer fully realize the awkwardness of his position. He sprang up and rushed to the door. Thought better of it and came back to the desk. Babbled an unintelligible apology. Rushed to the door again, knocking over a chair on the way. Continuing to babble apologies, picked up the chair and replaced it with the greatest of care, as if it were made of crystal and porcelain. Backed away, bowing, pressed the door open with his rear end, and spilled out into the hallway.

I carefully closed the door and stood there for a bit, kneading my stiffened facial muscles with the back of my hand. Shame and self-loathing filled me with nausea.

JUNE 2, '78

OSINUSHKA: DR. GOANNEK

From the eastern bank, Osinushka looked like a collection of white and red roofs buried in green thickets of red-berried mountain ash. It also had a narrow strip of beach and a seemingly wooden pier that was surrounded by a school of colorful boats. There wasn't a soul on the entire sunlit slope, and the only person in sight was sitting on the pier, dressed all in white and dangling his bare feet off the pier. Given how still he was, I assumed he was fishing.

I threw my clothes onto the seat and quietly got into the water. The water in Lake Velyo was good—it was fresh, clear, and a pure pleasure to swim in.

When I scrambled out onto the pier and, shaking the water out of my ears, started hopping on one foot on the hot boards, the man dressed in white finally looked away from his fishing line and, examining me over his shoulder, inquired with interest,

"So, did you come all the way from Moscow in your underwear?"

This was yet another old man—this one was a bit less than a hundred years old, dried-up and thin like his bamboo fishing rod, except that his face wasn't yellow but brown, or maybe even almost black. Then again, it may have only seemed that way because of the contrast with his spotless white clothing. However, his eyes looked young—small, blue, and cheerful. A dazzling white cap with a gigantic sun visor covered his obviously bald head and gave him a look of either a retired jockey or one of Mark Twain's schoolboys playing hooky from Sunday school.

"They say that there's an extraordinary quantity of fish here," I said, squatting next to him.

"They lie," he said. He said this curtly. Impressively.

"They say there's a good time to be had here," I said.

"Depends who you are," he said.

"This is a fashionable resort, they say," I said.

"It was once," he said.

I ran out of steam. We were silent for a bit.

"This resort was fashionable, young man," he pronounced didactically, "three seasons ago. Or as my great-grandson puts it, 'three seasons long ago.' You see, young man, nowadays no one can imagine a vacation without ice-cold water, gnats, raw food, and deep wilderness . . . 'Immovable rock, my resting place' . . . They need Taymyr and Baffin Land, believe it or not . . . Astronaut?" he asked suddenly. "Progressor? Ethnologist?"

"I was once," I said, not without some malice.

"And I'm a doctor," he said without batting an eyelash. "I don't suppose you need me? I've rarely been needed the last three seasons. However, in my experience, patients come in waves. For example, someone needed me yesterday. So I ask, why not today, too? Are you sure you don't need me?"

"Only as a pleasant companion," I said sincerely.

"Well, thank you for that," he responded readily. "Then let's go have some tea."

And off we went to have tea.

Dr. Goannek resided in a large log cabin next to the medical pavilion. The cabin had all the expected amenities: a balustered porch, windows with carved wooden trim, a decorative rooster on the roof, an automatically configured ultrasonic Russian oven, a deep bathtub, and a double bed, as well as a two-story cellar—the last, however, was connected to the Supply Line. There was a null-T booth behind the house, skillfully disguised as a wooden outhouse and surrounded by a mighty outcrop of nettles.

The doctor's tea consisted of ice-cold beetroot soup, millet porridge with pumpkin, and very bubbly raisin kvass. There was actually no tea as such—Dr. Goannek firmly believed that the consumption of strong tea contributed to the formation of kidney stones, while weak tea was a culinary travesty.

Dr. Goannek was a veteran of Osinushka—he took over the practice twelve seasons ago. He had seen Osinushka when it was an ordinary resort, one of thousands like it, as well as during its absolutely breathtaking heyday, when balneologists were temporarily convinced that only a moderate climate could make the vacationer happy. Nor had he abandoned it now, in its period of seemingly hopeless decline.

The current season, which, as always, had begun in April, had only brought three travelers to Osinushka. In mid-May, there had arrived a married pair of impossibly healthy sanitation workers, who were coming straight from the North Atlantic, where they had been cleaning up a giant pile of radioactive garbage. This couple—a Bantu man and a Malaysian woman—mixed up the hemispheres and came here, believe it or not, for some skiing. After roaming the surrounding forests for a few days, they disappeared one fine night, decamping for parts unknown. And only a week later did a telegram originating in the Falkland Islands arrive from the pair, containing a suitable apology.

And their only other visitor had been a strange young man—he turned up yesterday in the early morning, completely out of the blue. What made him so strange? First of all, they couldn't figure out how he had gotten here. He didn't have means of either air or ground transportation—Dr. Goannek could vouch for this himself, due to his insomnia and his excellent hearing. And he didn't seem to have walked, either—Dr. Goannek could unerringly identify all walkers by their odor. The only remaining possibility was null transportation. But as everyone knew, null connections have been unreliable for a few days now because of neutrino field fluctuations, which meant that someone could only get to Osinushka via null transportation by pure chance. However, then the question is: If this young man had come here by pure chance, then why did he immediately latch onto Dr. Goannek, as if he'd been looking for Dr. Goannek his entire life?

This last point seemed somewhat nebulous to the underwear-clad tourist Kammerer, and Dr. Goannek didn't hesitate to give the requisite explanations. The strange young man didn't need Dr. Goannek per se. He simply needed a doctor, but the sooner the better. The young man was complaining of nervous exhaustion—and the nervous exhaustion was indeed present, and, moreover, it was so serious that an experienced doctor like Dr. Goannek could see it with the naked eye. Dr. Goannek thought it necessary to immediately perform a scrupulous and thorough examination, which fortunately didn't reveal any pathology. It's noteworthy that this favorable diagnosis had a downright therapeutic effect on the young man. He visibly perked up and in two or three hours was receiving guests as if nothing had ever happened.

No, no, the guests had arrived in the most ordinary of ways—using a standard glider . . . As a matter of fact, they weren't guests but rather a single female guest. And that's exactly as it should be, for there is not and could not be better therapy for a young man than a charming young woman. During the many years of his extensive practice, Dr. Goannek had often seen analogous cases. For example . . . Dr. Goannek provided his first example. Or, say . . . Dr. Goannek provided his second example. And similarly, the best therapy for a young woman . . . And Dr. Goannek provided his third, fourth, and fifth examples.

To keep his end of the conversation up, tourist Kammerer hastened to provide an example from his personal experience—back when he was a progressor, he had once been on the verge of nervous exhaustion himself. However, this pitiful and poorly chosen example was indignantly rejected by Dr. Goannek. It turned out that progressors were a completely different matter: in some ways, they were much more complicated, and in other ways, they were actually much simpler . . . In any case, Dr. Goannek would have never felt comfortable using any psychotherapeutic methods on the strange young man if he had been a progressor—not without first consulting a specialist.

But the strange young man was clearly not a progressor. Noting parenthetically that he probably would have been unable to become one; he didn't have the right temperament for it. No, he wasn't a progressor but an actor or an artist, and one who had suffered a major creative failure. And this was far from the first or even the tenth such case Dr. Goannek had encountered in the course of his wide-ranging practice. I remember one time . . . And Dr. Goannek began to spout case histories, each one finer than the last, using an assortment of As, Bs, Cs, and even alphas in place of the patients' real names.

Tourist Kammerer, a former progressor and a naturally coarse man, rudely interrupted this edifying narration to declare that he would personally never consent to share a resort with some cracked-up artist. This was a rash remark, and tourist Kammerer was immediately put in his place. First of all, the term *cracked-up* was analyzed, criticized to smithereens, and tossed aside as not only medically illiterate but also vulgar. And only then did Dr. Goannek, his words dripping with extraordinary venom, inform him that the aforementioned cracked-up artist, likely anticipating the invasion of former progressor Kammerer with all of its ensuing inconveniences, had himself given up the idea of staying at the same resort, and therefore had left this morning using the first available glider. In fact, he was in such a hurry to avoid meeting tourist Kammerer that he didn't even have the time to say good-bye to Dr. Goannek.

Former progressor Kammerer, however, turned out to be completely insensible to venom. He took everything at face value and expressed complete satisfaction with the fact that the resort was free of nervously exhausted artistic types, and that there was now nothing stopping him from finding a sweet spot to relax in style.

"Where did this neurotic stay, anyway?" he asked bluntly, and immediately clarified: "I'm asking so I don't waste my time there."

In the course of the conversation, we had come out onto the balustered porch. The slightly scandalized doctor silently pointed to a picturesque cabin decorated with a big blue 6—right on the cliff, a bit separated from the other buildings.

"Excellent," declared tourist Kammerer. "Then we won't go there. We'll start out right over *there* . . . I like that dense thicket of ash trees . . ."

It was certain that initially, the sociable Dr. Goannek had intended to offer—and in case of resistance to insist—to serve as tour guide and glowing reference for Osinushka. But tourist and former progressor Kammerer now seemed much too rude and callous to him. "Certainly," he said coldly. "I suggest you take this path right here. You'll find Cottage Twelve . . ."

"Huh? What about you?"

"You'll have to excuse me. You see, I'm in the habit of relaxing in my hammock after tea . . ."

It was certain than a single plaintive glance would have sufficed to get Dr. Goannek to relent and forgo his habit in the name of hospitality. So the insensitive and vulgar Kammerer hastened to put the last nail into the coffin. "Old age, huh?" he said sympathetically, and the job was done.

Seething with silent indignation, Dr. Goannek started walking toward his hammock, while I disappeared into the thicket of mountain ashes, skirted the medical pavilion, and crossed the hillside toward the neurotic's cabin.

JUNE 2, '78
COTTAGE SIX

It was clear to me that Osinushka would, in all likelihood, never see Lev Abalkin again and that I wouldn't find anything useful in his temporary abode. However, there were two things that were completely unclear to me. How, indeed, had Lev Abalkin come to this Osinushka and why? From his perspective, if he really is in hiding, it would be much safer and more logical to see a doctor in any big city. For example, in Moscow, which is a ten-minute flight away. Odds are that he came here completely by accident: either he ignored the neutrino storm warning, or he didn't care where he was going. He needed a doctor, urgently, desperately. Why?

And another strange thing. Could an experienced hundred-year-old doctor really be so far off the mark as to declare a seasoned progressor unfit for his profession? Doubtful. Especially as Abalkin's career trajectory has come to my attention before . . . This looks rather unprecedented. It's one thing to steer a man to become a progressor in spite of his professional inclinations, and a very different thing to make a progressor out of a man whose nervous system cannot handle it. Heads ought to roll for this—and I mean permanently—because this reeks not only of wasted human potential but of the loss of human life . . . By the way, Tristan died already . . . And I thought that after I found Lev Abalkin, I absolutely had to find the people whose fault it all was in the first place.

As I had expected, the door of Lev Abalkin's temporary abode was unlocked. The small entrance hall was empty—there was only a toy panda cub solemnly sitting on a low circular table beneath a fluorescent light, gravely nodding its head, its ruby eyes glowing.

I looked to the right, into the bedroom. It looked like no one had entered this room in two years, if not all three—even the automatic lights weren't on, and there were cobwebs full of dead spiders in the corner above the neatly made bed.

I went around the table and walked into the kitchen. The kitchen showed signs of use. There were dirty dishes on the folding table, the Supply Line window was open, and the receiving side contained an unopened package of bananas. It looked as if Lev Abalkin had gotten used to having the services of an orderly during his years at Headquarters C. Then again, it was quite possible that he simply didn't know how to start the cybercleaner . . .

The kitchen had given me a bit of a hint of what I would find in the living room. But only a bit. The entire floor was strewn with torn pieces of paper. The wide sofa had been pulled to pieces, and its floral cushions had been scattered all over—I even found one on the floor in the farthest corner of the room. The chair by the table was overturned, and the table was in complete disarray—food-encrusted serving platters were mingling on its surface with more dirty dishes, and an open wine bottle was presiding in the middle of the chaos. Another such bottle had rolled to the wall, leaving a sticky trail on the rug. There was a wineglass containing dregs of wine on the table—oddly enough, there was only one, but as someone had torn off the window curtain, which was now hanging by a thread, I somehow immediately assumed that the second glass had been hurled through the wide-open window.

The crumpled paper was scattered all over, not just on the floor—nor was all the paper crumpled. I could see a few pieces of paper on the couch, a few scraps had somehow gotten into the food on the serving platters, and, what's more, the platters and dishes had been pushed slightly aside, and a whole stack of paper lay in the cleared space.

I took a few tentative steps and something sharp immediately bit into my bare foot. It was a piece of amber resembling a molar with two roots. It had a hole drilled through it. I crouched down, looked around, and found a few other such pieces, as well as the rest of the amber necklace, which was lying under the table right by the couch.

Still crouching down, I picked up the nearest piece of paper and flattened it out on the rug. This was half a sheet of ordinary writing paper containing a drawing of a face in stylus. A child's face. A chubby-cheeked boy of about twelve. In my opinion, a tattletale. The drawing was executed in a few precise, bold strokes. A very, very decent drawing. It suddenly occurred to me that I might be wrong, and that the person who had left all this mayhem behind him may not have been Lev Abalkin—it could actually have been some professional artist who had suffered some creative failure.

I picked up all the scattered paper, flipped the chair right side up, and sat down in it.

Again, it all looked rather odd. Someone had quickly and confidently covered the sheets of paper with drawings of faces—mostly children's faces—as well as Earth animals, buildings, landscapes, and even something resembling clouds. There were also several rough maps, carried out with the sure hand of a professional topographer, depicting groves, streams, swamps, and crossroads—and for some reason, there among the laconic topological symbols were two tiny human figures, sitting, lying down, and running, and also tiny images of animals—either wolves, or dogs, or deer, or moose, and for some reason, some of these had been crossed out.

I couldn't understand any of this—at any rate, it didn't match the mayhem in the room or the image of a staff officer of the Empire who hadn't yet undergone reconditioning. One of the pieces of paper contained an excellent portrait of Maya Glumova, and I was amazed by the expression of either bewilderment or dismay very skillfully captured on this smiling and overall cheerful face. There was also a caricature of his teacher, Sergei Pavlovich Fedoseyev, and a masterful one at that: this was probably exactly what Sergei Pavlovich had looked like a quarter century ago. When I saw this caricature, something finally clicked, and I realized what the buildings in the drawings had been—a quarter century ago, this was the typical architectural style of Eurasian boarding schools . . . These were quick, accurate, confident drawings that had been almost immediately torn up, crumpled, and thrown away.

I put away the pieces of paper and looked around the living room again. A light blue cloth lying under the table caught my attention. I picked it up. It was a wrinkled and torn woman's handkerchief. Of course, I immediately remembered the short story by Akutagawa, and I imagined Maya Toivovna sitting in this exact same chair in front of Lev Abalkin, looking at him and listening to him, a smile hovering on her lips that concealed the merest hint of either bewilderment or dismay, while her hands beneath the table ruthlessly pulled apart and ripped her handkerchief . . .

I had a clear image of Maya Glumova, but I had no idea what she was seeing and hearing. The drawings were the stumbling block. If it were not for the drawings, it would have been easy to imagine a typical staff officer of the Empire sitting on this destroyed couch, fresh from the barracks and savoring his well-deserved vacation. But I couldn't get away from the drawings, and they concealed something very important, very complicated, and very deep . . .

There was nothing more for me to do here. I reached for the videophone and dialed Excellentz's number.

JUNE 2, '78

EXCELLENTZ'S UNEXPECTED REACTION

He heard me out without a single interruption, which was a fairly bad sign in and of itself. I tried to console myself with the possibility that he wasn't unhappy with me but with some other circumstances that had nothing to do with me. However, having heard me out to the end, he said morosely, "Your visit to Glumova was almost a complete waste."

"My hands were tied by the cover story," I said coldly.

He didn't argue. "What do you plan to do next?" he asked.

"I don't think he'll come back here."

"I don't think so, either. What about Glumova?"

"It's hard for me to say. Or rather, I can't say anything at all. I don't understand anything. But there's a chance, of course."

"In your opinion, why did he meet with her at all?"

"That's just what I don't understand, Excellentz. As far as I can tell, they met here for love and nostalgia. Except the love wasn't exactly love and the nostalgia wasn't just nostalgia. Otherwise, Glumova wouldn't have reacted like that. Of course, if he got really drunk, he could have offended her in some way . . . Especially when you remember how strange their childhood relationship had been . . ."

"Don't exaggerate," grumbled Excellentz. "Many years have passed since they were children. Let me put it like this: If he sent for her again or came to her himself, would she take him back?"

"I don't know," I said. "I would guess yes. He still means a lot to her. She wouldn't have been in a state of such despair over a man she was indifferent to."

"Very poetic," Excellentz grumbled, then suddenly barked: "You should have found out why he wanted to see her! What they talked about! What he told her!"

I got angry. "I couldn't do any of that!" I said. "She was hysterical, and when she came to, there was an idiot of a journalist sitting in front of her, his hide an inch thick—"

He interrupted me. "You'll have to see her again."

"Then let me change the cover story!"

"What do you propose?"

"Here's one possibility. I'm from COMCON. There was a tragedy on a certain planet. Lev Abalkin was a witness. But he was so traumatized by this tragedy that he fled to Earth and is now avoiding everybody and everything . . . He's very unwell—on the verge of a nervous breakdown. We need to find him in order to find out what happened."

Excellentz was silent; my proposal clearly wasn't to his taste. I spent some time staring at the irritated speckled pate taking up the whole screen, then I spoke again, controlling myself: "You have to understand, Excellentz—we can't keep repeating the same lies. She already figured out that my visit wasn't a coincidence. I convinced her otherwise, I think, but if I appear in the same role again, it will clearly defy common sense! Either she believed that I was a journalist, in which case she'll have nothing to say to me and will simply send that thick-skinned idiot to hell, or she didn't believe me, in which case she'll do the same thing, only more so. But if I'm a COMCON representative, then I have the right to ask her questions, and I'll do my best to make sure she answers them."

I thought this all sounded fairly logical. In any case, I couldn't think of anything else. And besides, I wasn't willing to visit her in the character of the idiot journalist again. At the end of the day, it was up to Excellentz to decide whether he cared more about finding a man or keeping the reason for the search secret.

He asked me without looking up, "Why did you need to go to the museum in the morning?"

I was surprised. "What do you mean, why? To talk to Glumova."

He slowly looked up, and then I saw his eyes. His pupils were the size of his irises. I physically recoiled. It was obvious that I had said something terrible. I started babbling like a schoolboy: "But that's where she works . . . Where else could I talk to her? I didn't find her at home . . ."

"Glumova works at the Museum of Extraterrestrial Cultures?" he asked, carefully enunciating the words.

"Yes, yes, what's wrong?"

"In the Special Department for Artifacts of Unknown Purpose," he said quietly. I couldn't tell whether this was a question or a statement. And then a chill ran down my spine—I saw the left corner of his thin-lipped mouth begin to creep left and down.

"Yes," I said in a whisper.

I could no longer see his eyes. His shiny bald pate was taking up the entire screen again.

"Excellentz . . ."

"Quiet!" he barked. And we were both silent for a while.

"All right," he said at last in his usual voice. "Go home. Stay at home and don't go out. I may need you at any moment. But it'll most likely be at night. How long will it take you to come back?"

"Two and a half hours."

"Why so long?"

"I still have to swim across the lake."

"Fine. Report to me when you're back. And hurry."

And the screen went blank.

FROM LEV ABALKIN'S REPORT

The rain is coming down harder again and the fog is getting even thicker, making it almost impossible to make out the buildings along both sides of the street from the center of the road. The experts panic—it seems to them that this time, the bio-optical converters are failing. I calm them down. Having calmed down, they become brazen and start pestering me to turn the fog lamp on. I turn on the lamp. The experts are temporarily jubilant, until Puppen sits on his tail in the middle of the road and declares that he will not take another step until they get rid of this stupid rainbow, which is making his ears hurt and the skin between his fingers itch. He, Puppen, can see perfectly well without these ridiculous lamps, and if the experts can't see something, that doesn't matter—they don't need to see anything, anyway. Let them do something useful instead, like, say, prepare Puppen's oatmeal and bean chowder for his return. There's an outburst of indignation. As a matter of fact, the experts are a bit afraid of Puppen. Any earthling who meets a bighead sooner or later becomes a bit afraid of him. But at the same time, paradoxical as it may seem, that very same earthling isn't able to treat a bighead as something other than a big talking dog (a wonder of zoopsychology, a circus sideshow, etc. . . .).

One of the experts is imprudent enough to warn Puppen that if he digs his heels in, he may have to go without his supper. Puppen raises his voice. It turns out that he, Puppen, has managed perfectly well without experts his whole life. What's more, we were having a particularly good time out here precisely when we could neither see nor hear the experts. As for the specific expert who seems to have his eye on his, Puppen's, oatmeal and bean chowder . . . And so on and so forth.

I'm standing in the rain, which is coming down harder and harder, listening to this expert-and-bean gibberish, and I can't manage to shake off some kind of deep torpor. It keeps seeming to me that I'm attending an extremely silly theatrical production without beginning or end, in which all the characters have forgotten their lines—and now all the actors are feverishly ad-libbing in the forlorn hope that this gets them through. Someone has put on this production just for me, to keep me rooted to the spot as long as possible, to keep me from taking a single step, and meanwhile, someone behind the scenes is hurriedly trying to make it clear to me that I can't do anything, that everything is pointless, and that I should just go home . . .

I make an immense effort, pull myself together, and turn off the damn lamp. Puppen breaks off in the middle of a long, carefully crafted insult and continues forward as if nothing had happened. I follow, listening to Vanderhuze restore order on board: "Shame on you! . . . Interfering with the field team! . . . I'll kick you out of the cockpit! . . . On your ass! . . . You should know better!"

"Having some fun?" I ask Puppen quietly.

He only glances sideways at me with one protuberant eye.

"You're a troublemaker," I say. "All you bigheads are troublemakers and agitators."

"It's wet," Puppen responds irrelevantly. "Frogs everywhere. No room to walk . . . More trucks up ahead," he informs me.

There's a distinct, sharp stink of wet iron wafting out of the fog, and a minute later, we find ourselves in the middle of a vast disorganized herd of miscellaneous vehicles.

We see ordinary trucks, and caravan trucks, and giant platform trucks, and teardrop-shaped passenger cars, and even self-propelled monsters with eight wheels of human height. They are carelessly parked in the middle of the street and on the sidewalks—helter-skelter, randomly, bumper to bumper, sometimes even on top of one another. They are impossibly rusty and dilapidated, disintegrating at the slightest touch. We can no longer walk quickly, because we have to go around them, squeeze between them, and climb over them, and they are all filled with people's belongings, and these belongings have also long since rotted, decayed, and rusted beyond all recognition . . .

Somewhere at the edge of my consciousness, the chastened experts are mumbling plaintively and Vanderhuze is droning on anxiously, but I'm in no mood to pay attention to them. I curse and pull my foot out of a stinking quagmire of partially decayed rags, then I curse and immediately plummet into some huge wooden box, in which naked pink baby rats nestled in heaps of musty paper are squeaking frantically, then I break down some decayed wooden wall with my shoulder and roll out into the street, right into a puddle, scattering the frogs . . . Broken glass crunches and creaks underneath our feet, some round objects—either tin cans or ball bearings—roll away from us in different directions, a piece of seemingly solid nickel-plated iron disintegrates into dust when I try to rest a hand on it, and one time, the side of a gigantic caravan truck—as big as an international cargo container—suddenly splits all the way across by itself with a groan of decay, dumping out rivers of unrecognizable garbage shrouded in thick clouds of disgusting, stinking dust . . .

And then suddenly this repulsive labyrinth ends.

Actually, we're still surrounded by vehicles, hundreds of them, but they are parked in relative order on the sidewalks and along the curbs, and the middle of the street is now completely empty.

I look at Puppen. Puppen is furiously shaking himself off, scratching himself with all four paws at once, licking his back and spitting—then he sputters out some curses and again begins to shake off, scratch, and lick.

Vanderhuze anxiously inquires why we went off course and asks what that warehouse was. I explain that there was no warehouse. We discuss the following: If these are the signs of an evacuation, then why was the native population being evacuated from the outskirts into the center of the city?

"I'm not going back that way," Puppen announces, and furiously smashes a frog that was trying to sneak past us into the pavement.

At 2:00 PM, headquarters circulates its first summary report. There was an ecological disaster, but the civilization perished in some other way. The population disappeared overnight, so to speak, but it neither exterminated itself in wars nor evacuated itself into space—they didn't have the technology for that, and anyway, the planet looks like a landfill rather than a cemetery. The pitiful remnants of the native population are languishing in the countryside, halfheartedly working the land. They have no culture whatsoever, but they do excel at operating repeater rifles. The upshot for me and Puppen is that the city ought to be completely empty. I'm skeptical about this conclusion. So is Puppen.

The street gets wider, the houses and cars on the sides of the road recede entirely into the fog, and I feel an open space in front of me. After another few steps, a square, squat silhouette materializes from the fog. This is another armored vehicle—it's exactly like the one under the collapsed wall, but this one was abandoned a long, long time ago, has sagged under its own weight, and seems to have grown into the asphalt. All of its hatches are wide open. Two short machine gun barrels, which must have once pointed menacingly at anyone who entered the square, are now drooping dejectedly, lazily oozing rusty water droplets onto the windshield. I mechanically give the open side door a shove as we pass by, but it's rusted tightly in place.

I can't see anything in front of me. There's something special about the fog in this square—it's unnaturally dense, as if it's been sitting here for many, many years, and in that time has clumped, curdled like milk, and sagged under its own weight.

"Watch your step!" Puppen orders suddenly.

I look down but I don't see anything. However, it suddenly dawns on me that instead of asphalt, there's something soft, springy, and slimy beneath my feet—it feels like a thick, wet carpet. I crouch down.

"You can turn on your fog lamp," grumbles Puppen.

But I can already see without any lamp that the asphalt here is almost completely covered with some sort of disgusting thick crust—a compressed, moist mass overgrown with a profusion of colorful mold. I take out a knife and jab it into this crust, then I pry off a piece that looks like either a scrap of fabric or a fragment of a strap, and then something round and muddy green (a button? a buckle?) peeks out in the gap, and I can see either wires or springs slowly uncoiling in the same place . . . .

"They all walked here," says Puppen in a strange tone of voice.

I get up and keep walking along the soft, slippery surface. I try to tame my imagination, but I no longer succeed. They all walked here, along this road, abandoning their now unneeded cars and trucks—millions poured in from the avenue into this square, and the human stream flowed around the armored vehicle, and they dropped the few things they had attempted to bring, they stumbled and dropped them, and maybe they even fell down themselves, and then they were unable to get back up, and everything that fell was trampled, trampled by millions of feet. And for some reason, I imagine all this happening at night—the mass of humans is illuminated by a dim, lifeless light, and it's silent, like in a dream . . .

"A pit," says Puppen.

I turn on the fog lamp. There's no pit.

As far as the light can reach, the square is flat and smooth and glowing with countless faint dots of bioluminescent mold—except for a damp black rectangle of bare asphalt two feet in front of us, about fifty by a hundred feet in size. It looks as if someone had carefully cut it out of this moldy, shimmering carpet.

"Stairs," says Puppen, as though in despair. "Full of holes! Deep stairs! I can't see . . ."

My skin crawls: I've never heard Puppen speak in such a strange voice before. I lower my hand without looking, and my fingers come to rest on the large bulbous head, and I feel the nervous trembling of the triangular ear. The fearless Puppen is afraid. The fearless Puppen is pressing against my leg in exactly the same way as his ancestors had pressed against the legs of their masters when they sensed something unfamiliar and dangerous outside the cave . . .

"There's no bottom," he says in despair. "I don't know how to understand. There's always a bottom. They all left through there, but there's no bottom, and no one came back . . . Do we have to go there?"

I crouch down and hug him around the neck. "I don't see a pit," I say in the bighead tongue. "I only see a smooth rectangle of asphalt."

Puppen is breathing hard. All of his muscles are tense, and he is pressing closer and closer to me.

"You can't see it," he says. "You don't know how. There are four staircases, and the stairs are full of holes. Worn down. Shiny. They go deeper and deeper. They go nowhere. I don't want to go there. Don't order me to."

"Buddy," I say. "What's wrong? How could I order you to do anything?"

"Don't ask me to," he says. "Don't tell me to. Don't suggest it."

"We're going to leave now," I say.

"Yes. Quick!"

I dictate the report. Vanderhuze has already connected my channel to headquarters, and by the time I'm finished, the entire expedition has been briefed. There's a babel of voices. People suggest hypotheses and propose measures. It's loud. Puppen is slowly recovering—he's glancing sideways with a yellow eye

and constantly licking himself. Finally, Komov himself decides
to step in. The babel ceases. We're ordered to continue, and we
gladly obey.

We go around the terrible rectangle, cross the square, pass
the second armored vehicle blockading the avenue from the other
side, and then we again find ourselves between two rows of abandoned vehicles. Puppen is again briskly trotting up ahead, and
he's again energetic, grumpy, and arrogant. I chuckle to myself,
thinking that in his place I would now be deeply embarrassed
about my fit of unmanageable, childish panic in the square. But
that's not the kind of thing that bothers Puppen. Yes, he felt fear
and was unable to hide it, but he doesn't see anything shameful
or embarrassing about that.

He's now thinking out loud: "They all went underground. If
there was a bottom, I'd be telling you that they now live deep
underground where we can't hear them. But there's no bottom.
I don't understand where they could live down there. I don't
understand why there's no bottom and how that could be."

"Try to explain it," I tell him. "This is very important."

But Puppen can't explain it. It's very frightening, he insists.
Planets are round, he says, and this planet is also round, I saw
that myself, but over there, in that square, it's not at all round.
Over there, it is like a plate. And the plate has a hole in it. And
this hole goes from an emptiness where we are, straight into
another emptiness, where we aren't.

"And why didn't I see this hole?"

"Because it's sealed. You don't know how. It's sealed against
ones like you, not ones like me . . ."

Then he suddenly informs me that there's danger again. Typical, moderate danger. There hadn't been any danger at all for a
long time, and now it's back.

A minute later, a third-story balcony falls down from the
facade of a building to the right. I quickly ask Puppen whether
the danger has decreased. Without hesitation, he answers that it
has, but not much. I want to ask him which direction it's coming

from, but then a jet of dense air hits me in the back, my ears begin to ring, and Puppen's fur stands on end.

Something like a small hurricane sweeps through the avenue. It's hot and smells like iron. A few more balconies and cornices crash down on both sides of the street. The wind tears a roof off a long, squat house, and this roof—old, leaky, and crumbling—floats over the pavement, slowly spinning and breaking into pieces, then disappears in a cloud of foul yellow dust.

"What's going on over there?" wails Vanderhuze.

"Some kind of wind," I respond through gritted teeth.

A new gust of wind forces me to run forward against my will. This is kind of humiliating.

"Abalkin! Puppen!" thunders Komov. "Stay in the center of the street! Keep away from the walls! I'm flushing out the square and things may fall down."

And for the third time, a short, hot hurricane sweeps along the avenue, just as Puppen is trying to position himself with his nose to the wind. He's knocked off his feet and dragged along the pavement in the embarrassing company of some careless rat.

"Are you done?" he asks irritably when the hurricane is over. He doesn't even try to get back on his feet.

"I'm done," says Komov. "You may continue."

"Thank you very much," says Puppen, with as much venom as the most venomous snake.

I hear someone giggling on the air, unable to help himself. Sounds like Vanderhuze.

"My apologies," says Komov. "I needed to drive away the fog."

In response, Puppen hurls the longest and most intricate curse in the bighead tongue at him, gets up, violently shakes himself off, then suddenly freezes in an uncomfortable position. "Lev," he says. "The danger's gone. Completely. It blew away."

"Thank goodness for small mercies," I say.

Some information from Espada. An extremely emotional description of the Chief Gattauch. I can see him as if he were here in front of me: an unimaginably dirty, smelly, lichen-covered old man, looking about two hundred years old but claiming that he's twenty-one, constantly wheezing, coughing, clearing his throat, and blowing his nose. He keeps a repeater rifle on his knees throughout the conversation, and he occasionally fires it into the air above Espada's head. He doesn't want to answer questions but instead keeps attempting to ask questions of his own, and he listens to the answers with ostentatious inattention, publicly declaring every second answer to be a lie . . .

The avenue goes through another square. Actually, this isn't exactly a square—there's just a semicircular pocket park on the right side of the street, and behind it a long yellow building with a concave facade lined with decorative columns. The facade is yellow, and the bushes in the park are also a kind of muted pre-autumn yellow, and that's why I don't immediately notice another "glass" standing in the middle of park.

This time it's intact and looks shiny and brand new, as if someone had placed it between these yellow bushes this very morning—a seven-foot-tall cylinder three feet in diameter, made from a translucent, amber-like material. It's standing completely upright and its oval door is tightly shut.

There's a burst of enthusiasm aboard Vanderhuze's ship, whereas Puppen uses this as another opportunity to demonstrate his indifference and even contempt for these objects, which "do not interest his people": he immediately begins to scratch himself with his rear end to the glass.

I walk around the glass, grab the protrusion on the oval door with two fingers, and peer inside. One glance is plenty—in there, taking up the entirety of the glass with its articulated legs, holding its three-foot-long spiked claws in front of it, sits a gigantic crawspider from Pandora in all its glory, grimly goggling at me with its two rows of olive-green eyes.

It isn't fear that saves me, but a reflexive reaction to something completely unexpected. In the blink of an eye, I'm bracing my shoulder against the closed door, and my feet are braced against the ground, and I'm bathed in sweat, and I'm shaking like a leaf.

And Puppen is already here, ready for an immediate, fierce battle—he's swaying back and forth on spring-loaded legs, expectantly moving his bulbous head from side to side. His dazzling white teeth gleam wetly in the corners of his mouth. This only lasts for a few seconds, then he peevishly inquires, "What's the matter? Who upset you?"

I fumble for the handle of my scorcher, peel myself away from the door by force of will, and start to back away, holding my scorcher at the ready.

Puppen retreats with me, getting more and more annoyed. "I asked you a question!" he declares indignantly.

"Don't tell me," I say through gritted teeth, "you don't smell it yet."

"Where? In that booth? There's nothing in there!"

Vanderhuze and the experts are droning anxiously in my ear. I'm not listening to them. I know myself that I could, for example, prop the door closed with a log—if I could find one—or that I could incinerate it whole with my scorcher. I keep backing away without taking my eyes off its door.

"There's nothing in there!" Puppen repeats insistently. "And there's no one in there. It's been empty for years. Do you want me to open the door and show you that there's nothing in there?"

"No," I say, somehow managing to control my vocal cords. "Let's get out of here."

"Let me just open the door—"

"Puppen," I say. "You're wrong."

"My people are never wrong. I'm going. You'll see."

"You're wrong!" I bark. "If you don't come with me this instant, you aren't my friend and you don't give a damn about me!"

I turn abruptly on my heel (the scorcher is in my lowered hand, the safety is off, and it's set on continuous discharge) and walk away. My back feels huge, the entire width of the avenue, and it's completely unprotected.

Puppen, looking extremely disgruntled and ill-tempered, trots behind me to the left, his paws pitter-pattering on the sidewalk.

He's grumbling and picking fights. And when we're two hundred paces away, when I've almost entirely calmed down and am starting to think about how to make peace, Puppen suddenly disappears. There's only the sound of claws scraping along the pavement and then he's gone. And now he's right by the booth, and it's too late to rush after the idiot and drag him away by his hind legs, and my scorcher is now completely useless, and the damned bighead cracks open the door and looks into the booth for a very long, an infinitely long time . . .

Then, without having ever made a sound, he closes the door and returns. A humiliated Puppen. A crushed Puppen. A Puppen who unequivocally admits his complete uselessness and is therefore prepared to endure any ensuing treatment. He comes back to my leg and sits down next to me, dejectedly hanging his head. We're silent. I avoid looking at him. I look at the glass, feeling the trickles of sweat on my temples drying up and tightening my skin, and noticing the agonizing tremors draining out of my muscles and giving way to a dreary, lingering pain. What I most want right now is to hiss *You bastard!* at him, expel a deep, shuddering breath, and box the ears of this dejected, idiotic, stubborn, brainless bulbous head as hard as I can. But I only say, "We got lucky. For some reason, they don't attack here."

A message from headquarters. They speculate that "Puppen's rectangle" is an entrance to an interdimensional tunnel that was used to evacuate the population of the planet. Presumably by the Wanderers . . .

We're walking through an unusually empty region. There are no living things here; even the mosquitoes have disappeared. I rather dislike this, but Puppen doesn't show any signs of anxiety.

"This time you got here too late," he grumbles.

"Yes, it looks like it," I readily reply.

This is the first time Puppen has spoken since the crawspider incident. He seems to be in the mood to chat about something unrelated. This is rare for him.

"The Wanderers," he grumbles. "I keep hearing: the Wanderers, the Wanderers . . . Do you know nothing about them?"

"Very little. We know that they are a supercivilization and that they are much more powerful than we are. We infer that they aren't humanoid. We infer that they're familiar with our entire galaxy and have been for a very long time. We also infer that they don't have a home—in our or your understanding of this word. That's why we call them the Wanderers."

"Would humans like to meet them?"

"What can I say? . . . Komov would give his right hand to do so. Whereas I, personally, would prefer to never meet them."

"Are you afraid of them?"

I don't want to discuss this. Especially right now. "You know, Puppen," I say, "that's a longer conversation. Keep your eyes peeled—I've noticed you've become a bit absentminded."

"I'm keeping them peeled. Everything is fine."

"Have you noticed that all the living things are gone?"

"That's because there are often people here."

"Oh yeah?" I reply. "That's very reassuring . . ."

"There are none here now. Almost."

We're coming to the end of District 42 and approaching an intersection. Puppen suddenly announces, "There's a man around the corner. He's all alone."

It's a decrepit old man in a long black coat down to his feet and a fur hat with ear flaps tied under a dirty, tousled beard, wearing cheerful bright yellow gloves and silly-looking cloth-top boots. He's moving with extreme difficulty, barely managing to drag his feet. He's about sixty feet away, but even at this distance, you can clearly hear that he's wheezing, breathing heavily, and occasionally groaning from the strain.

He's filling up a cart with tall, thin wheels that looks like a stroller. He shuffles through a broken shop window, disappears for a long time, and then clambers out at the same slow way, holding on to the wall with one hand and using the other bent and gnarled hand to clutch two or three brightly labeled cans to his chest. Every time he gets sufficiently close to his cart, he collapses onto a three-legged folding chair, sits still for a while and rests, and then starts just as slowly and carefully transferring the cans from his bent hand into the cart. Then he takes another rest, as if taking a nap sitting down, and he again rises to his trembling feet and heads toward the shop window—a long black figure bent almost in half.

We're standing on the corner, almost not bothering to conceal ourselves, because it's obvious to us that the old man can't see or hear anything around him. According to Puppen, he's all alone here; there is no one else around, unless they're maybe very far way. I have no desire whatsoever to make contact with him, but it looks like we'll have to, if only to help with those cans. But I'm afraid to scare him. I ask Vanderhuze to show him to Espada, so that Espada can determine what kind of person he is—*sorcerer, soldier,* or *human.*

The old man has unloaded his tenth armful of cans and is again resting, slumping over in the three-legged chair. His head is jiggling and is drooping closer and closer to his chest. It looks as if he's falling asleep.

"I've never seen anything like this," declares Espada. "Talk to him, Lev."

"He's so old," Vanderhuze says doubtfully.

"He's going to die," grumbles Puppen.

"Exactly," I say. "Especially if I appear before him in this rainbow robe—"

I don't have time to finish the thought. The old man suddenly jerks forward, then softly topples sideways onto the sidewalk.

"It's over," says Puppen. "Go take a look if you're interested."

The old man is dead—he's not breathing, and we can't feel his pulse. He seems to have had a massive heart attack on top of complete bodily depletion. He didn't die from hunger, however. It's just that he's impossibly, incredibly decrepit. I'm on my knees, staring into his greenish-white face—gaunt, with bristly gray eyebrows, a half-open toothless mouth, and sunken cheeks. A very human face. A face that wouldn't look out of place on Earth. The first normal person in this city. And he's dead. And I can't do anything about it, because I only have field equipment with me.

I inject him with two vials of necrophage and tell Vanderhuze to send in the medics. I don't plan to stay here. There's no point. He won't speak. And if he does speak, then it won't be anytime soon. Before I leave, I stand over him for another minute, look at the cart half full of cans and at his overturned chair, and I think about the fact that this old man probably dragged this chair with him everywhere and constantly sat down on it to rest . . .

At about 6 PM, it starts to get dark. According to my calculations, we still have two hours left until the end of the route, and I suggest to Puppen that we rest and eat. Puppen isn't in need of rest, but as usual, he won't pass up the chance for a snack.

We sit down on the edge of a large empty fountain, in the shadow of some mythological winged monster, and I open the food packets. The walls of abandoned houses glow dimly around us, there's a dead silence, and it's nice to think about the fact that the dozens of miles we've traversed are no longer dead and empty but are filled with people working.

Puppen never talks while he's eating, but when he's full, he likes to chat. "That old man," he says, meticulously licking a paw clean, "did they really bring him back to life?"

"Yes."

"He's alive again, he's walking and talking?"

"I doubt he's talking, much less walking, but he's alive."

"Too bad," grumbles Puppen.

"Too bad?"

"Yes. It's too bad he's not talking. It'd be interesting to know what's over *there* . . ."

"Where?"

"Where he went when he became dead."

I chuckle. "You think there's something there?"

"There must be. I have to go somewhere when I'm gone."

"Where does the electrical current go when it's turned off?" I ask.

"I could never understand that," admits Puppen. "But it's not exactly the same thing. You're right that I don't know where the electrical current goes when it's turned off. But I also don't know where it comes from when it's turned on. But I do know and understand where I come from."

"And where were you when you weren't here yet?" I ask craftily.

But this doesn't stump Puppen. "I was in the blood of my parents. And before that, in the blood of the parents of my parents."

"So when you're not here, you'll be in the blood of your children."

"And if I don't have children?"

"Then you'll be in the ground, in the grass, in the trees . . ."

"That's not true! Only my body will be in the grass and in the trees. But where will I be myself?"

"It was your body in the blood of your parents, too—not you yourself. After all, you don't remember what it felt like to be in the blood of your parents."

"What do you mean, I don't remember?" Puppen replies in surprise. "I remember a lot!"

"Oh, right, you do . . ." I mutter, vanquished. "You have genetic memories . . ."

"Call it whatever you like," grumbles Puppen. "But I really don't understand where I'd go if I died right now. I don't have children, after all."

I decide to end this argument. It's clear to me that I'll never be able to prove to Puppen that there's nothing *there*. So I silently roll up my food packet, put it away in my backpack, and get more comfortable, stretching my legs.

Puppen meticulously licks another paw clean, gets the fur on his cheeks into perfect order, and starts talking again. "You surprise me, Lev," he announces. "All of you surprise me. Aren't you tired of being here?"

"We're working," I contradict him lazily.

"Why do pointless work?"

"Why is it pointless? You can see yourself how much we've learned in a single day."

"That's exactly what I'm asking: Why learn pointless things? What are you going to do with it? You keep learning and learning, and you don't do anything with it."

"Do you have an example in mind?" I ask.

Puppen is a champion debater. He just attained one victory and he's now clearly gunning for another one. "For example, the bottomless pit I found. What could someone want a bottomless pit for?"

"It's not exactly a pit," I say. "It's more like a door into another world."

"Can you go through this door?" inquires Puppen.

"No," I admit. "We can't."

"What's the point of a door that you can't go through?"

"We can't go through it today, but we may be able to tomorrow."

"Tomorrow?"

"Figuratively speaking. The day after tomorrow. In a year . . ."

"Another world, another world . . ." grumbles Puppen. "Isn't there enough room in this one for you?"

"What can I say? . . . I guess our imaginations need more room."

"Sure they do!" Puppen says venomously. "Except that as soon as you made it to another world, you'd immediately begin to remake it in the image of your own. And your imaginations would again run out of room, and then you'd look for another world, and you'd begin to remake that one, too."

He abruptly ends this philippic, and at the very same moment I sense the presence of a stranger. Here. Nearby. Two steps away. Next to the pedestal with the mythological monster.

This is a completely ordinary local—as far as I can tell, belonging to the *human* category—a strong, well-built man wearing canvas pants and a canvas jacket over bare skin, with a repeater rifle on a sling around his neck. A mop of messy hair is falling over his eyes, but his cheeks and chin are smoothly shaven. He's standing completely still near the pedestal—only his eyes are slowly moving back and forth between me and Puppen. Apparently, he sees no less well in the dark than we do. I can't understand how he managed sneak up on us without making any noise or otherwise alerting us.

I discreetly reach behind my back and flip the translator's lingan on.

"Come here and have a seat—we're friends," I mouth soundlessly. Half a second later, the lingan emits soft and rather appealing guttural sounds.

The stranger flinches and takes a step back.

"Don't be afraid," I say. "What's your name? My name is Lev, and his name is Puppen. We aren't enemies. We want to talk to you."

No, it's not working. The stranger takes another step back and partially conceals himself behind the pedestal. His face is still expressionless, and I can't even tell whether he understands what's being said to him.

"We have good food." I don't give up. "Maybe you are hungry or thirsty? Have a seat with us, and I'll be happy to share with you—"

It suddenly occurs to me that this man must find the words *we* and *us* rather strange, and I hastily switch to the singular. But this doesn't help. He disappears behind the pedestal, and now I can neither see nor hear him.

"He's leaving," grumbles Puppen.

And I immediately see the man again—he's crossing the street, walking completely silently and taking long, gliding steps. He reaches the sidewalk on the opposite side of the street, then he disappears into an alley without looking back once.

JUNE 2, '78

LEV ABALKIN FIRSTHAND

At about 6 PM, Andrei and Sandro barged in on me unannounced. I put the folder into my desk and immediately told them sternly that I wouldn't countenance any work-related conversations, as they now answered to Claudius and not to me. And what's more, I was busy.

They began plaintively whining that they hadn't come because of work, that they had missed me, and that I was being unfair. Whatever else you might say about them, they are excellent whiners. I softened. We started in on my liquor, and for a while we happily discussed my cacti. Then I suddenly discovered that, completely unbeknownst to me, we were no longer discussing cacti but Claudius, and this was at least somewhat logical, since Claudius is so prickly and lumpy that he even reminds me of a cactus. However, before I even knew it, these two young provocateurs very cleverly and naturally changed the subject to bioreactors and Captain Nemo.

Pretending to play along, I let them get really excited, and then, at the climactic moment, when they had already decided that their boss was going to be a soft touch, I kindly suggested that they get the hell out of here. And I really would have kicked them out, because I had gotten very angry both at them and at myself, but then Alena showed up, also unannounced. It's fate, I thought, and I headed to the kitchen. Either way, it was already supper time, and even young provocateurs know that they aren't supposed to talk shop in front of others.

It turned out to be a very pleasant supper. The provocateurs, forgetting about everything in the world, strutted before Alena. When she'd cut them down to size, I started to strut myself, just to maintain the mood. This peacock parade ended with a great debate: What should we do next? Sandro demanded that we go see the Octopi, and that we go right now, because they play the best things at the very beginning. Andrei got as worked up as a real music critic; his attacks on the Octopi were passionate and astonishingly baseless, and his theory of modern music was striking in its originality and boiled down to the fact that this was the perfect night to try sailing his new yacht, the *Philosopher*. I was for charades or, at the very most, forfeits. Alena, on the other hand, having realized that I wasn't going anywhere and was busy anyway, got upset and began to make mischief. "Dump the Octopi in the river!" she demanded. "Man the tip-topsails! Let's make some noise!" And so on and so forth.

At the very height of this discussion, at 7:33 PM, we heard the buzzing of the videophone. Andrei, who was sitting closest to the device, jabbed a finger into the button. The screen lit up, but it wasn't showing an image. And I couldn't hear anything, either, because Sandro was wailing, *"Oh fair isles, fair isles!"* at the top of his lungs, at the same time performing ridiculous contortions in an attempt to imitate the inimitable B. Tuareg, while Alena, who had gone completely off the deep end, was facing off against him with the Song Without Words by Glière (or perhaps not Glière).

"Shush!" I barked, making my way to the videophone.

It became a bit quieter, but the device was still silent, its empty screen shimmering. As it was unlikely to be Excellentz, I calmed down. "Please wait, I'll take this somewhere else," I said into the bluish shimmer.

When I got to my study, I put the videophone on the desk, collapsed into a chair, and said, "There, that's better . . . But just so you know, I can't see you."

"I'm sorry, I forgot . . ." said a deep male voice, and a face appeared on the screen—a narrow, extremely pale face, with deep lines from nose to chin. A low, wide forehead, large deep-set eyes, and straight black hair down to his shoulders.

The interesting thing is that I immediately realized I knew him, but I didn't immediately realize who it was.

"Hello, Mak," he said. "Do you recognize me?"

I needed a few seconds to collect myself. I was completely unprepared for this. "Wait, wait . . ." I stalled, feverishly trying to figure out how I was supposed to behave.

"Lev Abalkin," he reminded me. "Remember? Saraksh, the Blue Serpent—"

"My God!" cried journalist Kammerer, formerly Mak Sim, Earth resident on Saraksh. "Lyova! And they told me you weren't on Earth and that they didn't know when you'd be back . . . Or are you still over there?"

He was smiling: "No, I'm back . . . But I'm interrupting you, I think?"

"You're very welcome to interrupt me!" said journalist Kammerer earnestly. This wasn't the same journalist Kammerer who had visited Maya Glumova—it was more like the one who had visited his teacher. "I need you! After all, I'm writing a book about bigheads!"

"Yes, I know," he cut me off. "That's exactly why I'm calling you. But, Mak, it's been a long time since I've worked with bigheads."

"That doesn't matter," objected journalist Kammerer. "What matters is that you were the first to work with them."

"Actually, you were the first."

"No. All I did was find them. Anyway, I've already written about myself. And I've picked out material on Komov's recent projects. So, as you can see, I have a prologue and an epilogue, I'm only missing a little thing—the main body . . . Listen, Lyova, we have to meet. How long are you planning to be on Earth?"

"Not too long," he said. "But we definitely have to meet. Not today, though. I—"

"Frankly, today doesn't work for me, either," broke in journalist Kammerer. "How about tomorrow?"

He gazed at me silently for a while. I suddenly realized that I couldn't make out the color of his eyes—they were set so deeply beneath his overhanging eyebrows.

"Amazing," he said. "You haven't changed at all. How about me?"

"Honestly?" asked journalist Kammerer, to say something.

Lev Abalkin smiled again. "Yes," he said. "It's been twenty years. And you know, Mak, when I look back, those were the happiest days of my life . . . My whole life ahead of me, so much to look forward to . . . And when I look back on that time, I think about how lucky I was to start out with bosses like Komov and like you, Mak."

"Now, now, Lev, don't exaggerate," said journalist Kammerer. "What did I have to do with it?"

"What do you mean, what did you have to do with it? Komov was in charge, Rawlingson and I did the legwork, but you were the one coordinating everything!"

Journalist Kammerer goggled at him. So did I, but I also became suspicious. "Now, Lev," said journalist Kammerer, "I see that you were too young, buddy, to understand a damn thing about our chain of command. The only thing I did for you back then was provide shelter, food, and transportation . . . And even those—"

"And you came up with ideas!" inserted Lev Abalkin.

"What ideas?"

"The expedition beyond the Blue Serpent—that was your idea!"

"Only in the sense that I infor—"

"See? That's thing one. And the idea that progressors should be working with bigheads instead of zoopsychologists—that's thing two!"

"Wait, Lev! That was Komov's idea! I didn't give a damn about any of you back then! I was dealing with an uprising in Pandeia! And the first large-scale assault landing by the Ocean Empire! You of all people must understand—My God! To be honest, I wasn't thinking about you at all at the time! Zef was the one responsible for you, Zef, not me! Remember the red-haired native?"

Lev Abalkin was laughing, baring his even white teeth.

"And wipe that grin off your face!" said journalist Kammerer angrily. "You're putting me in a very awkward position. This is ridiculous! No, no, I see it's way past time I wrote this book. I can't believe the stupid stories going around!"

"OK, OK, I'll stop," said Abalkin. "We'll have to continue this debate in person."

"Exactly," said journalist Kammerer. "Except there won't be a debate. There's nothing to debate. Let's do it like this. . ." Journalist Kammerer fiddled with the buttons of his desk pad. "Let's meet at my place at ten in the morning . . . Or maybe you'd rather—"

"I prefer my place," said Lev Abalkin.

"Then give me your address," ordered journalist Kammerer. He was still a bit piqued.

"The Osinushka Resort," said Lev Abalkin. "Cottage Six."

JUNE 2, '78

A FEW HYPOTHESES ABOUT
LEV ABALKIN'S INTENTIONS

I told Sandro and Andrei that they were at liberty. Completely officially. I had to assume an official expression and speak in an official tone—however, I managed this without difficulty, because I really wanted to be left alone with my thoughts.

Having instantly gauged my mood, Alena piped down and unquestioningly agreed not to enter my study and, in general, to act as a guardian of my peace. As far as I can tell, she has an absolutely incorrect impression of my work. For example, she is convinced that my work is dangerous. But she has an unshakeable grasp of some of the fundamentals. In particular, she knows that if I'm suddenly busy, it doesn't mean that I've been visited by inspiration or had a brilliant idea—it simply means that I've been given an urgent problem that requires an urgent solution.

I tweaked her ear and shut myself up in my study, leaving her to tidy up the living room.

How did he get my number? That's easy. I gave the number to his teacher. And besides, Maya Glumova could have told him about me. Therefore, either he talked to Maya Toivovna again, or he decided to see his teacher after all. In spite of everything. He's been out of touch for twenty years, and now he suddenly decides to visit. Why?

What was he trying to achieve by calling me? He may have called for sentimental reasons. Nostalgia about his first real job. His youth, the happiest time of his life. Hmm. Doubtful . . . Or the altruistic desire to help out a journalist (and the person who discovered his beloved bigheads) with his work, with a liberal dash of, say, wholesome ambition. Nonsense. Why would he then give me a fake address? Or maybe it's not fake? But if it's not fake, then he's not in hiding, which means that Excellentz got something wrong. . . Actually, how do we know that Lev Abalkin is in hiding?

I quickly loaded the informatorium, found the number, and called Cottage Six at the Osinushka Resort. No answer. As expected.

Okay, let's leave this for now. Moving on. What was the most important part of our conversation? By the way, one time, I almost let the cat out the bag. I could have bitten my tongue off. *You of all people must understand what an assault landing by Fleet Group C means!*

I wonder how you know about Fleet Group C, Mak, and more important, why you think I know anything about this? Of course, he wouldn't have said any of this, but he would have thought it and he would have figured everything out.

After such a mortifying blunder, there'd be nothing remaining for me but to actually go into journalism . . . All right, let's hope that he didn't notice anything. He didn't have the time to evaluate and analyze my every word, either. He was clearly trying to achieve something by calling me, and chances are he was ignoring everything else.

But what exactly was he trying to do? Why did he try to attribute his accomplishments—and Komov's, too—to me? And what's more, why did he do this point blank, right after saying hello . . . You might think that I'd really been telling tales, taking credit for his work, passing off fundamental ideas about bigheads as my own—and that he had found me out and was letting me know I was a piece of shit . . . His grin was certainly suggestive . . . But that's ridiculous! Only the narrowest of specialists currently know that I was the one to discover bigheads, and even they may have forgotten this fact due to its irrelevance . . .

This is all absurd, of course. But the fact remains that I just received a call from Lev Abalkin, who informed me that in his opinion, I, journalist Kammerer, was the founding father of big-head science and its leading light. Our conversation contained nothing else of significance. Everything else was empty pleasant-ries. Well, there was also the (probably) fake address at the end . . .

Of course, another possibility does suggest itself. It didn't mat-ter to him what we talked about. He said whatever nonsense came into his head, because he only called to take a look at me. He was told by his teacher or by Maya Glumova that a certain Maxim Kammerer was asking about him. "Oh yeah?" thinks Lev, who is in hiding. How very odd! I just came back to Earth and already a Maxim Kammerer is asking about me. Wait a minute, I know a Maxim Kammerer! What's this? A coincidence? Lev Abalkin doesn't believe in coincidences. Let's call this person and see if he is really Maxim Kammerer, formerly known as Mak Sim . . . And if it really is him, then let's see how he acts . . .

I felt that I had put my finger on it. He calls and turns off his video just in case. In case I'm *not* Maxim Kammerer. He sees me. Probably not without surprise, but at the same time with obvious relief. This is just your run-of-the-mill Maxim Kammerer, he has guests over, they are eating, drinking, and making merry, there's nothing at all suspicious about it. Well, might as well exchange some empty pleasantries, make an appointment, and sign off . . .

But! This is neither the whole truth nor nothing but the truth. There are two stumbling blocks. First of all, in this case, why did he talk to me at all? He could have watched and listened for a bit, made sure that I was really me, and successfully rung off. Wrong number, happens all the time. And that'd be the end of that.

And second, I wasn't born yesterday either. I could see that he wasn't merely talking to me. He was also observing my reactions. He wanted to make sure that I was me and that I would react to something he said in a specific way. He was saying deliberate nonsense and carefully monitoring my reactions to it . . . That's strange, too. Everyone reacts to deliberate nonsense in the same way. Therefore, either something's wrong with my logic, or . . . Or else from Abalkin's point of view, he wasn't saying nonsense at all. For instance, it could really be the case that for some completely unbeknownst-to-me reason, Abalkin actually thinks it's possible that I played a pivotal role in bighead research. He calls me to verify this, and my reaction convinces him that he's wrong.

That makes sense, but it's rather odd. What do bigheads have to do with it? Then again, come to think of it, bigheads really have played a fundamental role in Abalkin's life. Wait a minute!

If someone asked me to briefly summarize this man's biography, I would probably tell them the following: he liked working with bigheads, he wanted to work with bigheads more than anything in the world, he was already successfully working with bigheads, but for some reason, he wasn't allowed to work with bigheads . . . Damn it all, would it really be so surprising if he had finally run out of patience, given up on COMCON and Headquarters C, abandoned his military discipline, and come back to Earth to sort things out? If he'd come back to find out, once and for all, why he hadn't been allowed to do what he loves, who has been getting in his way his whole life, who he could hold responsible for it all—the collapse of his cherished plans, and his bitter lack of understanding, and the fifteen years he spent doing immeasurably difficult and unrewarding work . . . So he came back!

He came back and immediately ran across my name. And he remembered that I was in essence his supervisor the first time he worked with bigheads, and he wanted to find out whether I had been involved in this unprecedented, forced separation of a man from the work he loves. And he found out (using a simple trick) that no, I hadn't been involved—as it happens, I'd been dealing with invasions and hadn't been in the loop.

That's one possible way to explain our recent conversation. But only this conversation and nothing else. This hypothesis doesn't help explain either the strange business with Tristan or the strange business with Maya Glumova, nor does it shed any light on why Lev Abalkin has gone into hiding. For God's sake, if this hypothesis were correct, Lev Abalkin ought to be roaming the halls of COMCON and kicking his tormentors' asses, as befits a hothead with an artistic temperament . . . On the other hand, there was something to this, and it did give rise to certain practical questions. I decided to pose them to Excellentz; however, first I had to give Sergei Pavlovich Fedoseyev a call.

I checked the time: 9:51 PM. Let's hope that the old man hadn't gone to bed yet.

Indeed, it turned out that the old man hadn't gone to bed yet. He stared at journalist Kammerer from the screen with a certain bewilderment, as if he didn't recognize him. Journalist Kammerer apologized profusely for calling at such an inopportune hour. The apology was accepted, but the bewildered expression remained.

"I have a couple of questions for you, Sergei Pavlovich, that's all," said journalist Kammerer anxiously. "You saw Abalkin, right?"

"Yes. I gave him your number."

"I'm so sorry, Sergei Pavlovich . . . He just gave me a call . . . and he sounded a bit strange . . ." Journalist Kammerer was having a bit of trouble choosing his words. "I got the impression . . . I'm probably wrong, of course, but these things do happen . . . After all, he may have misunderstood you . . ."

The old man became alarmed. "What's wrong?" he asked.

"You did tell him about me, right? . . . I-I-I mean, about our conversation? . . ."

"Naturally. I don't understand. Was I not supposed to?"

"No, no, that's not it. He must have misunderstood you, I guess. Picture this: We haven't seen each other in fifteen years. And now he calls me, and as soon we say our hellos, he starts heaping painfully sarcastic praise on me for . . . Well, to cut a long story short, he practically accuses me of taking credit for his bighead work! And, I swear to you, there's no reason, there isn't the slightest reason for it . . . Believe me, I'm only interested in this subject as a journalist, as a popularizer, nothing more—"

"Wait, wait, young man!" The old man raised his hand. "Please calm down. Of course I didn't tell him anything of the sort. If for no other reason than that I don't know anything about it."

"Well, but . . . maybe . . . you weren't clear . . ."

"I couldn't have been unclear, because we didn't talk about it! I told him that a journalist, Kammerer, was writing a book about him and had contacted me for material. The journalist's number is such and such. Give him a call. That's it. That's all that I told him."

"Then I don't get it," said journalist Kammerer, almost in despair. "I thought he must have misunderstood you at first, but if not . . . then I don't even know . . . He must be unwell. It has to be a delusion. You know, these progressors have to keep it together at work, but I've seen very strange behavior from them on Earth . . . Must be their nerves . . ."

The old man frowned, curtaining his eyes with his eyebrows. "W-Well, you know . . . At the end of the day, it's possible that Lyova did misunderstand me . . . Or misheard me, to be exact . . . We only spoke for a bit, I was in a hurry, the wind was howling in the pine trees, the branches were were rustling, and I only remembered about you at the very last moment."

"No, no, I don't want to insist . . ." backtracked journalist Kammerer. "Maybe I was the one who misunderstood him . . . You know, his appearance shocked me too . . . He's changed a lot, he's become unfriendly . . . Didn't you think so, Sergei Pavlovich?"

Yes, Sergei Pavlovich had thought so as well. Encouraged and prompted by the barely concealed hurt feelings of the naive and talkative journalist Kammerer, ashamed of his student and probably of certain thoughts of his own, he gradually and very haltingly explained what had happened.

At approximately 5 PM, Sergei Pavlovich Fedoseyev left the Midges by glider and set a course for Sverdlovsk, where he was due at a meeting of a certain club. Fifteen minutes later, he was literally attacked and forced to land in a wild pine forest by a glider that came out of nowhere and turned out to be piloted by none other than Lev Abalkin. In a clearing amid the rustling pines, the student and teacher had a brief conversation constructed along the lines already familiar to me.

Having barely said hello and almost not allowing his aged teacher open his mouth, he ambushed the old man with words of sarcastic gratitude. He sardonically thanked poor Sergei Pavlovich for the herculean efforts he supposedly expended to convince the Appointments Board to send applicant Abalkin not to the Institute of Zoopsychology, where the applicant, due to his callowness and stupidity, had intended to apply, but to progressor school. These efforts had, of course, been crowned with astonishing success, and were the reason the rest of Lev Abalkin's life had been so happy and serene.

Hearing such a blatant perversion of the truth, the shocked old man naturally boxed his former pupil's ear. Having thus made him appropriately quiet and receptive, he calmly explained that he had gotten everything backward. It had been he, S. P. Fedoseyev, who had intended for Lev Abalkin to be a zoopsychologist, having already reached an agreement with the institute and made the appropriate recommendations to the board. It had been he, S. P. Fedoseyev, who reacted to what seemed to him to be a nonsensical decision of the board by protesting against it, both in person and in writing, all the way up to the regional council of education. And it had been he, S. P. Fedoseyev, who was eventually summoned to the Eurasian Sector and whipped like a schoolboy for attempting to oppose the decision of the Appointments Board without sufficient qualifications. ("They presented me with the conclusions of four experts and proved to me that if two and two make four, then I'm an old ass, and that the chairman of the Appointments Board—a certain Dr. Serafimovich—is completely correct . . .")

When he got to this point, the old man fell silent.

"And then what happened?" hazarded journalist Kammerer.

The old man made a sad chewing motion with his lips. "The little idiot kissed my hand and rushed to his glider."

We stayed silent for a bit. Then the old man added, "And that's when I remembered about you. Frankly, I thought he wasn't listening . . . Maybe I should have told him more, but I didn't feel up to it. For some reason, I felt like I'd never see him again . . ."

JUNE 2, '78

A BRIEF CONVERSATION

Excellentz was at home. Dressed in a severe black kimono, he sat in state at his desk, doing what he loved best: examining some ugly collectible figurine through a magnifying glass.

"Excellentz," I said. "I need to know whether during his time on Earth, Lev Abalkin has contacted anyone else."

"He has," said Excellentz, and looked at me with what seemed to be interest.

"May I ask whom?"

"You may. It was me."

I stopped short. Excellentz waited a bit, then commanded, "Report."

I gave my report. I repeated both conversations word for word, briefly presented my deductions, and concluded by stating that, in my opinion, we should expect Abalkin to shortly contact Komov, Rawlingson, Goryachev, and other people in one way or another connected with his work with the bigheads. And same went for this Dr. Serafimovich, the then chairman of the Appointments Board. Since Excellentz was staying silent and wasn't looking down, I allowed myself one question: "May I ask what he talked to you about? I'm very surprised he got in touch with you at all."

"You're surprised . . . I am, too. But there was no conversation. He pulled the same stunt with me as he did with you: he didn't turn on his video. He admired me for a bit, probably recognized me, and hung up."

"So then why do you think it was him?"

"Because he contacted me via a channel only known to one person."

"Maybe this person—"

"No, that's impossible . . . As for your hypothesis, it's untenable. Lev Abalkin had become an excellent resident—he loved his work and wouldn't have traded it for the world."

"Although given his temperament, becoming a progressor—"

"This is outside your area of expertise," said Excellentz sharply. "Stay focused. Get back to work. I'm rescinding the order to find and watch Abalkin. Follow him instead. I want to know where he goes, whom he meets, and what they talk about."

"Understood. And if I do come across him?"

"Interview him for your book. And then report back to me. No more and no less."

JUNE 2, '78

A COUPLE THINGS ABOUT SECRETS

At about 11:30 PM, I took a quick shower, peeked into the bedroom, and made sure that Alena was sleeping like a log. Then I came back to my study.

I decided to start with Puppen. Puppen was of course neither an earthling nor even a humanoid, and I have to say, modesty aside, that it took all of my skill in handling information channels to find the facts I needed. Let me note in parentheses that most of my planetmates are completely unaware of the true capabilities of that eighth (or is it now ninth?) wonder of the world, the Great Worldwide Informatorium. It's quite possible, however, that even I, with all my skill and experience, cannot claim complete mastery over its boundless memory.

I submitted eleven queries—three of which, as it turned out, were superfluous—and as a result received the following information about the bighead Puppen.

His full name was, it turns out, was Puppen-Itrich. Starting in '75 and to this day, he's been a member of the permanent delegation from the bighead people to Earth. Judging by the tasks he performed with respect to Earth administrators, he was something like the translator-interpreter of the mission—however, his true position was unknown, since the relationships internal to the delegation had remained a completely closed book to earthlings. Certain evidence suggested that Puppen was the head of something like a family unit within the mission, but so far it has proved impossible to figure out either the size or the composition of this unit, and yet, from the looks of things, these factors played a rather important role in deciding a wide range of important diplomatic issues.

On the whole, we'd gathered a sizable number of facts about both Puppen himself and the mission as a whole. Some of them were astonishing, but all of them eventually either came in conflict with new data or were completely refuted by subsequent observations. It looked like our xenologists were inclined to throw up their hands (or, if you prefer, throw in the towel) when faced with this mystery. And certain very respectable xenologists had come to concur with the opinion of Rawlingson, who, in a moment of weakness, said some ten years back, "I think they are just messing with us!"

Then again, none of this had much to do with me. The only takeaway from this was I ought to be heedful of Rawlingson's words.

The delegation was located in Canada, on the banks of the Thelon River, northwest of Baker Lake. The bigheads, it turned out, enjoyed complete freedom of movement, and they made good use of it, although they did not recognize any means of transportation other than null-T. The delegation residence had been constructed in strict accordance with a blueprint provided by the bigheads themselves—however, the bigheads had politely declined the pleasure of actually inhabiting it, and instead made themselves comfortable in makeshift underground chambers, or to put it simply, in burrows. They didn't believe in telecommunication, which meant that the efforts of our engineers, who had created video equipment tailored specifically to their hearing, vision, and ease of manipulation, had been in vain. The bigheads only believed in face-to-face meetings. Therefore, I'd have to fly to Baker Lake.

Having finished with Puppen, I decided that I may as well find Dr. Serafimovich. I managed this without much difficulty—that is, I managed to find information about him. It turned out that he had died twelve years ago at the age of 118. Valery Markovich Serafimovich, doctor of pedagogy, a permanent member of the Eurasian Council for education, and a member of the World Council for pedagogy. A pity.

I applied myself to the problem of Korney Jasmaa. For two years now, Korney Janovich Jasmaa's address had been the Camp Jan villa in the Volga steppe, six miles north of Antonov. He had a lengthy employment history, which made it clear that all his professional activities had been connected to the planet Giganda. He appeared to be a very distinguished theoretician and a prominent practitioner in the field of experimental history, but all the details of his career flew out of my head as soon as I was struck by two inconspicuous facts:

First of all, Korney Janovich Jasmaa was a posthumous son.

Second, Korney Janovich Jasmaa was born on October 6, '38.

The only difference between him and Lev Abalkin was that Korney Jasmaa's parents were not members of the Yormala group but a married couple who had died tragically during the Mirror experiment.

I couldn't believe my memory and opened the folder. Everything was as I had remembered. And of course, there was still the note of the back of the Arabic text: " . . . two of our twins met on Giganda. A complete coincidence . . ." A coincidence. I suppose that over there, on Giganda, there really had been a kind of coincidence: Lev Abalkin, a posthumous son born on October 6 of '38, had met Korney Jasmaa, a posthumous son born on October 6 of '38 . . . And is this a coincidence, too? Twins. From different parents. "If you don't believe me, check 07 and 11." Right. I'm looking at 07 right now. Therefore, somewhere in the bowels of our department, there also exists an 11. And it'd be logical to assume that there also exists a 01, and a 02, and so on, so forth . . . By the way, shame on me for not immediately paying attention to that strange code—07. Our cases (stored on crystallorecords and not in folders, of course) are usually designated either by whimsical phrases or by the names of objects . . .

By the way, what was this Mirror experiment? I've never even heard of it . . . This thought passed through my subconscious mind, and I entered the query into the GWI almost without thinking about it. The answer surprised me: "THIS INFORMATION IS RESTRICTED TO SPECIALISTS. PLEASE ENTER PROOF OF SECURITY CLEARANCE." I typed in the relevant information and resubmitted the query. This time, the answer card popped out after a few seconds. "THIS INFORMATION IS RESTRICTED TO SPECIALISTS. PLEASE ENTER PROOF OF SECURITY CLEARANCE." I leaned back in my chair. Wow! Never before in my life has COMCON-2 security clearance been insufficient to get information from the GWI.

And that's when I had the distinct feeling that I had gone outside the bounds of my area of expertise. For some reason, it was suddenly crystal clear to me that I was faced with a huge, grim secret, that Abalkin's mysterious, incomprehensible fate didn't simply end with the secret of Abalkin's identity—it was intertwined with the fates of many others, and I had no right to interfere with those fates, neither as a COMCON employee nor as a human being.

And of course, the issue wasn't the fact that the GWI refused to give me information about some Mirror experiment. I was certain that this experiment had nothing whatsoever to do with the secret. The GWI's intransigence was simply a clarifying blow that caused me to look back. And the blow made the scales fall from my eyes, so that I immediately connected everything—the strange behavior of Yadviga Lekanova, and the exceptional level of secrecy, and the unusual nature of this "document receptacle," and the unusual case code, and Excellentz's refusal to fully brief me, and even his original order not to interact with Abalkin . . .

And now there was also the fantastical coincidence of the circumstances and the dates of birth of Lev Abalkin and Korney Jasmaa.

There was a secret. Lev Abalkin was only one part of this secret. And I finally understood why Excellentz had chosen me for this job. There must have been people completely privy to the secret, but for some reason or another, they weren't suited to this search. And there must have been lots of people who would do this job no worse and maybe even better than I would, but Excellentz had doubtlessly understood that the search would sooner or later lead to the secret, and it was important that the person in question had the discretion to stop before they uncovered it. And in case the secret was revealed in the course of the search after all, it was important that Excellentz trust the person in question unconditionally.

And on top of everything, Lev Abalkin's secret is a secret of identity! That's even worse. It's the gravest of all possible secrets—one that a person isn't allowed to know about himself . . . A simple example is information about a person's incurable disease. A more complicated example is a secret misdeed that was committed in ignorance but had irreversible consequences—as in the case of King Oedipus in times immemorial . . .

Well, Excellentz had made the right choice. I don't like secrets. In my opinion, the secrets of our time and planet all have a certain unsavory stink to them. I admit that many of them are quite sensational and are capable of astonishing someone, but I personally always find being initiated into them unpleasant, and I find initiating innocent bystanders into them even more so. Most COMCON-2 employees feel the same way, which might be why we so rarely have issues with leaks. But my distaste for secrets probably does exceed the average. I don't even use the idiom "to clear up a secret"—rather, I always talk about *cleaning* it up, and feel myself to be a sanitation worker in the original sense of word.

Like right now, for example.

FROM LEV ABALKIN'S REPORT

In the dark, the city looks flat, like an antique engraving. Deep within the windows, we can see the glow of bioluminescent mold, and there are small pearly rainbows glimmering above the rare green spaces—some unknown phosphorescent flowers blossoming at night. Faint but irritating aromas waft toward us. The first moon creeps out from behind the rooftops and hangs over the avenue—a giant serrated sickle that floods the city with an unpleasant orange light.

For some reason, Puppen is inexplicably disgusted by this celestial body. He constantly glances at it with disapproval, and each time, he convulsively opens and closes his mouth, as if he wants to howl but is restraining himself. This is all the stranger because on his native Saraksh, the moon is invisible due to atmospheric refraction, and he has always treated the Earth's Moon with complete indifference—at least as far as I know.

Then we notice the children.

There are two of them. They are holding hands and slowly plodding along the sidewalk, looking like they're trying to stay hidden in the shadows. They are walking in the same direction we are. Judging by their clothing, they are boys. One is taller, about eight years old, and the other one is very young—maybe four or five. They've probably just come out of some side alley, otherwise I would have seen them from a distance. They've been walking for a long time, for hours—they are exhausted and are barely managing to trudge forward . . . The younger of the two isn't walking at all anymore but hanging off the old older one's hand and dragging himself along. The older boy has a flat bag with a wide strap slung across his body; he's constantly adjusting it, and it keeps hitting him in the knees.

The translator drones on in a flat, emotionless voice: "I'm tired, my legs hurt . . . Go on, keep walking . . . Go on . . . Bad man . . . You're the bad man . . . You big-eared snake . . . You rotten rat tail . . ." Aha. They stop. The younger one wrenches his hand out of the older one's grasp and sits down. The older boy lifts him up by the collar, but the younger one sits down again, and the older one lets him have it. Rats, snakes, foul-smelling beasts, and other fauna come pouring out of the translator. Then the younger boy starts loudly bawling, and the translator goes silent in bewilderment. It's time to get involved.

"Hi, boys," I silently mouth.

I've come right up to them, but they only notice me now. The younger one immediately stops crying—he's looking at me, his mouth open wide. The older one is also looking at me, but he's glowering sullenly, and his lips are squeezed tightly shut. I crouch down in front of him and say, "Don't be scared. I'm nice. I won't hurt you."

I know that lingans don't convey tone and am therefore trying to select simple, soothing words.

"My name is Lev," I say. "I see that you are tired. May I help you?"

The older boy doesn't answer. He's still glowering at me, looking extremely suspicious and wary, while the younger one has suddenly become interested in Puppen and can't take his eyes off him—you can see that he's both scared and fascinated. Puppen is on his best behavior—he's sitting off to the side, turning his bulbous head away.

"You're tired," I say. "You're hungry and thirsty. I'll give you something good to eat . . ."

And then the older boy explodes. They aren't the least bit tired, and they don't want anything good to eat. He's about to take care of this rat-eared snake, and then they'll keep walking. And anyone who gets in their way will get a bullet to the belly. Got it?

No problem. No one's planning to get in their way. Where are they going?

Where they're supposed to be going.

But where's that? Maybe we're going the same way? Then the rat-eared snake could get a ride on my shoulders . . .

Everything is eventually sorted out. The boys eat four bars of chocolate and drink two bottles of sparkling water. I squeeze half a tube of fruit paste into each small mouth. There's a thorough examination of Lev's rainbow suit, and (after a short but extremely energetic dispute), Puppen gives permission to pet him—but just the once, and only on the back, definitely not on the head. Everyone on Vanderhuze's ship is overwhelmed by the cuteness and is loudly cooing.

We subsequently learn the following. The boys are brothers; the older one is called Iyadrudan and the younger Pritulatan. They used to live quite far away (we fail to get more precise information) with their father in a large white house with a pool in the yard. Until recently, they also lived with two aunts and another brother—he was the oldest, eighteen years old—but they all died. After that, their father stopped taking them with him to get food; he started going all alone, by himself, even though the whole family used to go together. There are lots of places to get food—you can get it here, and here, and here, and here (we fail to get more precise information). Whenever he went out alone, their father always ordered them: if he didn't come back by evening, they needed to take the Book, come out onto the avenue, and keep walking until they got to the pretty glass house that lights up in the dark. But they weren't supposed to go into this house—they were supposed to sit outside and wait for people to come and take them to their mom and dad, and that's it. Why at night? Because there are no bad people on the streets at night. They only come out during the day. No, we've never seen them, but we've often heard them jingling their bells, playing their songs, and trying to get us to come out of the house. Then our father and older brother would take out their rifles and sink a bullet into their bellies . . . No, they've never seen and don't know anyone else. Well, long ago, some people with rifles did come to their house and argued with their father and older brother all day, then their mother and both aunts also joined in. They were all shouting loudly, but their father managed to outargue everyone, of course, and those people left and never came back . . .

Little Pritulatan falls asleep as soon as I pick him up. Iyadru-dan, on the other hand, refuses any help. He lets me adjust the bag containing the Book, and now he's walking next to us, look-ing self-sufficient, his hands in his pockets. Puppen is running up ahead, not participating in the conversation. He's doing his best to project an air of complete indifference to what is happening, but he's in fact as intrigued as the rest of us by the obvious pos-sibility that the boys' destination—this lit-up building—is none other than Object Patch 96 . . .

Iyadrudan doesn't know how to retell what's written in the Book. The adults used this Book to write down everything that happened to them. How Pritulatan was bitten by a poisonous ant. How the water started suddenly draining out of the pool, but their father prevented it. How their aunt died—she was open-ing a can, their mother looked over at her and she was already dead . . . Iyadrudan hasn't read this book—he isn't a good reader and doesn't like to read, he isn't advanced. Pritulatan, on the other hand, is very advanced, but he's just a baby and doesn't understand anything. No, they were never bored. How can you be bored in a house that has 507 rooms? And every room is full of all sorts of strange things, including things that even their father didn't know the names of, nor what their purpose was. But there wasn't a single rifle. Rifles are hard to find nowadays. They might have been able to find a rifle in the house next door, but their father had strictly forbidden them to go outside . . . No, their father didn't let them use his rifle. He said there was no need for that. But when we get to the house that lights up and the nice people who meet us there take us to our mom, we'll be allowed to shoot all we want . . . Are you maybe the man who'll take us to our mom? Why don't you have a rifle, then? You're a nice man, but you don't have a rifle, and our father said that all nice people have rifles . . .

"No," I say. "I don't know how to take you to your mom. I'm a stranger here myself and I'd like to meet the nice people, too."

"That's too bad," says Iyadrudan.

We come out into the square. Up close, Object Patch 96 looks like a giant antique jewelry box made of blue crystal—vulgarly resplendent and gleaming with countless precious stones and gems. It's permeated with an even blue-white light, which emanates from the building and illuminates the cracked asphalt overgrown with bristly black weeds and the dead facades of the houses ringing the square. The walls of this amazing building are completely transparent, and the interior is a cheerful riot of sparkling, shimmering colors: reds, golds, greens, and yellows. As a result, you don't immediately notice the door—as wide as a gate and welcomingly open—or the couple of shallow steps leading up to it.

"Toys!" Pritulatan whispers reverently and begins to wriggle, trying to slide down out of my arms.

Only now do I realize the box isn't filled with jewelry but with colorful toys—an assortment of hundreds, no, thousands of colorful, extremely crudely fashioned toys: grotesquely large, brightly painted dolls, ugly wooden cars, and a great variety of multicolored trinkets that are hard to make out at this distance.

The small but advanced Pritulatan immediately starts whining and begging everyone to go inside this magical house, it's OK that Dad told them not to, we'll just go in for a second, grab that truck, then we'll come right out and wait for the nice people . . . Iyadrudan tries to get him to cut it out, first verbally and then, when this doesn't work, by twisting his ear, and the whining becomes unintelligible. The translator dispassionately spews out a whole bag of "rat-eared snakes" into the air. Vanderhuze and company are filled with indignation and demand that we soothe and comfort him, and then suddenly we all—even the advanced Pritulatan—go quiet at once.

The native from before, the one with the rifle, suddenly appears at the corner nearest to us. Stepping softly and sound-lessly over the patches of blue light, his hands resting on the rifle slung across his chest, he walks right up to the children. He firmly takes the suddenly quiet Pritulatan by the left hand and the beaming Iyadrudan by the right hand, and he leads them away, across the square, toward the illuminated building—tak-ing them to their mother and father and the countless chances to shoot all they like.

I watch them go. Everything seems to be going according to plan, but some small thing, some niggling detail, is spoiling the entire picture. Some drop of tar . . .

"Did you figure it out?" asks Puppen.

"What are you talking about?" I respond irritably, since I just can't shake off the feeling that some unknown speck of dust is spoiling the entire picture.

"Turn off the light in that building and shoot it a dozen times . . ."

I barely hear him. I suddenly identify my speck of dust. The native is walking away, holding the children's hands, and I see the rifle swinging in time with his footsteps, like a pendulum—left to right, then right to left . . . It couldn't possibly swing like that. A heavy magazine rifle weighing no less than fifteen pounds couldn't possibly swing back and forth at this rate. Only a toy rifle, made of wood or plastic, could swing like that. This "nice man" doesn't have a real rifle . . .

I don't have time to think this through. A native with a toy rifle. The natives are snipers. Maybe the toy rifle is from this toy pavilion. Turn the light off and blast it to bits . . . This pavilion looks just like . . . No, I don't have the time to think anything through.

There's a shower of bricks on the left side of the street, then a wooden frame crashes to the sidewalk and smashes to pieces. A large yellow shadow is gliding down the ugly facade of a six-story building—the third one from the corner—moving diagonally, across the gaping black windows, so smoothly and weightlessly that it's hard to believe that the layers of plaster and pieces of brick are raining down from the facade in its wake. Vanderhuze is shouting something, the children are shrieking horribly in unison, and in the meantime, the shadow is already on the pavement, just as weightless, translucent, and giant as before. Its dozens of legs are moving so quickly that they blur together, the long articulated body is rhythmically swelling and deflating amid the flickering motion, and its grasping pincers are raised high in front of it, shining with a motionless varnished gleam . . .

The scorcher appears in my hand by itself. I turn into an automatic distance gauge, concerned only with measuring the distance between the crawspider and the figures of the children, fleeing diagonally across the square. (The native with the fake rifle is somewhere nearby, too, running with all his might, lagging slightly behind the children, but I'm not watching him.) The distance is rapidly decreasing, everything is perfectly clear, and when the crawspider is in my sights, I shoot.

At the moment I pull the trigger, it's about sixty feet away. I rarely have the opportunity to use my scorcher, and I'm astonished by the result. The reddish-purple flash temporarily blinds me, but I manage to see that the crawspider seems to explode. Instantly. All at once, from its pincers to the ends of its hind legs. Like an overheated boiler. There's a brief thunderclap, a rumbling echo reverberates around the square, and then a dense, almost solid-seeming cloud of steam puffs up where the monster used to be.

It's all over. The cloud of steam is diffusing with a soft hiss, I no longer hear panicked screams and sounds of pounding feet coming from the dark alley, and the glittering, vulgarly resplendent jewelry box of a pavilion is still standing there like nothing happened . . .

"Damn, what a scary monster . . ." I mumble. "What the hell are they doing here, a hundred parsecs from Pandora? And I guess you didn't smell it again, huh?"

Puppen doesn't have the time to answer. We hear the crack of a rifle shot. It echoes around the square and is immediately followed by a second shot. The sounds are coming from somewhere nearby. Somewhere right around the corner. Ah, they're coming from that alley they all ran into . . .

"Puppen, stay on my left and keep your head down!" I order him as I begin to run.

I don't understand what's happening in that alley. The children are probably being attacked by another crawspider . . . So it's not a toy rifle after all? And then three people step out of the darkness of the alley and stop, blocking our path. And two of them are armed with real repeater rifles, and the two barrels are aimed squarely at me.

I can see everything clearly in the bluish-white light: a tall, gray-haired old man wearing a gray uniform with shiny buttons and two stocky young men with rifles at the ready—they are flanking the old man from behind, dressed in the same gray uniforms and wearing belts loaded down with ammunition bags.

"Very dangerous," clicks Puppen in the bighead tongue. "I repeat, this is very dangerous."

I slow down and, despite some inner resistance, force myself to put my scorcher back in its holster. I stop in front of the old man and ask, "How are the children?"

The muzzles of the rifles are aimed straight at my stomach. At my belly. The young men's faces are grim and completely ruthless.

"The children are fine," replies the old man.

His eyes are bright and even rather cheerful. He doesn't have the same sullen, gloomy expression as the two armed men. It's an ordinary wrinkled old man's face, not even without a certain dignity. However, it's possible it only seems that way to me; it's possible I only have this impression because he isn't holding a rifle but a shiny, polished cane that he keeps using to casually and lightly tap the leg of his tall boot.

"Who did you shoot?" I ask.

"A bad man." The translator communicates the answer.

"So you're probably the nice men with rifles?" I ask.

The old man hikes up his eyebrows: "Nice men? What do you mean?"

I explain what Iyadrudan told me. The old man nods. "I see. Yes, we're those nice men." He looks me over from head to toe. "And you're doing well, I see . . . A translating machine behind your back . . . We had those once, but they were huge, as big as a room . . . And we never did have weapons like that. You really made short work of that bad man! As if you blasted him from a cannon. When did you fly here?"

"Yesterday," I say.

"And we haven't fixed our flying machines. No one left to fix them." He openly looks me over again. "Yes, I'm impressed. And as you can see, everything here has broken down. How did you manage? Did you fight them off? Or did you find another way?"

"It does look like everything has broken down," I say carefully. "I've spent a whole day here already, but I still don't understand a thing . . ."

He has clearly taken me for someone else. As a matter of fact, that may initially come in handy. But I need to be careful—very careful . . .

"I can see that you don't understand a thing," says the old man. "And that's at the very least strange . . . Didn't you have the same thing?"

"No," I say. "We didn't have the same thing."

The old man suddenly produces a long sentence, which the translator immediately responds to with "This language cannot be decoded."

"I don't understand," I say.

"You don't understand . . . And I thought I spoke the language of the people from beyond the mountains quite well."

"That's not where I'm from," I object. "I've never even been there."

"So where are you from?"

I make my decision. "This doesn't matter right now," I say. "We won't talk about us. We're doing well. We don't need help. We'll talk about you. I haven't understood much, but one thing is clear: you need help. How can we help you? Where do we start? And what's happening here, anyway? These are the things we'll talk about. And let's sit down, because I've been on my feet all day. Is there a place where we could sit down and have a calm conversation?"

He spends a while silently searching my face with his eyes. "You don't want to say where you're from," he finally says. "Well, that's your right. You've got the strength. Except this is silly. I already know—you're from the Northern Archipelago. They spared you only because they didn't notice you. Lucky you. But I have to ask: Where have you been while they've been rotting us alive over here? Enjoying your lives, damn your hides!"

"You aren't the only ones in trouble," I object quite sincerely. "It's now your turn."

"We're very glad," he says. "Let's go sit down and talk."

We walk into the house across the street, go up to the second floor, and find ourselves in a dirty room with very little furniture— a table in the middle of the room, a huge couch against the wall, and two stools by the window. The windows overlook the square, and the room is illuminated by the blue-white light of the pavilion. Someone is sleeping on the couch, wrapped in a glossy raincoat up to the very top of his head. There are tins of canned food and a large metal flask on the table.

The old man begins to clean house as soon as he enters the room. He wakes up the sleeper and sends him out of the house. He orders one of the grim young men to take a position on a stool by the window, and the man stays there from then on, his eyes fixed on the square. The second young man nimbly opens some tins, then takes a position by the door, leaning on the doorjamb with his shoulder.

I am invited to sit on the couch, after which I'm boxed in by the table and surrounded by tins of canned food. The flask turns out to contain ordinary water—relatively clean, although with a metallic aftertaste. They also don't forget about Puppen. The soldier who'd been chased off the couch puts an open tin in front of him on the floor. Puppen doesn't object. Then again, he doesn't eat—instead, he prudently walks over to the door and sits down next to the sentry. At the same time, he takes great care to keep snorting, sniffing, and scratching himself, diligently pretending to be an ordinary mutt.

Meanwhile, the old man grabs the second stool, sits down opposite to me, and our conversation begins.

First of all, the old man introduces himself. Of course, he turns out to be a gattauch, and, what's more, not just a gattauch but a gattauch-okambomon, which should apparently be translated as "the ruler of the entire territory and all adjoining regions." The entire city and port, as well as the approximately dozen tribes living within a thirty-mile radius, are under his command. He has little idea of what's happening outside this region, but he supposes it's about the same as here. The total population of his region is currently no more than five thousand persons. It contains neither industry nor any kind of halfway sensibly organized agriculture. On the other hand, there's a lab in the outskirts. A good lab, at one time one of the best in the world, and to this day, Drowdan himself runs it ("I'm surprised you've never heard of him . . . He was also lucky—he turned out to be a long-liver, like myself . . ."), but they've been working for forty years and gotten nowhere. And they probably never will.

"And that's why," concludes the old man, "let's not beat around the bush or haggle. I just have one condition: if you cure us, then cure everyone. No exceptions. If that works for you, then everything else is up to you. Everything. I accept unconditionally. And if not, then leave us be. We'll all die, of course, but you'll have no peace while a single one of us lives."

I stay silent. I keep waiting for a hint from headquarters. Any hint at all! But they don't seem to understand anything, either.

"Let me remind you," I finally say, "that I still have no idea what's going on here."

"Then ask questions!" says the old man sharply.

"You spoke of curing you. Is there an epidemic?"

The old man's face turns stony. He stares into my eyes for a long time, then he wearily rests his elbows on the table and rubs his forehead with his fingers. "I told you not to beat around the bush. We're not going to haggle. Just spell it out for me: Do you have a universal cure? If yes, then set the terms. If not, then we have nothing to talk about."

"We'll never get anywhere like this," I say. "Proceed from the assumption that I know absolutely nothing about you. As if I've been asleep for the last forty years. I know nothing about your disease, nothing about the cure you need—"

"And you know nothing about the invasion?" says the old man without opening his eyes.

"Almost nothing."

"And you know nothing about the Global Abduction?"

"Almost nothing. I know that everyone left. I know that space aliens are involved. That's all."

"*Spay-ce . . . a-lee-ens . . .*" the old man repeats with difficulty in Russian.

"People from the moon . . . People from the sky . . ." I say.

He grins, baring strong yellow teeth. "They didn't come from the sky or the moon. They came from underground!" he says. "So you do know some things."

"I walked across the city. And I saw a lot."

"And nothing like this happened where you're from? Nothing at all?"

"We didn't have anything like this," I say firmly.

"And you didn't notice anything? You didn't notice the end of mankind? Stop lying! What are you trying to achieve with these lies?"

"Lev!" Komov's voice rustles beneath my helmet. "Use the Idiot Gambit!"

"I'm just a subordinate," I sternly declare. "I only know what I'm supposed to know! I only do what I'm ordered to do! If I were ordered to lie, I'd lie, but I haven't received such an order."

"And what have you been ordered to do?"

"To conduct reconnaissance in your region and report back."

"How ridiculous!" the old man says with weary disgust. "Fine. Have it your way. You seem to need to be told things that everyone knows . . . Very well. Listen up."

It turned out that everything was the fault of a race of odious subhumans that had proliferated in the bowels of the planet. Forty years ago, these subhumans attempted to invade the surface. The invasion began with an unprecedented pandemic that the subhumans unleashed on the entire planet at once. The pathogen responsible for the pandemic had not yet been found. The symptoms of the disease were as follows: starting from twelve years of age, otherwise normal children began rapidly aging. The rate of development of the human body upon reaching this critical inflection point would accelerate exponentially. Sixteen-year-old boys and girls looked forty, old age began at eighteen, and the number of people who survived past twenty could be counted on the fingers of one hand.

The pandemic raged for three years, after which the subhumans made their first appearance aboveground. They offered every government the opportunity to organize a transfer of their populations "to the neighboring world"—that is, to their world, under the ground. They promised that there, in the neighboring world, the pandemic would abate by itself—and that's when millions and millions of terrified people rushed into their special wells, from which, of course, none had ever returned. And that was how, forty years ago, the local population had perished.

Of course, not everyone believed them and not everyone was terrified. Entire families and clusters of families, as well as whole religious communities, remained. Amid the appalling conditions of the pandemic, they continued their doomed fight for the right to exist and live as their ancestors had. However, the subhumans couldn't even leave this pitifully small percentage of the original population alone. They made it their mission to hunt down all the children—humanity's last hope. They flooded the planet with "bad people." At first, these were fake people disguised as cheerful painted clowns jingling their bells and playing merry songs. Silly children would happily follow them and disappear forever into the amber glasses. At the same time, illuminated toy stores like the one we just saw had appeared in the main squares of the town—a child would enter one and disappear without a trace.

"We did everything we could. We armed ourselves—the abandoned arsenals were full of weapons. We taught the children to be afraid of 'bad people,' and then we even taught them to use rifles to destroy them. We blew up the stalls and blasted the toy stores to smithereens until we realized that it'd be better to put sentries by their doors to intercept careless children. But that was just the beginning . . ."

The subhumans, with inexhaustible inventiveness, kept churning out more and more kinds of child hunters. There had appeared monsters. It was almost impossible to hit one with a rifle as it was attacking a child. Then there were the giant, colorful butterflies—one would fall upon a child, envelop it in its wings, and disappear together with it. These butterflies were completely immune to bullets. And most recently, they had invented fake humans that were impossible to tell apart from ordinary soldiers. These would simply take an unsuspecting child by the hand and lead them away. Some of them even knew how to talk . . .

"We are well aware that we have practically no chance of surviving. The pandemic isn't ending, although we'd hoped at first that it would. Only one person in a hundred thousand hasn't been infected. For example, I myself, Drowdan . . . and one more boy—I watched him grow up, he is eighteen now, and he looks eighteen . . . If you didn't know all this, you know it now. If you did know this, then keep in mind that we understand our situation perfectly. And we're prepared to agree to all of your conditions—we'll work for you, we'll obey you . . . There's just one thing we won't agree to: if you cure us, cure everyone. No elites, no chosen ones!"

The old man stops, reaches for a mug of water, and sips from it greedily. The soldier at the door shuffles his feet and yawns, covering his mouth with his hand. He looks twenty-five. How old is he really? Thirteen? Fifteen? A teenager . . .

I sit perfectly still, trying to keep my face expressionless. I had subconsciously expected something like this, but for some reason I'm still struggling to fit the victim's eyewitness account into my conscious mind. I have no doubts about the veracity of the old man's story, but it's like a dream—each individual piece makes sense, but if you put it all together, it looks completely ridiculous. Maybe the issue is that I have deep-seated preconceived notions about the Wanderers—ones unconditionally accepted on Earth?

"How do you know that they are subhumans?" I ask. "Have you seen them? Personally?"

The old man grunts. There's a terrible expression on his face. "I'd give half my worthless life to see one of them in front of me," he rasps out. "I'd take him . . . With these hands . . . But I've never seen them, of course. They are too careful and too cowardly . . . Anyway, probably no one's ever seen them except those filthy government traitors forty years ago . . . And rumor has it they have no shape at all—like water or, say, steam . . ."

"Then I don't understand," I say. "Why should beings that have no form lure a few billion people into their underground caverns?"

"Damn you!" says the old man, raising his voice. "They are *subhumans!* How could you and I judge what subhumans might need? Maybe they need slaves. Maybe they need food . . . Or maybe they need building blocks for their fake people . . . What difference does it make? They've destroyed our world! And they still won't leave us alone, they hunt us down like vermin—"

And then his face suddenly contorts into a terrible grimace. With astonishing vigor for his age, he leaps all the way back to the opposite wall, throwing the stool aside with a crash. In the blink of an eye, he's holding a large nickel-plated revolver with both hands and pointing it at straight at me. The sleepy guards are now awake and are now erratically fumbling for their rifles, their suddenly childlike faces showing very similar expressions of mingled horror and suspicion.

"What's going on?" I say, trying not to move.

The nickel-plated barrel is shaking, and the guards, having successfully groped for their weapons, cycle their bolts at the same time.

"Your silly clothes finally turned on," Puppen clicks in his own language. "We can barely see you. Just your face. You have no shape, like water or steam. Then again, the old man has already decided not to shoot. Should I take him out anyway?"

"No need," I say in Russian.

The old man finally finds his voice. He is whiter than the wall and stammering—but out of hatred and not fear, of course. A formidable old man. "Damn underground shapeshifter!" he says. "Put your hands on the table! The right hand, then the left! That's right . . ."

"This is a misunderstanding," I say angrily. "I'm not a changeling. I have special clothes. They can make me invisible, they just haven't been working well."

"Clothes, huh?" the old man says mockingly. "They've learned how to make invisibility cloaks in the Northern Archipelago!"

"We've learned to do a lot of things in the Northern Archipelago," I say. "Put your weapons away, please, and let's sort this out calmly."

"You're an idiot," says the old man. "You should have at least taken a look at our maps. There's no Northern Archipelago . . . I had you pegged from the start, I just couldn't believe such impudence."

"Don't you find this humiliating?" clicks Puppen. "Why don't you take the old man, and I'll deal with the young ones . . ."

"Shoot the dog!" the old man orders the guards without taking his eyes off of me.

"Watch who you call a dog!" Puppen says in the clearest possible local dialect. "You garrulous old fart!"

Then the boys' nerves give out and the shooting begins . . .

JUNE 3, '78

MAYA GLUMOVA AGAIN

I really overdid it with the videophone volume. The instrument by my ear let out a melodious roar, much like the stranger in small-clothes in the midst of wooing Mrs. Nickleby. I shot out of my chair like a cannonball, fumbling to press the correct button to receive the incoming call.

Excellentz was calling. It was 7:03 AM.

"Time to get up," he said fairly good-naturedly. "When I was your age, I never slept."

I wonder how long I'll have to keep hearing from him about my age? I'm already forty-five . . . And, by the way, he did plenty of sleeping at my age. And he's no slouch at it now, either.

"I wasn't sleeping," I lied.

"Even better," he said. "That means you can start working immediately. Find this Glumova. Find out the following from her. Has she seen Abalkin since yesterday? Did Abalkin talk to her about her work? If he did, what exactly was he interested in?

Had he expressed an interest in seeing her at the museum? That's all. No more and no less."

I responded to this code phrase. "I must find out from Glumova whether she has seen him again, whether they talked about her work, and if it turns out they did, I must find out what he was interested in and whether he had expressed a wish to visit her at the museum."

"Correct. You proposed changing the cover story. I don't object. COMCON is looking for Progressor Abalkin in order to obtain information about a certain tragic accident. The investigation is related to a secret of identity and is thus being carried out in a clandestine fashion. I don't object. Any questions?"

"I wish I knew what the museum had to do with anything . . ." I muttered under my breath.

"Did you say something?" inquired Excellentz.

"Let's say that they didn't talk about that damn museum. In that case, may I attempt to figure out what did happen between them during that first meeting?"

"Do you really care?"

"How about you?"

"I don't, no."

"It's the strangest thing," I said, looking off to the side. "We know what Abalkin wanted from me. We know what he wanted from Fedoseyev. But we have no idea what he was trying to do with Glumova."

Excellentz said, "Fine. Figure it out. But only if it doesn't get in the way of investigating the central questions. And don't forget to wear a radio wristband. Put it on right now, so I can see."

With a sigh, I took the wristband out of my desk drawer and put it on my left wrist. It felt tight.

"Very good," said Excellentz, and hung up.

I headed to the shower. There were sounds of banging and clanging coming from the kitchen—Alena was operating the utilizer. I took a shower, then we had breakfast. Alena sat across from me, wearing my dressing gown and resembling a Chinese

Buddha. She announced that she was supposed present a report today, and offered to read it to me for practice. I begged off, citing the circumstances.

"Again?" she asked, sympathetically and aggressively at the same time. "Again," I admitted with some defiance. "Hell and damnation," she said. "I can't argue with that," I said. "How long will it take?" she asked. "I have three more days," I said. "What if you run out of time?" she asked. "Then it's all over," I said. She gave me a quick glance, and I realized that she was again imagining all sorts of horrors. "I'm sick of it all," I said. "I'm bored. Let me get this case out of the way, and then let's you and I take a trip to some far-off place." "I can't," she said sadly. "Aren't you sick of it all?" I said. "After all, your work doesn't matter much . . ." That's the right tack to take with her. She immediately got her hackles up and started to prove to me that her work did matter, and that she works on devilishly fascinating and important projects. Eventually, we decided that in a month we would take a trip to Novaya Zemlya. That's the fashion nowadays . . .

I came back to my study and dialed Glumova's home phone number without sitting down. No one answered. It was 7:51 AM. A bright sunny morning. Only someone like our Elephant could sleep in until eight in this weather. Maya Glumova had probably already left for work, and the freckled Toivo must have returned to his boarding school.

I made a rough outline of today's schedule. Right now it's late evening in Canada. If I remember correctly, bigheads are primarily nocturnal, so it shouldn't be a problem to go there in three or four hours . . . By the way, how's null-T working today? I looked it up. Null transportation has been working normally since around four in the morning. Therefore, I had the time for both Puppen and Korney Jasmaa today.

I went to the kitchen, had another cup of coffee, and walked Alena to the roof, where she got into her glider. We said exaggeratedly warm good-byes—she was starting to feel the prepresentation jitters. I diligently waved to her until she disappeared from view, then I returned to my study.

I wonder what it is about Excellentz and this museum. It's just a museum . . . Of course, it does have something to do with progressors, and in particular, their work on Saraksh . . . Then I remembered Excellentz's pupils, dilated to the size of his irises. Was he actually scared? Did I really manage to scare Excellentz? And with what?! With the ordinary and, what's more, accidental statement that Abalkin's girlfriend works in the Museum of Extraterrestrial Cultures . . . In the Special Department for Artifacts of Unknown Purpose . . . No, wait! He named the department himself. I told him that Glumova works at the Museum of Extraterrestrial Cultures, and he announced: *in the Special Department for Artifacts of Unknown Purpose* . . . I recalled the suites of rooms crammed, stuffed, barricaded, and hung with curios resembling either sculptures or topological models . . . And Excellentz considers it possible that an imperial officer who's been up to some mischief a hundred parsecs away may be interested in something in these rooms . . .

I dialed Glumova's work number and was slightly dumbfounded. There on the screen, smiling pleasantly at me, was Grisha Serosovin, nickname Aquarius, from the fourth subgroup of my department. For a few seconds, I watched a succession of expressions on Grisha's rosy-cheeked face. A pleasant smile, confusion, official willingness to receive orders, and then finally, a pleasant smile again. This time a slightly strained one. It wasn't hard to understand. If I felt rather dumbfounded myself, it only stood to reason that he'd be a bit flustered. The head of his department must have been the last person he expected to see on the screen. However, on the whole, he handled it quite well.

"Hello," I said. "May I speak to Maya Toivovna?"

"Maya Toivovna . . ." Grisha looked around. "You know, she's not here. I don't think she's been in today yet. Would you like to leave her a message?"

"Tell her she got a call from Kammerer, journalist. She should remember me. By the way, are you new? I don't recall—"

"Yes, I only started yesterday . . . Actually, I'm not employed by the museum; I'm only here to work with the exhibits . . ."

"Ah, I see," I said. "Well, all right . . . Thank you. I'll call back later."

Well, well, well. Excellentz is taking action. It looks like he's absolutely sure that Lev Abalkin will make an appearance at the museum. And in this very department. Let's try to understand why he chose Grisha specifically. Grisha has been working for us for a week less than a year. A bright kid with good reflexes. An exobiologist by training. Maybe that's all it is. A young exobiologist begins his first independent research project. Something like *The relationship between the topology of an artifact and the biostructure of a sentient being.* Everything is easy, relaxed, discreet, and appropriate. By the way, Grisha is also the departmental subacc champion . . .

All right. I think I now understand. Very well. Glumova is presumably delayed for some reason. For instance, she may be off somewhere, having a conversation with Lev Abalkin. By the way, he did make an appointment with me for 10:00 AM. He was almost certainly lying, but if I were really planning to fly to that appointment, now would be the time to give him a call and confirm that his plans hadn't changed. And without further ado, I dialed Osinushka.

Cottage Six picked up immediately, and Maya Glumova appeared on the screen. "Oh, it's you," she said with disgust.

It was impossible to convey the hurt and disappointment on her face. She had really wilted in the last twenty-four hours—her cheeks had sunk in, her lips were parched, and there were dark circles under her wistful, sick-looking, and very wide-open eyes. And only a second later, when she slowly leaned away from the screen, did I notice that her beautiful hair was carefully and becomingly styled, and that she was wearing that same amber necklace over her severely elegant gray dress with a high neck.

"Yes, it's me . . ." said journalist Kammerer in confusion. "Good morning. Actually, I . . . Is Lev there?"

"No," she said.

"You see, we had an appointment . . . I wanted to . . ."

"Here?" she asked eagerly, moving closer to the screen again. "When?"

"At ten o'clock. I wanted to confirm . . . but he's not there, I guess . . ."

"Are you sure you had an appointment? What exactly did he say?" she asked, sounding completely childlike and looking avidly at me.

"What exactly did he say?" journalist Kammerer repeated slowly. Except that the person speaking was no longer journalist Kammerer—it was me. "Here's the thing, Maya Toivovna. Let's not kid ourselves. He probably won't come."

Now she was looking at me as if she couldn't believe her eyes. "What? . . . How could you know that?"

"Wait for me," I said. "I'll explain everything. I'll be there in a few minutes."

"What happened to him?" she screamed in a piercing and terrible voice.

"He's alive and well. Don't worry. Wait, I'll be there soon . . ."

Two minutes to get dressed. Three minutes to the nearest null-T booth. Damn, there's a line at the booth. Guys, please, let me go ahead of you, this is very urgent . . . Thank you very much, thank you! . . . One minute to find the code. Oh, those crazy provincial codes! . . . Five seconds to enter the code. And now I'm stepping out of the booth into the deserted timbered lobby of the holiday club. One more minute and I'm standing on the wide porch and looking this way and that. Aha, it's over there . . . I burst straight through the thickets of nettles and mountain ashes. I hope I don't run into Dr. Goannek . . .

She was waiting for me in the entrance hall, sitting at the low table with the panda cub, the videophone on her knees. As

I came in, I gave an involuntary glance at the living room door, which was ajar, and she hurriedly said, "We'll talk right here."

"As you wish," I replied.

I took a look around the living room, kitchen, and bedroom in an ostentatiously unhurried manner. Everything had been carefully tidied up, and there was of course no one there. Out of the corner of my eye, I could see her sitting motionless with her hands on the videophone, staring straight ahead.

"Who were you looking for?" she said coldly.

"I don't know," I admitted honestly. "It's just that we're about to have a sensitive conversation, and I wanted to make sure we were all alone."

"Who are you?" she asked. "But please don't tell any more lies."

I related my second cover story, explained about the secret of identity, and added that I wasn't going to apologize for lying—I had simply been trying to do my job without subjecting her to unnecessary worry.

"So you aren't going to pull punches with me anymore, I take it?" she said.

"What do you propose I do?"

She didn't answer.

"You sit here, waiting for him," I said. "And he won't come, you know. He's stringing you along. He's stringing all of us along, and there's no end in sight. And the clock is ticking."

"Why do you think he won't come back?'

"Because he's in hiding," I said. "Because he's been lying to everyone he speaks to."

"Then why did you call here?"

"Because I can't find him!" I said, slowly growing fiercer. "I have to take every chance, no matter how unlikely."

"What did he do?" she asked.

"I don't know what he did. Maybe nothing. I'm not looking for him because he did something. I'm looking for him because he's the only witness to a terrible tragedy. And if we can't find him, we'll never know what happened . . ."

"Where did it happen?"

"It doesn't matter," I said impatiently. "Where he was working. Not on Earth. On a planet called Saraksh."

You could see on her face that she'd never heard of Saraksh before. "Why is he in hiding?" she asked softly.

"We don't know. He is on the verge of a mental breakdown. You could say he's unwell. He may be imagining things. It could be an idée fixe . . ."

"Unwell . . ." she said with a very mild shake of the head. "Maybe . . . But then again, maybe not . . . What do you want from me?"

"Have you met with him again?"

"No," she said. "He promised to call again, but he never did."

"So then why are you waiting for him here?"

"Where else could I wait for him?" she asked.

Her voice was so bitter that I averted my eyes and stayed silent for some time. Then I asked, "Where was he going to call you? At work?"

"Probably . . . I don't know. He called me at work before."

"He called you at the museum and told you he'd meet you there?"

"No. He immediately invited me to join him. Right here. I found a glider and flew to him."

"Maya Toivovna," I said. "I'm interested in all the details of your meeting . . . You told him about yourself, about your work. He told you about his . . . Try to remember how it was."

She shook her head. "No. We didn't talk about things like that . . . You're right, of course—that's strange . . . I hadn't seen him in so long . . . It was only later, when I got home, that I realized I hadn't learned anything about him . . . I did ask him: where have you been, what have you been doing . . . but he waved it all away, as if it were all trivial, irrelevant."

"So then he was the one asking questions?"

"No, no! He wasn't interested in anything like that . . . Who I am, what I'm like . . . Whether I'm alone or whether I have someone . . . What gives my life meaning . . . He was like a boy . . . I don't want to talk about it."

"Maya Toivovna, we don't need to talk about anything you don't want to talk about . . ."

"I don't want to talk about anything!"

I got up, went to the kitchen, and brought her some water. She greedily drank the whole glass, spilling water on her gray dress.

"This is nobody's business but our own," she said, handing me the glass.

"Don't tell me about things that aren't my business," I said, sitting down. "What questions did he ask you?"

"I'm telling you, he didn't ask me anything! He told stories, reminisced, drew, debated . . . like a boy . . . It turns out he remembers everything! Almost every single day! Where he stood, where I stood, what Rex said, how Wolff had looked . . . I didn't remember a thing, and he kept shouting at me, forcing me to remember, and then I would . . . And he was so happy when I remembered something he hadn't! . . ."

She fell silent.

"This was all about your childhood?" I asked, having waited a bit.

"Of course! That's what I'm telling you—it's no one's business but our own, it was all about the two of us! . . . He really did seem like a madman. . . I was completely exhausted, I was falling asleep, and he'd wake me up, shouting in my ear: *And then who fell off the swings?* And if I'd remember, he'd grab me, pick me up, and run around the house with me in his arms, shouting, 'Yes, you got it, that's right!'"

"And he didn't ask you about your teacher or your school friends?"

"I'm telling you, he didn't ask me about anyone or anything! Can't you get that through your head? He told stories, remembered things, and demanded that I remember them, too . . ."

"Yes, I see, I see," I said. "And, in your opinion, what was he planning to do next?"

She looked at me as if I were journalist Kammerer. "You don't understand anything," she said.

And of course, on the whole, she was right. I'd gotten answers to Excellentz's questions: Abalkin had *not* been interested in Glumova's work, Abalkin had *not* been intending to use her to gain entry to the museum. But I really had no idea what Abalkin was trying to do when he arranged these twenty-four hours of nostalgia. Sentiment . . . an homage to childhood love . . . a return to his youth . . . I didn't believe this. There had been a practical goal, one that had been carefully thought out, and Abalkin had achieved it without arousing Glumova's suspicions. I was sure that Glumova herself knew nothing about this goal. After all, she didn't understand what really happened between the two of them herself . . .

And there was one more question I had to ask. All right. Say they reminisced, loved each other, had a drink, reminisced again, fell asleep, woke up, loved each other again, and again fell asleep . . . What then drove her to such despair, verging on hysteria? Of course, there was a wide variety of very different possibilities. For example, it could be something related to the habits of a staff officer of the Island Empire. But it could be something else. And this thing could well prove to be quite valuable to me. Here I hesitated in indecision; either I'd have to chance leaving something potentially very important behind, or I'd have to risk being appallingly tactless, accepting the possibility that I might still not learn anything of significance . . .

I decided to risk being tactless.

"Maya Toivovna," I said, trying as hard as I could to make my voice sound firm, "do tell me, what caused the state of despair that I accidentally witnessed during our last meeting?"

I forced out this sentence, not daring to look her in the eye. I wouldn't have been surprised if she immediately told me to go to hell, or even thwacked me over the head with the videophone. However, she didn't do either.

"I was an idiot," she said fairly calmly. "A hysterical idiot. I felt like he had squeezed me out like a lemon and thrown me out the door. And now I see that he had other things to worry about. He didn't have the time or energy for tact. I kept demanding explanations, but he really couldn't explain anything. After all, he probably knows you're looking for him . . ."

I got up. "Thank you very much, Maya Toivovna," I said. "I think you've misunderstood our intentions. No one is planning to hurt him. If you see him again, please try to impress that upon him."

She didn't answer.

JUNE 3, '78

A FEW THINGS ABOUT EXCELLENTZ'S IMPRESSIONS

I could see from the cliff that, in the absence of patients, Dr. Goannek was fishing. This was lucky, because his null-T booth was nearer than the one at the resort club. Alas, there did turn out to be an apiary along the way, a fact I had rashly overlooked during my first visit, and I was forced to save myself by jumping over certain decorative wicker fences and knocking down similarly decorative earthenware pots and jugs. However, everything turned out fine in the end. I ran up onto the balustered porch, entered the familiar parlor, and, without sitting down, called Excellentz.

I thought I could get away with a short report, but the conversation turned out to be rather long, and I was forced to take the videophone out onto the porch so that the talkative and touchy Dr. Goannek wouldn't be able to take me by surprise.

"Why does she stay there?" asked Excellentz thoughtfully.

"She's waiting."

"Do they have a rendezvous?"

"As far as I understand, no."

"Poor thing . . ." grumbled Excellentz. Then he asked, "Are you coming back?"

"No," I said. "I still have this Jasmaa and the bighead compound."

"What for?" he asked.

"This compound," I answered, "currently contains a certain bighead named Puppen-Itrich, the very same one who worked with Abalkin during Operation Dead Word."

"I see."

"From what I understood from Abalkin's report, the relationship that developed between them over there wasn't entirely ordinary."

"In what way was it extraordinary?"

I hesitated, choosing my words with care. "I might venture to call it a friendship, Excellentz . . . Do you remember the report?"

"I do. I understand what you're trying to say. But tell me this: How did you figure out that Puppen is on Earth?"

"Hmm . . . It was rather difficult. First, I—"

"That will do," he interrupted me, and paused expectantly.

I got it. It took me a moment, but I got it. He had a point. Even I, an employee of COMCON-2, with all of my considerable experience with the GWI, had found it quite difficult to locate Puppen. What then of simple Progressor Abalkin, who had, moreover, been stuck in Deep Space for the last twenty years, and whose understanding of the GWI was akin to a twenty-year-old's?

"I see your point," I said. "You're right, of course. But you have to admit that it's doable. Given the will."

"I admit it. But it's not only that. Did it ever occur to you that he may be casting stones into bushes?"

"No," I replied honestly.

Casting stones into bushes, translated from our specialized language, means to lead someone on a wild goose chase and to scatter red herrings—in short, to take someone for a ride. Of course, it was theoretically possible that Lev Abalkin was pursuing a certain well-specified goal, and that all of his stunts with Glumova, his teacher, and myself were merely masterfully orchestrated false trails—fake clues we were supposed to puzzle over in vain, wasting our time and energy and getting hopelessly distracted from the main point. "It doesn't look like it to me," I said confidently.

"And my impression is that it does," said Excellentz.

"You know best, of course," I said coolly.

"No doubt," he agreed. "But unfortunately, it's only an impression. I don't have any facts. However, if I'm *not* wrong, then I think it's unlikely that in his situation, he'd have remembered about Puppen, spent a lot of effort to find him, rushed to another hemisphere, and done another song and dance over there—all to cast one more stone into a bush. Don't you think so?"

"You see, Excellentz, I don't know what situation he's in, and that's probably why I don't have the same impression."

"And what impression do you have?" he asked with unexpected interest.

I tried to figure out how to say it. "Definitely not casting stones. There's a logic to his actions. They are interconnected. What's more, he keeps using the same technique. He's not wasting time and energy coming up with new techniques—he keeps making statements to shock people, then he listens to their stunned sputtering . . . He's trying to find something out, something about his life . . . or rather, about his fate. Something that's been hidden from him . . ." I trailed off, then said, "Excellentz, he must have figured out that there's a secret of identity connected with him."

Now we were both quiet. The speckled bald pate was swaying on the screen. I felt like I was living through a historic moment. This was one of the rare occasions when my reasoning (not the facts I'd unearthed, but my actual reasoning, my logical deductions) were making Excellentz reconsider his ideas.

He lifted his head and said, "All right. Go see Puppen. But keep in mind that you're most needed here, by my side."

"Understood," I said, and asked, "What about Jasmaa?"

"He's not on Earth."

"Says who?" I said. "He's on Earth. He's at Camp Jan near Antonov."

"He's been on Giganda for three days."

"I see," I said, making an effort to be ironic. "What a coincidence! Born on the same day as Abalkin, another posthumous child, also referred to by a number—"

"All right, all right," grumbled Excellentz. "Stay focused."

The screen went dark. I returned the videophone and went down into the yard. Then I cautiously made my way through the thickets of giant nettles and stepped straight out of Dr. Goannek's wooden outhouse into the night rain on the banks of the Thelon River.

JUNE 3, '78

AN OUTPOST ON THE THELON RIVER

Through the pattering of the rain, I could hear the rushing of the invisible river beneath the cliff—it was very close at hand. There was a softly glimmering lightweight metal bridge in front of me, the illuminated display above it proclaiming this to be THE TERRITORY OF THE BIGHEAD PEOPLE in Lincos. Strangely, the end of the bridge was sunk in the tall grass—not only was there no road leading up to the bridge, there wasn't even a lousy little path. A few steps away, a squat circular building that looked like a fortified barracks gazed at me with its lone glowing window. There was a hint of the unforgettable odor of Saraksh: the scent of rusty iron, carrion, and lurking death. Even here on Earth you can come across some strange spots. You might think that you're home, that you know everything here, that everything is pleasant and familiar, but no—sooner or later, you're sure to stumble on something totally bizarre . . . All right. What does journalist Kammerer think about this building? Aha! It turns out that he has already formed a very definite opinion about it.

Journalist Kammerer found a door in the round wall, gave it a hard shove, and found himself in a vaulted room. This room was empty except for a desk, and behind it sat a young man resting his chin on his hands. The young man's curls and long, gentle face gave him a distinct resemblance to Alexander Blok—that is, if the poet had decided to whimsically deck himself out in a bright, multicolored Mexican poncho. The young man looked into journalist Kammerer's eyes with an utterly disinterested and slightly weary blue-eyed gaze.

"This is some building!" said journalist Kammerer, brushing the raindrops from his shoulders.

"They like it," objected Alexander B. indifferently, without changing position.

"No way!" said journalist Kammerer sarcastically, looking around for a place to sit.

There were no empty chairs in the room, nor were there armchairs, sofas, couches, chaise longues, or benches. Journalist Kammerer looked at Alexander B. Alexander B. kept looking at him with the same indifferent expression, showing no inclination to be gracious or even merely polite. This was strange. Or rather, it was unusual. But you could tell that in this place, it was the norm.

Journalist Kammerer was about to open his mouth to introduce himself, but then Alexander B. suddenly lowered his wondrous eyelashes onto his pale cheeks with a certain weary resignation and, with all the emotion of a transport robot, began to recite his memorized script: "Dear friend! Unfortunately, you have traveled here in vain. You will find absolutely nothing of interest here. The rumors that have led you here are grossly exaggerated. The territory of the bighead people cannot in any way be considered a recreational-educational complex. The bigheads—a remarkable, very distinctive people—like to say this about themselves: 'We're inquisitive but not curious.' The members of the bighead delegation are here as representatives of their people—they are not here to participate in unofficial contacts, and they absolutely must not

be treated as objects of idle curiosity. Esteemed friend! The most
appropriate course of action would be for you to immediately set
off on your return journey and to convince all of your friends and
acquaintances of the true state of affairs."

Alexander B. fell silent and languidly lifted his lashes. Journalist
Kammerer was still there, which apparently didn't surprise him
in the least. "Of course, before we say farewell, I will answer all
your questions."

"Aren't you supposed to do that standing up?" inquired journalist Kammerer.

There was a flicker of something like animation in the blue
eyes. "To be honest, I am," admitted Alexander B. "But I busted
up my knee yesterday, and it still really hurts, so you'll have to
excuse me."

"Gladly," said journalist Kammerer, perching himself on the
edge of the desk. "I see you're overrun by sensation-seekers."

"You're the sixth party of my shift."

"I'm all alone!" objected journalist Kammerer.

"'Party' is a measure word," objected Alexander B., becoming
even more animated. Like, say 'stack.' A stack of books. A piece
of cotton. A box of chocolates. After all, it's possible that there's
only one piece of chocolate left in the box. All alone."

"Your explanations have fully satisfied me," declared journalist
Kammerer. "But I'm not a sensation-seeker. I'm here on business."

"Eighty three percent of all parties," immediately responded
Alexander B., "are here on business. The last party—five units
in number, counting small children and a dog—was looking to
discuss the possibility of lessons in the bighead tongue with the
leaders of the delegation. But the vast majority of people are collecting xenofolklore. It's a fad! Everyone's collecting xenofolklore.
I collect xenofolklore myself. But bigheads don't have any folklore!
It's a hoax! That joker Long Mueller published a little book in
the style of Ossian, and everyone lost their heads over it . . . 'Oh
shaggy, thousand-tailed trees, harboring your sorrowful thoughts
in fluffy warm trunks. Thousands upon thousands of tails you

have, but not a single head! . . . ' And, by the way, the bighead tongue doesn't have the concept of a tail! Their tail is their organ of direction, and a faithful translation would be 'compass' rather than 'tail' . . . 'Oh shaggy thousand-compassed trees!' But I see you are not a folklorist."

"No," admitted journalist Kammerer honestly. "I'm much worse. I'm a journalist."

"Writing a book about bigheads?"

"In a manner of speaking. Why?"

"No reason. Be my guest. You won't be the first or the last. Have you ever even seen a bighead?"

"Yes, of course."

"On the screen?"

"No. The thing is, I was the one to discover them on Saraksh . . ."

Alexander B. even stood up a bit. "So you're Kammerer?"

"At your service."

"No, I'm the one at your service, doctor! I await your orders, instructions, requests . . ."

I immediately remembered Kammerer's conversation with Abalkin and hastily explained: "I just discovered them, nothing more. I'm not an expert on bigheads. And right now I'm not interested in bigheads in general—I need one bighead in particular, the translator of the mission. So, if you don't mind . . . May I go across the bridge?"

"Good gracious, doctor!" Alexander B. threw up his hands. "I see you think we're here to guard the entrance? Not in the least! Please go ahead! A lot of people do that. You know, you explain to them that the rumors are grossly exaggerated, they nod and say good-bye, then they go outside and slip right across the bridge . . ."

"And?"

"They come back after a while. Very disappointed. They didn't see anyone or anything. Well, they saw forests, hills, ravines, charming scenery—but no bigheads. First of all, bigheads are nocturnal, second, they live underground, and most important—they only see the people they want to see. That's actually what we're here for—to serve as liaisons, so to speak."

"Who are you, exactly?" asked journalist Kammerer. "COMCON?"

"Yes. Trainees. We take turns working here. We can communicate both ways. . . Which of the translators did you need, exactly?"

"Puppen-Itrich."

"Let me give it a try. Does he know you?"

"I doubt it. But tell him that I want to speak to him about Lev Abalkin, whom he certainly knows."

"Of course!" said Alexander B., and pulled the selector toward him.

Journalist Kammerer (as did I, I have to confess) watched with a fascination turning to awe as this young man with the gentle face of a romantic poet all of a sudden bizarrely bulged out his eyes, formed an impossible-seeming tube with his delicate lips, and started to click, quack, and hoot like thirty-three bigheads put together (in the middle of a forest, in the dead of the night, by a torn-up concrete road, beneath Saraksh's dimly phosphorescing sky)—and these sounds seemed very appropriate in this empty, barrack-like, vaulted room with its rough and bare walls. Then he fell silent and bowed his head, listening to the series of answering clicks and hoots—and in the meantime, his lips and lower jaws kept moving strangely, as if they were being held in constant readiness to continue the conversation. This spectacle was rather unpleasant, and journalist Kammerer, despite his awe, decided it would be more tactful to look away.

However, the conversation didn't last too long. Alexander B. leaned back in his chair and, gently massaging his lower jaw with his long pale fingers, said, sounding slightly out of breath, "It sounds like he agreed. However, I don't want to give you false hope: I'm not at all sure that I understood everything correctly. I picked up two layers of meaning, but I think there was also a third . . . Anyway, go across the bridge—there's a path on the other side. The path goes into the forest. He'll meet you there. Or rather, he'll take a look at you . . . No. How can I put it? You know, it's a lot easier to understand a bighead than it is to translate his words. For instance, take their slogan: 'We are inquisitive but not curious.' This happens to be an example of a good translation. 'We're not curious' can be understood both as 'We don't indulge in vain curiosity' and at the same time as 'We aren't of interest to you.' Do you understand?"

"I understand," said journalist Kammerer, climbing down from the desk. "He'll take a look at me, and only then will he decide whether he should talk to me. Thank you for all your trouble."

"No trouble at all. It was my pleasure . . . Wait, take my raincoat, it's raining . . ."

"Thank you, but no thanks," journalist Kammerer said, and went out into the rain.

JUNE 3, '78

PUPPEN-ITRICH, BIGHEAD

It was 3 AM local time, the sky was covered with clouds, and the forest was dense, making this night world seem gray, flat, and hazy, like a blurry old photograph.

Of course, he noticed me first, and for at least five minutes, if not for all ten, he followed a parallel course to mine, hiding in the dense underbrush. When I finally became aware of him, he realized it almost immediately and instantly materialized on the path in front of me.

"I'm here," he announced.

"I can see that," I said.

"We'll talk here," he said.

"OK," I said.

He immediately sat down, looking for all the world like a dog talking to his master—a large, fat, bigheaded dog with small triangular ears sticking straight up and big round eyes beneath a massive broad forehead. His voice was hoarse, and he spoke without the slightest accent, so that only the short, choppy sentences and a certain exaggerated clarity of articulation gave him away as a nonnative speaker. And he also smelled. But he didn't smell of wet dog, as one might have expected, but rather something inorganic, like heated resin. It was a strange smell—more reminiscent of a machine than a living creature. If memory serves, the bigheads on Saraksh smelled completely different.

"What do you need?" he asked bluntly.

"Did they tell you who I am?"

"Yes. You're a journalist. You're writing a book about my people."

"That's not exactly right. I'm writing a book about Lev Abalkin. You know him."

"All my people know Lev Abalkin."

This was news to me. "And what do your people think about Lev Abalkin?"

"My people don't think about Lev Abalkin. They know him."

This seemed to be the beginning of some linguistic quagmire. "I was trying to ask you how your people feel about Lev Abalkin."

"They know him. All of them. From birth to death."

Journalist Kammerer and I conferred and decided to abandon this topic for the time being. We asked, "What can you tell me about Lev Abalkin?"

"Nothing," he replied curtly.

This was the thing I feared most. I feared it so much that my subconscious had rejected the very possibility, and I was completely unprepared. I was at a total, pathetic loss, and in the meantime, he brought his front paw to his mouth and started to noisily bite between his claws. Not like an Earth dog—more like one of our cats.

However, thankfully my self-control didn't desert me. I managed to realize that if this *Canis sapiens* had really wanted nothing to do with me, he would have simply refused to see me. "I know that Lev Abalkin is your friend," I said. "You lived and worked together. A lot of earthlings would like to know what Lev Abalkin's bighead friend and colleague thinks about him."

"Why?" he asked, just as curtly as before.

"It's experience," I answered.

"Useless experience."

"There's no such thing as useless experience."

He started in on the other paw, then in a few seconds grumbled indistinctly, "Ask specific questions."

I thought about it. "I know that you last worked with Abalkin fifteen years ago. Have you worked with other earthlings since?"

"I have. Many earthlings."

"Did you feel the difference?"

I didn't mean anything in particular by this question. But Puppen suddenly froze, slowly lowered his paw to the ground, and raised his bulbous head. A gloomy red light briefly flashed in his eyes. However, it didn't take more than a second for him to start gnawing his claws again. "Hard to say," he grumbled. "Jobs are different; people are also different. Hard question."

He dodged the question. Why? My innocent inquiry seemed to fluster him. He was at a loss for a good second. Or was it linguistics again?

Come to think of it, linguistics can also be a good tool. Let's go on the attack. Face this head on. "So you meet with him," I declared, "and he asks you to work with him again. Is it a yes or a no?"

This could have meant, *If you meet him and he asks you to work with him again, would you say yes or no?* Or instead, *You met with him, and (as I've found out) he asked you to work with him again. Did you say yes or no?* Linguistics. I admit that this was a rather pathetic maneuver, but what else was there left for me to do?

And linguistics saved me. "He didn't ask me to work with him," objected Puppen.

"Then what did you talk about?" I said in surprise, continuing the successful gambit.

"The past," he mumbled. "It's not interesting."

"Did you think," I asked, wiping the metaphorical sweat off my brow, "that he'd changed a lot in the intervening fifteen years?"

"That's not interesting, either."

"No. That's very interesting. I saw him recently myself and found that he'd changed a lot. But I'm an earthling and I need to know your opinion."

"In my opinion, yes."

"There we go! How did you think he changed?"

"He doesn't care about the bighead people anymore."

"Really?" I said with genuine surprise. "And when we talked, he spoke of nothing else."

His eyes glowed red again. I interpreted this to mean that my words had disconcerted him once more. "What did he say to you?" he asked.

"We were arguing about which earthling has done the most to improve our relationship with the bighead people."

"What else?"

"That's it. We only talked about this."

"When was this?"

"The day before yesterday. What made you think that he doesn't care about the bighead people anymore?"

He suddenly announced, "We're wasting time. Don't ask empty questions. Ask real questions."

"All right. I'll ask a real question. Where is he now?"

"I don't know."

"What is he planning to do?"

"I don't know."

"What did he say to you? I want to know every word."

And then Puppen assumed a strange pose, one I might even call unnatural: he crouched on spring-loaded paws, stretched out his neck, and stared at me from below. Then, rhythmically swaying his heavy head back and forth, he spoke, carefully enunciating the words: "Listen to me carefully, understand me correctly, and remember this for a long time. The people of Earth do not interfere in the affairs of the bighead people. The bighead people do not interfere in the affairs of the people of Earth. So it was, so it is, and so it always will be. The Lev Abalkin affair is an affair of the people of Earth. This has been decided. And therefore. Don't look for something that isn't there. The bighead people will never give asylum to Lev Abalkin."

Wow! I blurted out, "He requested asylum? From you?"

"I said only what I did: the bighead people will never give asylum to Lev Abalkin. That's it. Do you understand?"

"I understand. But I'm not interested in this. I'm asking you again, what did he say to you?"

"I'll answer. But first repeat the important thing I told you."

"All right, I'll repeat it. The bighead people won't interfere in the Abalkin affair and would refuse him asylum. Right?"

"That's right. And that's the important thing."

"Now answer my question."

"I'll answer it. He asked me whether there was a difference between him and the other people I worked with. The exact same question you asked me."

As soon as he finished speaking, he turned around and slipped into the underbrush. Not a single branch or leaf had flickered, and he was already gone. He had disappeared.

Damn, Puppen! . . . *I taught him how to speak our language and use the Supply Line. I stayed by his side when he got sick with his strange illnesses . . . I tolerated his bad manners, put up with his blunt remarks, forgave him things that I don't forgive anyone else . . . If it came down to it, I'd fight for Puppen like I would for another earthling, like I'd fight for myself. And Puppen? I don't know . . .* Damn, Puppen-Itrich!

JUNE 3, '78

EXCELLENTZ IS PLEASED

"Very curious!" said Excellentz when I finished my report. "You were right to insist on a visit to this menagerie, Mak."

"I don't understand," I replied, irritably tearing the burrs off my wet pants. "Does this make any sense to you?"

"Yes."

I goggled at him. "Do you honestly believe that Lev Abalkin may have requested asylum?"

"No. I don't believe that."

"Then how does this make sense? Or do you think he was casting another stone?"

"Maybe. But that's not the point. It doesn't matter what Lev Abalkin was doing. The bigheads' reaction—that's what matters. You don't need to worry about it, though. You brought me important information. Thank you. I'm happy. And you should be happy, too."

I began to tear off the burrs again. There was no doubt about it—he was certainly happy. Even in the dim light of the office,

155

I could see his green eyes blazing. This was just how he had looked when I—young, cheerful, and out of breath—had informed him that Goody-Goody Presht had finally been caught red-handed and was sitting downstairs in the car, gagged and ready. I had caught Goody-Goody myself, but at the time, I hadn't yet understood something perfectly clear to Wanderer: the sabotage had come to an end, and by the following day, trains full of grain would be heading to the capital . . .

And this was another thing that was obviously clear to him and I didn't understand, but I didn't feel the least bit satisfied. I hadn't caught anyone; no one was waiting, gagged, to be questioned—there was only a mysterious man with a mutilated fate rushing around our gentle giant of a planet, rushing around without finding a place for himself, flailing as if he'd been poisoned and, in his turn, poisoning everyone he met with resentment and despair, betraying others and getting betrayed himself . . .

"Let me remind you, Mak," Excellentz suddenly said softly. "He's dangerous. And he's all the more dangerous because he doesn't know it."

"What the hell is he, for God's sake?" I asked. "An insane android?"

"Androids can't have secrets of identity," said Excellentz. "Stay focused."

I stuffed the burrs into my jacket pocket and sat up straight.

"You can go home now," said Excellentz. "You're free until 7 PM. After that, I'll need you nearby—stay within city boundaries and wait for my call. He may try to break into the museum tonight. We'll take him there."

"All right," I said without any enthusiasm.

He gave me a frank once-over. "I hope you're in good shape," he said. "It'll only be the two of us, and I'm too old for this."

JUNE 4, '78

THE MUSEUM OF
EXTRATERRESTRIAL CULTURES, NIGHT

At 1:08 AM, the radio bracelet on my wrist beeped, and Excellentz's muffled voice rapidly mumbled, "Mak, museum, main entrance, quick . . ."

I banged the cockpit canopy shut so I wouldn't get hit with a blast of air and put the engine straight into overdrive. The glider soared vertically into the starry sky. Three seconds to brake. Twenty-two seconds to hover and orient myself. Star Square is empty. And there's no one in front of the main entrance, either. That's strange . . . Aha. A skinny black figure appears from the null-T booth by the corner of the museum. It slips toward the main entrance. Excellentz.

The glider silently landed in front of the main entrance. A warning light immediately flashed on the control panel, and the mild voice of the cyberinspector reproachfully informed me that "gliders may not be landed on Star Square . . ." I flipped the canopy open and leaped out onto the sidewalk. Excellentz was already fiddling with the door using a magnetic lockpick. "Gliders may not be landed . . ." solemnly repeated the cyberinspector.

"Shut him up," mumbled Excellentz through gritted teeth, without turning around.

I slammed the canopy shut. And at that very moment, the door of the main entrance swung open.

"Follow me!" Excellentz threw out, and dived into the darkness.

I dived in behind him. It was just like old times.

He was taking huge bounds in front of me—long, gaunt, and angular, once more nimble and light on his feet, all in black and looking like the shadow of a medieval demon—and it flashed through my head that none of our current pipsqueaks had ever seen this Excellentz, and that the only ones left who had were Peter Angelov, old man Elephant, and myself, and that it was a good fifteen years ago.

He led me on a complicated winding path from room to room, from hallway to hallway, maneuvering flawlessly between wall displays and glass cases, between statues and scale models that looked like misshapen machines, and between machines and instruments that looked like misshapen statues. There was no light anywhere—apparently the automatic switches had been turned off in advance—but he never made a mistake or lost his way, even though I knew that his night vision was much worse than mine. He had really prepared for this night escapade, our Excellentz, and he wasn't doing badly, he wasn't doing badly at all, if you didn't count his breathing. His breathing was too loud, but there was nothing to be done about that. That was age. Those damn years.

He suddenly came to a halt and, as soon as I caught up to him, gripped my shoulder with his fingers. At first I was afraid that he was having a heart spasm, but I almost immediately realized that we had arrived and that he was simply catching his breath.

I looked around. Empty tables. Shelves along the walls crammed with alien curios. Xenographic projectors by the far wall. I had seen all this before. We were in Maya Toivovna Glumova's workshop. This was her desk, and that was the chair that journalist Kammerer had sat in . . .

Excellentz let go of my shoulder, took a step toward the shelves, bent down, and walked parallel to them without standing up straight—he was looking for something. Then he stopped, picked something up with a visible effort, and walked toward the table in front of the door. He was carrying the object—a long, thin slab with rounded corners—out in front of him, his arms sinking under the weight, and leaning back slightly to compensate. He carefully and very quietly placed the object on the table, went still for a moment, then suddenly pulled a very a long, colorful fringed shawl out of his breast pocket like a magician. He spread it out with a flick of the wrist and threw it over his slab. Then he bent down to me, put his lips to my ear, and said in a barely audible whisper, "As soon as he touches that piece of cloth, take him. And if sees us before that, take him. Stand right here."

I took a station on one side of the door, with Excellentz on the other.

I didn't hear anything at first. I was standing with my back against the wall, mechanically evaluating the possible scenarios and staring at the cloth spread out on the table. I wonder why Lev Abalkin would want to touch it. Even if he needs that slab, how would he know that it's hidden under the cloth? What is this slab, anyway? It looks like a case for a portable intravisor. Or for some kind of musical instrument. But that seems unlikely. It's too heavy. I don't understand a thing. It's clearly bait, but if it's bait, it's not meant for a human . . .

Then I heard a noise. It must be said that this wasn't a small noise—something large and metallic had crashed in the depths of the building, coming apart in the fall. I immediately remembered the giant ball of barbed wire the museum girls had worked so diligently on with their molecular soldering irons. I glanced at Excellentz. Excellentz was also listening and also looking perplexed.

The banging and clanging gradually died down, and all was silent again. That's strange. A progressor—a professional, a master of stealth—blindly crashing into such a bulky object? Unthinkable. Of course, he could have caught his sleeve on a single protruding barb . . . No, he couldn't have. Not a progressor. Or has being back on our safe Earth already caused the progressor to loosen up? . . . Doubtful. Then again, we'll see. Either way, he must now be frozen still on one leg, listening intently, and he'll do that for at least five minutes . . .

He didn't even think to stand on one leg and listen. He was clearly getting closer to us, and his perambulations were accompanied by a whole cacophony of different noises, all completely inappropriate for a progressor. He shuffled his feet and scraped the soles of his shoes loudly against the floor. He bumped into the lintels and the walls. One time he crashed into the furniture and burst into a series of unintelligible, mostly sibilant curses. And when I saw the faint glimmers of an electric light reflected in the projector screens, my doubts turned to certainty.

"It's not him," I said to Excellentz almost out loud.

Excellentz nodded. He was looking bewildered and sullen. He no longer had his back to the wall—he was now facing me, legs apart and scowling, and it was easy to imagine that in a minute, he'd grab the pseudo-progressor by the lapels, evenly shake him, and snarl into his face, "Who are you and what are you doing here, you irrelevant bastard?"

And this image was so vivid in my mind that at first I wasn't even surprised when he pulled one side of his black jacket open with his left hand and began to shove his favorite twenty-six-caliber Duke pistol into it with his right hand—it was as if he was freeing his hands for the upcoming grabbing and shaking.

But when it finally dawned on me that this entire time, he had been standing there holding this eight-shot sure death in his hand, I was completely stunned. This could only mean one thing: Excellentz was ready to kill Lev Abalkin. It couldn't mean anything else, because Excellentz never drew a weapon to frighten, threaten, or make an impression on someone—only to kill.

I was so shocked that I forgot about everything else. But then a beam of bright white light burst into the workshop, followed by the pseudo-Abalkin, after the latter bumped into one last lintel.

He actually even looked a bit like Lev Abalkin: he was stocky, short, and had long black hair down to his shoulders. He was wearing a large white raincoat and holding an electric Tourist flashlight in front of him in one hand, while gripping either a small suitcase or a large briefcase in the other. After he came into the room, he paused, shone his flashlight around the shelves, and said, "Hmmm, ought to be here."

His voice was raspy, and his tone was exaggeratedly chipper. This is the tone that people speak to themselves in when they are a bit scared, embarrassed, and guilty—in other words, when they are ill at ease. *One foot in the ditch*, as the Hontians say.

I could now see that this was actually an old man. Maybe even older than Excellentz. He had a long, pointed aquiline nose, a long, pointed chin, hollow cheeks, and a high, very white forehead. On the whole, he looked more like Sherlock Holmes than Lev Abalkin. The only thing I could say with certainty about this man was that I had never seen him before in my life.

After taking a quick look around, he walked up to the table, put his briefcase-suitcase on the colorful cloth next to our slab, then began to search the shelves, illuminating them with his flashlight—slowly and methodically, shelf by shelf, section by section. The entire time, he kept mumbling things under his breath, although I could only make out the occasional word: ". . . Well, as everyone knows . . . hmm-hmm-hmm . . . A real illisium . . . hmm-hmm-hmm . . . Junk, junk, and more junk . . . hmm-hmm . . . Not in its place . . . All crammed and hidden away . . . hmm-hmm-hmm . . ."

Excellentz was watching these maneuvers with his hands behind his back and a very unfamiliar and uncharacteristic expression plastered on his face—hopeless weariness or maybe weary boredom. It was as if he was looking at something that he was impossibly sick of—a barnacle clinging to him that had grown hateful over the course of his life, but one he had long resigned himself to and despaired of freeing himself from. To be honest, I was initially somewhat surprised that he had given up on that most natural of intentions—to take this man by his lapels and gleefully shake him. But now, looking at his face, I realized that it would have been pointless. Whether he shook him or not, it made no difference, everything would come back full circle: this man would always crawl and root around, mumble under his breath, stand with one foot in ditches, upset museum exhibits, and disrupt carefully planned and thought-out operations . . .

When the old man got to the section farthest from us, Excellentz gave a deep sigh, came up to the table, perched on an edge by the briefcase, then said peevishly, "Come on, what are you looking for, Bromberg? Detonators?"

Old man Bromberg let out a thin squeal and jumped sideways, knocking over a chair. "Who's there?" he shrieked, frantically scanning the room with his flashlight. "Who is it?"

"It's me, it's me!" Excellentz responded even more peevishly. "Quit all that trembling!"

"Who? You? What the hell?!" He shone the light on Excellentz. "Aha! Sikorsky! I knew it!"

"Don't point that thing at me," ordered Excellentz, shading his face with his hand.

"I knew that these must be your monkey tricks!" shrieked old man Bromberg. "I immediately figured out who was behind this charade!"

"Stop pointing that thing at me or I'll smash it to pieces!" barked Excellentz.

"I'll ask you not to yell at me!" screeched Bromberg, but he did point the flashlight away. "And don't you dare touch my briefcase!"

Excellentz got up and walked toward him.

"Don't you dare get near me!" shrieked Bromberg. "I'm not a boy! Shame on you! You're an old man!"

Excellentz came up to him, took the flashlight away, and put it on the table closest to us with its reflector up. "Have a seat, Bromberg," he said. "We need to talk."

"You and your conversations . . ." Bromberg grumbled, and sat down.

Amazingly, he was now completely calm. A respectable, energetic old man. I might even call him cheerful.

JUNE 4, '78

ISAAC BROMBERG: BATTLE OF THE IRON ELDERS

"Let's try to have a calm conversation," suggested Excellentz.

"Let's try, let's try!" replied Bromberg energetically. "And who's the young man propping up the wall by the door? Have you acquired a bodyguard?"

Excellentz didn't immediately answer. It's possible that he was contemplating sending me away—*Maxim, you're free to go*—and then I would have left, of course. But that would have offended me, and Excellentz was certainly aware of that. However, I grant that he may have had other considerations. In any case, he gestured vaguely in my direction and said, "This is Maxim Kammerer, a COMCON employee. Maxim, this is Dr. Isaac Bromberg, a historian of science."

I bowed, and Bromberg immediately declared, "I knew it. Of course you were afraid you couldn't handle me alone, Sikorsky . . .

Have a seat, young man, have a seat, make yourself comfortable. If I know your boss, we'll be here a while."

"Have a seat, Mak," said Excellentz.

I sat down in the familiar visitor's chair.

"All right, I'm awaiting your explanations, Sikorsky," said Bromberg. "What's the meaning of this ambush?"

"We really scared you, I see."

"Nonsense!" Bromberg immediately flared up. "Don't be absurd! Thank goodness I don't frighten easily! And if anyone can scare me, Sikorsky—"

"But you let out that awful shriek and knocked over so much furniture."

"Well, you know, if you were all alone at night, in an absolutely empty building, and right in your ear—"

"There's absolutely no need to go into absolutely empty buildings at night."

"First, it's absolutely none of your business where I go and when I do it, Sikorsky! And second, when else am I supposed to come here? I'm not allowed in during the day. During the day, they're making some suspicious repairs, they're setting up some ridiculous new exhibition . . . Admit it, Sikorsky, it was your idea to close access to the museum! I urgently needed to refresh my memory on certain facts! I come here, I'm not allowed in! Me! A member of this museum's academic council! I call the director, I ask, what's happening? By the way, the director, the lovely Grant Khochikian, is in a certain sense a student of mine . . . The poor man stammers, the man turns crimson—he's ashamed of his behavior before me . . . But his hands are tied—he gave his word! He was asked by certain very respectable people, and he gave his word! May I inquire who asked him? Could it have been a certain Rudolf Sikorsky? No! Oh, no! No one here has even heard of Rudolf Sikorsky! But I can't be taken in like that! I immediately figured out whose ears were peeking out from behind the curtain! And I'd still like to know, Sikorsky, why you've been keeping mum for an hour instead of answering my questions! I'm asking you, what's behind

all this? Closing the museum! The disgraceful attempt to appropriate museum exhibits! And who the hell turned off the electricity? I
have no idea what I would have done if I hadn't happened to have
a flashlight in the glider. Look at this goose egg, damn you! And
I knocked something over back there! I sincerely hope—I want to
hope!—that it was only a model . . . And you should pray to God,
Sikorsky, that it was only a model, because if it was an original,
you'll be putting it together for me yourself, with your own two
hands! Down to the very last barb! And if the last barb is missing,
off you go to Tagora without a peep . . ."

His voice cracked and he began to hack with a painful-
sounding cough, thumping his chest with both his fists. "Am I
ever going to get answers to my questions?" he furiously croaked
through the coughing.

I was sitting there as if watching a play, finding this rather
comical, but then I glanced at Excellentz and was dumbfounded.

Excellentz, Wanderer, Rudolf Sikorsky—that block of ice,
that frost-covered granite monument to Equanimity and Self-
Possession, that infallible machine for getting information—was
flushed crimson to the very top of his head, breathing heavily, and
convulsively clenching and unclenching his bony, freckled fists,
while his famous ears were glowing red and ominously twitching.
However, he was still restraining himself—but only he knew what
this cost him. "I'd like to know, Bromberg," he said in a strangled
voice, "why you needed the detonators?"

"Oh, is that what you'd like to know?" Dr. Bromberg whis-
pered venomously, and leaned forward to peer into Excellentz's
face, getting so close that his long nose was in danger of winding
up between my boss's teeth. "And what else would you like to
know about me? Are you maybe interested in the consistency of
my stool? Or perhaps you'd like to hear about my recent conversation with Pilguy?"

I didn't like that Pilguy had been mentioned in this context.
Pilguy was interested in biogenerators, and for two months
now my department had been interested in Pilguy. However,

Excellentz paid no attention to Pilguy. He leaned sharply forward himself—so quickly that Bromberg barely had the chance to recoil. "I'll let you worry about your own stool!" he growled. "What I'd like to know is why you think you have the right to break into the museum, and why you're trying to get your paws on the detonators, when you were very clearly told that for the next few days—"

"Oh, you're planning to criticize my behavior, are you? Ha! Who? Sikorsky! Doing what? Criticizing me! Accusing me of breaking in! I wonder how you got into the museum yourself! Eh? Tell me that!"

"That's irrelevant, Bromberg!"

"You're a burglar, Sikorsky!" announced Bromberg, extending a long, gnarled finger toward Excellentz. "You've been reduced to breaking in!"

"You're the one who's been reduced to breaking in, Bromberg!" roared Excellentz. "You and no one else! You were given completely clear, unambiguous instructions: the museum is closed! Any normal person in your place—"

"When a normal person comes across yet another conspiracy, it's his duty to—"

"It's his duty to use his head a little, Bromberg! It's his duty to realize that he doesn't live in the Middle Ages! Mysteries and secrets don't exist because of someone's whim or ill will."

"No, they don't exist because of someone's whim or ill will—they're the result of your breathtaking arrogance, Sikorsky, your ridiculous, truly medieval, idiotically fanatical certainty that you should be able to determine what the public should and shouldn't know! You're a very old man, Sikorsky, but you still haven't realized that this is, above all, immoral!"

"I find it amusing to be lectured about morals by a man who, in order to satisfy his childish feelings of protest, decides to break in! You're not only an old man, Bromberg, you're a pathetic, senile old geezer!"

"Very well!" said Bromberg, suddenly calming down again. He stuck a hand into a pocket of his white raincoat, extracted a shiny object, and then banged it down on the table in front of Excellentz. "Here's my key. I, like every employee of this museum, am entitled to a key to the service entrance, and I used it to get in."

"In the dead of the night and in defiance of the director of the museum?" Excellentz didn't have a key, he had a magnetic lockpick, and there was nothing left for him to do but to keep attacking.

"In the dead of the night, but with a key! Where's your key, Sikorsky? Show me your key, please!"

"I don't have a key! I don't need one! I'm here in an official capacity, not because I have a bug up my ass, you doddering, hysterical idiot!"

And then all hell broke loose! I'm sure that the walls of that humble workshop had never heard such outbursts of hoarse roars interspersed with raspy screeches before. Such epithets. Such an orgy of emotion. Such absurd arguments and even more absurd counterarguments. And forget the walls! After all, these were merely the walls of a quiet academic establishment, far removed from worldly passions. But even I—a man no longer in his first youth, who you might think had seen it all—even I had never seen anything like this, at least when it came to Excellentz.

The battlefield would constantly become completely shrouded in smoke, and then you could no longer figure out what they were fighting about: you could only make out the epithets hurtling between them like white-hot cannonballs—the various "irresponsible windbags," "feudal knights of the cloak and dagger," "activist-provocateurs," "bald-headed secret service agents," "sclerotic demagogues," and "underhanded jailers of ideas." And, of course, the less exotic "old asses," "poisonous geezers," and "dotards" were raining down like shrapnel . . .

However, the smoke would occasionally clear, and then truly amazing retrospective vistas would appear before my astonished, spellbound eyes. That's when I realized that the battle I was accidentally witnessing was one of countless such battles in a silent, invisible war that had started back when my parents were just finishing school.

It didn't take me long to remember who this Isaac Bromberg was. I had heard of him before, of course—maybe even back when I was just a kid working in the Free Search Group. I had definitely read at least one of his books, *The Way It Really Was*, which told the story of the Massachusetts Terror. I recall not liking the book: the beginning sounded too much like a pamphlet, the author had worked too hard to strip the romance from this genuinely horrifying story, and he had devoted too many pages to a detailed discussion of the political underpinnings of various approaches to dangerous experiments—a discussion I wasn't at all interested in at the time.

However, in certain circles Bromberg's name was famous and commanded considerable respect. You might say that he belonged to the extreme left wing of the well-known Jiyuist movement— founded by Lamondois a long time ago and proclaiming that science has the right to develop without any restrictions. The extremists of this movement embrace principles that seem perfectly natural at first glance but in practice turn out to completely infeasible at any specific stage of human development. (I remember being completely astonished when I first became acquainted with the history of the Tagoran civilization, which had scrupulously observed these principles since the long bygone days of their First Industrial Revolution.)

Every scientific discovery that can be realized must be realized. It's difficult to argue with the principle itself, although even at this stage, it's hard to avoid a variety of caveats. What do you do with the discovery once it's realized? Answer: you keep its consequences under control. Very nice. And what happens if you don't foresee all the consequences? What happens if you overestimate some consequences and underestimate others? And finally, what happens when it's completely clear that you won't be able to keep even the most obvious and unpleasant consequences under control? What if this requires unimaginable energy resources and unthinkable moral strain? (By the way, that's exactly what happened with the Massachusetts machine, when, right under the eyes of the stunned researchers, a new, nonhuman Earth civilization emerged and rapidly began to gain in power.)

"Stop the experiment!" the World Council usually says in such cases.

"Not on your life!" the extremists declare in response. Do we increase oversight? Yes. Devote more resources to it? Yes. Do we risk it? Yes! After all, "If you never drink or smoke, you'll be hale and hearty when you croak" (from a speech by the patriarch of the extremists, J. G. Prenson). But no prohibitions! Ethico-moral prohibitions in science are worse than any ethical upheavals that have ever arisen or could ever arise because of the riskiest twists and turns of scientific progress. This stance can doubtlessly impress people with its dynamism and finds unapologetic evangelists among young scientists—but it is fiendishly dangerous when its principles are espoused by an eminent, talented expert, whose influence can be used to assemble a dynamic, talented team and to amass significant energy resources.

Our COMCON-2 was mainly concerned with handling these practical extremists. Old man Bromberg, on the other hand, was a theoretical extremist, which was probably why I hadn't come across him before. However, as I now saw, he had been a pain in Excellentz's neck and rear his entire life.

Due to the nature of its work, COMCON-2 never prohibits anyone anything. We aren't sufficiently conversant with modern science for that. The World Council issues the prohibitions. And our job is to implement these prohibitions and prevent information leaks, because in these cases, information leaks often lead to the direst consequences.

Bromberg evidently either wouldn't or couldn't understand this. The fight to remove each and every obstacle to the dissemination of scientific knowledge had literally become his idée fixe. He had an amazing temperament and inexhaustible energy. He had countless connections in the scientific world, and as soon as he heard that the results of promising research were being put on hold, he would start foaming at the mouth and raring to expose, reveal, and demystify.

There was absolutely nothing to be done about him. He didn't believe in compromises, so it was impossible to negotiate with him; he never admitted defeat, so it was impossible to beat him. He was as ungovernable as a cosmic cataclysm.

But apparently, even the most lofty and abstract idea requires a concrete point of application. And for him, this purpose was served by COMCON-2 in general and Excellentz in particular. These were the concrete embodiments of the forces of evil and darkness that he was doing battle with. "COMCON-2!" he'd hiss venomously, hopping up to Excellentz and immediately hopping back again. "How Jesuitical! . . . Take your famous acronym—the Commission for Contact with Other Civilizations. How noble! How respectable! And what's hiding behind this lofty phrase? Only your shady little shop! The Commission for Control, my foot! It's a Committee of Conservatives, not a Commission for Control! A Community of Conspirators! . . ."

He'd spent the last half-century irritating Excellentz past all endurance. What's more, as far as I could tell, he was irritating and nothing more—like a biting fly or an annoying mosquito. He was obviously in no position to significantly interfere with our work. It simply wasn't in his power. But, on the other hand, it was in his power to constantly mumble and grumble, chatter and jabber, distract us from our work, never leave us alone, aim poisonous gibes at us, demand strict compliance with all the forms and then agitate public opinion against excessive bureaucracy—in a word, to harass us until we collapsed from exhaustion. I wouldn't have been surprised if it turned out that twenty years ago, Excellentz immersed himself in the bloody mess on Saraksh in order to get a bit of respite from Bromberg. I felt especially bad for Excellentz, who was not only a principled man but also extremely fair-minded, and therefore was probably completely aware that

Bromberg's activities, if you ignored their form, did have a certain positive social function. They themselves were a type of social oversight: he oversaw the overseers.

But poisonous old Bromberg was apparently completely devoid of the most elementary feelings of justice—he tarred all our work with the same brush, considered it all indisputably harmful, and hated it with a sincere, ardent passion. And this hatred assumed such odious forms, and the behavior of this obnoxious old man was so unbearable, that Excellentz, despite his sangfroid and inhuman restraint, apparently lost face every time he confronted Bromberg and turned into a quarrelsome, foolish, and spiteful yeller. "You cowardly ignoramus!" he was rasping out in a broken voice. "You're nothing but a parasite that feeds on the mistakes of giants! You couldn't even invent pasta sauce yourself, yet you presume to sit in judgment on the future of science! You're discrediting the very cause you're trying to champion, you savorer of worthless gossip! . . ."

The old men apparently hadn't gone toe-to-toe in a long time and were now showering each other with their accumulated stores of venom and bile. In many ways, this spectacle was educational, even if it did flagrantly contradict the well-known thesis that man is by nature good and glorious. Right now, they resembled two old mangy fighting cocks more than they did human beings. For the first time, I realized that Excellentz was a very old man.

However, for all its unseemliness, this spectacle did dump a veritable avalanche of truly invaluable information on my head. There were a lot of allusions I simply didn't understand—they seemed to reference cases long since closed and forgotten. Others referred to stories I was already intimately familiar with. But there were also a few things I heard—or understood—for the very first time.

For example, I learned about Operation Mirror. It turned out that this was the code name for a set of highly classified global military exercises carried out decades ago to prepare for possible external aggression—presumably in the event of an invasion by the Wanderers. The number of people who had known about this had been in the single digits, and the millions of people who took part in it never even suspected it. Despite all the precautions, a few people died, as is usually the case with affairs of global scale. Excellentz had been one of the organizers of this operation and the person responsible for preserving its secrecy.

I learned about the origins of the Freak case. As everybody knows, Jonathan Pereira had stopped working in the field of theoretical eugenics of his own accord. In putting this area on hold, the World Council was essentially following his recommendations. Well, it turns out that our darling Bromberg had sniffed this out and, in his fervor, had spread the details of Pereira's theory far and wide—and as a result, five devilishly talented hotheads from the Schweitzer Laboratory in Bamako had started and, in fact, almost completed an experiment into a new variant of *Homo super*.

I was already familiar with the broad outlines of the android story, mostly because it is always cited as a classical example of an unsolvable ethical dilemma. However, I was fascinated to learn that Dr. Bromberg does not by any means consider the android question closed. The "subject or object?" issue doesn't interest him at all. He doesn't give a hoot about the secrets of identity of the scientists who worked with the androids, and the right of an android to a secret of identity he considers nonsensical and semantically meaningless. *The full details of this story should be published for the edification of future generations, and work with the androids should continue . . .*

And so on and so forth.

One story I hadn't heard before caught my ear. It was about a certain object that they sometimes called a sarcophagus and other times an incubator. In the course of their argument, they kept connecting this sarcophagus-incubator to the detonators— there was clearly some elusive link between the two—the very same detonators that Bromberg had come here for, and that were now lying on the table in front of me under a colorful shawl. However, the detonators mostly came up in passing—even if they did come up more than once—and the brawl mostly centered around the "veil of disgusting secrecy" that Excellentz had thrown over this sarcophagus-incubator. This secrecy was the exact reason that Dr. So-and-So, who had achieved unparalleled results on the anthropometry and physiology of the Cro-Magnons (how did the Cro-Magnons come into this?), had been forced to keep these results under wraps, thereby hindering the development of paleoanthropology. And another Dr. So-and-So, who had figured out the operating principle of the sarcophagus-incubator, had found himself in the equivocal and embarrassing position of a man erroneously credited with coming up with this principle himself, and as a result, he abandoned science entirely and now paints mediocre landscapes . . .

I pricked up my ears. The detonators were connected to the mysterious sarcophagus. Bromberg had come here for the detonators. Excellentz was using the detonators as bait for Lev Abalkin. I began to listen with redoubled attention, hoping that in the heat of the quarrel, the old men would blurt out something else, and I'd finally learn something significant about Lev Abalkin. But, as it turned out, this happened only after they finally calmed down.

JUNE 4, '78

LEV ABALKIN AT DR. BROMBERG'S

They calmed down suddenly and simultaneously, as if they had run out of steam at the same time. They fell silent. Stopped glaring fierily at each other. Bromberg, huffing and puffing, pulled out a large, old-fashioned handkerchief and began to wipe his face and neck. Excellentz, without looking at him, reached into his coat (for a second, I was afraid he was reaching for his gun), took out a pill pod, rolled a white ball into the palm of his hand, put it under his tongue, and offered the pod to Bromberg.

"I refuse!" said Bromberg, demonstratively turning away.

Excellentz kept offering him the pill pod. Bromberg gave it a furtive sidelong glance, like a rooster. Then he theatrically declared, "Dare to take poison from a sage's hand, but from a fool refuse an antidote . . ."

He took the pod and also rolled a white ball into the palm of his hand. "I don't need this!" he announced, tossing the ball into his mouth. "Yet . . ."

"Isaac," Excellentz said, smacking his lips, "what are you going to do when I die?"

"I'll do a jig," said Bromberg morosely. "Don't be silly."

"Isaac," Excellentz said, "what did you want the detonators for, anyway? Wait, wait, don't get going again. Far be it from me to interfere in your personal affairs. If you had become interested in the detonators a week ago or a week from now, I would have never asked you this question. But as it happens, you wanted them today. The very same day that a completely different person was supposed to come for them. If this is merely an incredible coincidence, just tell me so, and we'll say our good-byes. This is giving me a headache."

"Who was supposed to come for them?" asked Bromberg suspiciously.

"Lev Abalkin," said Excellentz wearily.

"Who's that?"

"You don't know Lev Abalkin?"

"First time I hear of him," said Bromberg.

"I believe you," said Excellentz.

"I should think so!" said Bromberg haughtily.

"You I believe," said Excellentz. "But I don't believe in coincidences . . . Listen, Isaac, would it really be so hard to tell me plainly, without any theatrics, why you chose today of all days to come for the detonators?"

"I don't like the word *theatrics!*" said Bromberg querulously, but without his former energy.

"I take it back," said Excellentz.

Bromberg started wiping his face again. "I don't have any secrets," he declared. "As you know, Rudolf, I hate any and all secrets. It was you who put me in the uncomfortable position of being dishonest and theatrical . . . When, in fact, it's all very simple . . . A certain person paid me a visit this morning . . . Do you absolutely need his name?"

"No."

"A certain young man. I don't suppose it matters what we talked about. The conversation was fairly personal. But in the course of this conversation, I noticed that he had a rather strange birthmark right over here"—Bromberg pointed to the crook of his right elbow. "I even asked him, 'What's this, a tattoo?' As you know, Rudolf, tattoos are my hobby . . . 'No,' he replied. 'It's a birthmark.' What it most resembled was the letter Ж in Cyrillic, or perhaps the Japanese character *sanju*—'thirty.' Does that ring a bell, Rudolf?"

"It does," said Excellentz.

It rang a bell for me, too—it reminded me of something I had seen very recently, something that had seemed both strange and unimportant.

"Did you figure it out right away, then?" Bromberg asked enviously.

"Yes," said Excellentz.

"And I didn't. The young man had been gone a long time and I was still sitting there, trying to recall where I'd seen that symbol before . . . One that was exactly like it, not just similar to it. I finally remembered. I had to check, don't you see? I didn't have a single reproduction at hand . . . I rushed to the museum—the museum was closed . . ."

"Mak," said Excellentz, "could you please hand us the object under the shawl?"

I obeyed.

The slab was heavy and warm to the touch. I placed it on the table in front of Excellentz. Excellentz slid it closer to himself, and then I could see that this was actually a case made out of a bright, amber-colored, smoothly polished material, with a barely noticeable, perfectly straight line separating the slightly convex lid from the heavy base. Excellentz tried to open the lid, but he was unsuccessful—his fingers kept losing their grip.

"Give it to me," Bromberg said impatiently. He shoved Excellentz away, grabbed the lid with both hands, lifted it off, and put it to the side.

These were apparently the things they had been calling detonators: round gray knobs about three inches in diameter, arranged in a straight line, each in its own neat groove. There were eleven detonators in total, and there were also two empty grooves, from which you could see that the bottoms of the hollows were lined with whitish hair that looked like mold, and that the hairs were wiggling, as if they were alive—as a matter of fact, they probably were actually alive in some way.

However, what first caught my eye were the fairly intricate hieroglyphs on the surfaces of the detonators—one per detonator, and each one different. They were large, pinkish brown, and slightly blurry, as if someone had applied colored ink to damp paper. And I instantly recognized one of them: a slightly blurry stylized Ж, or, if you prefer, the Japanese hieroglyph *sanju*—the miniature original of the magnified copy of the back of sheet 1 in case 07. From my perspective, the corresponding detonator was the third one from the left, and Excellentz hovered a long forefinger above it, saying, "Is that it?"

"Yes, yes," said Bromberg impatiently, shoving his hand aside. "Don't get in the way. You don't understand anything . . ."

He gripped the edge of the detonator tightly with his nails and began carefully taking it out of its hollow, twisting it as if he were unscrewing it, muttering, "That's not the point . . . Do you really believe I could be wrong about that? . . . How absurd . . ." He finally succeeded at extracting the detonator from its hollow and began carefully lifting it higher and higher above the case— and you could see the thin whitish hairs stretching behind the thick gray disk, getting thinner and thinner, then snapping one by one. And when the last hair had snapped, Bromberg turned the disk upside down, and there, surrounded by the translucent wiggling hairs, I saw the same hieroglyph, except it was small and black and had very crisp outlines, as if it was embossed into the gray material.

"Yes!" Bromberg said triumphantly. "An exact copy. I knew I couldn't be wrong."

"About what?" asked Excellentz.

"The size!" said Bromberg. "The size, the details, the proportions. You see, his birthmark doesn't just resemble this symbol—it's exactly the same." He stared at Excellentz. "Listen, Rudolf, one good turn deserves another. Did you mark them all or something?"

"No, of course not."

"So then they had these from the very beginning?" asked Bromberg, tapping the crook of his right elbow with a finger.

"No. These symbols appeared on their elbows between the ages of ten and twelve."

Bromberg carefully screwed the detonator back into its groove and collapsed contentedly into his chair. "Well, well, well," he said. "It's just as I thought . . . Well, Mr. Police President, what was the good of all this secrecy? I have his number, and as soon as golden-fingered Phoebus illuminates the tops of these architectural monstrosities of yours, I'll immediately get in touch with him, and we'll have a good talk . . . And don't you try to dissuade me, Sikorsky!" he cried, wagging a finger right under Excellentz's nose. "He came to me himself, and I figured out myself—you hear me? myself, with this old head—who was standing in front of me, and now he's mine! I didn't gain access to any of your silly secrets! A bit of acumen, a bit of luck—"

"All right, all right," said Excellentz. "Be my guest. I don't object. He's yours, meet with him and talk to him. But only to him, please. Not to anyone else."

"Wellllll . . ." drawled Bromberg with ironic hesitation.

"Actually, do as you like," said Excellentz suddenly. "Right now, none of this matters . . . Tell me, Isaac, what did you talk to him about?"

Bromberg rested his hands on his belly and twiddled his thumbs. The victories he had attained over Excellentz were so momentous and obvious that he could certainly allow himself to be magnanimous. "I have to admit, our conversation was a bit puzzling," he said. "Now, of course, I see that this Cro-Magnon man was simply pulling my leg."

This morning—or, rather, yesterday morning—he had a visit from a man of around forty or forty-five years of age, who introduced himself as Alexander Dimmock, a designer of agricultural machines. He was of medium height, with a very pale face and the long, straight black hair of a Native American. He complained that for many months, he had been trying and failing to figure out the circumstances of the disappearance of his parents. He told Bromberg an extremely enigmatic and therefore fiendishly seductive story, which he had supposedly collected bit by bit, not disdaining even the most apocryphal rumors. Bromberg had written the entire story down in full, but it hardly made sense to recount it now. In fact, there was precisely one reason for Alexander Dimmock's visit: he wanted to know whether Bromberg, the world's foremost expert on forbidden science, could shed any light whatsoever on this story.

Foremost expert Bromberg dived into his card catalog, but he couldn't find anything about the Dimmocks. The man was visibly disappointed by this outcome and was just about to leave when he had had a brainwave. It could very well be, he said, that his parents' last name hadn't been Dimmock at all. It could even be that the entire story that he put together had no basis in fact. Perhaps Dr. Bromberg could try to remember whether there had been any mysterious scientific occurrences that were subsequently banned from wide publication close to the date of Alexander Dimmock's birth (February '36), as he had lost his parents at either one or two years of age . . .

Expert Bromberg had made another foray into his card catalog, but this time into its chronological section. He discovered a total of eight different incidents between '33 and '39, the story of the sarcophagus-incubator among them. Together with Alexander Dimmock, they examined every one of these incidents, concluding that not a single one of them could be linked to the fate of the Dimmocks.

"And therefore, old fool that I am, I concluded that a story that had completely escaped my notice back in the day had fallen into my lap! Can you imagine? Not just one of your lousy bans, but the bona fide disappearance of two biochemists! I would have never forgiven you for this, Sikorsky!"

And Bromberg then interrogated Alexander Dimmock for a good two hours, demanding he remember every detail, no matter how small, and every rumor, no matter how outlandish. He had also extracted from Dimmock a solemn promise to undergo a deep mental probe—so that during the last hour of their conversation, the man was clearly dreaming of only one thing—to hightail it out of there . . .

Only at very end of the conversation did Bromberg completely accidentally notice the birthmark. This birthmark, which apparently had nothing to do with the problem, had unaccountably lodged itself in Bromberg's brain. The man had long since gone. Bromberg had already sent a few queries to the GWI and spoken (to no avail) to a few specialists about the Dimmocks, but the damned mark wouldn't get out of his head. First of all, Bromberg was absolutely sure that he had seen it somewhere before, and second, he couldn't shake the feeling that either this symbol or something related to this symbol had come up during his conversation with Alexander Dimmock. And it was only after he had scrupulously reproduced the entire conversation from memory sentence by sentence that he finally recalled the sarcophagus, remembered about the detonators, and had been struck by an astonishing conjecture about who Alexander Dimmock really was.

The very first thing he did was to immediately call Dimmock and tell him that the secrets of his origins had been revealed. But his, Bromberg's, innate scientific integrity demanded that he make absolutely sure and rule out other possible interpretations. He, Bromberg, had seen crazier coincidences. So, first, he rushed to call the museum—

"Say no more," Excellentz said gloomily. "Thank you, Isaac. So now he knows about the sarcophagus . . ."

"And why shouldn't he?" snapped Bromberg.

"Indeed," Excellentz said slowly. "Why shouldn't he?"

THE SECRET OF LEV ABALKIN'S IDENTITY

On December 21, '37, a team of pathfinders under the command of Boris Fokin landed on a rocky plateau of an unnamed planet in the EN 9173 system, with the mission of examining certain ruins discovered there in the previous century and attributed to the Wanderers.

On December 24, an intravision survey detected the presence of a large cavern beneath the ruins, carved out of the rock at a depth of ten feet.

On December 25, Boris Fokin attempted to enter this cavern and succeeded on his first attempt without running into any surprises. It was shaped like a hemisphere about sixty-six feet in diameter. The hemisphere was lined with amberine—a material very characteristic of the Wanderer civilization—and it contained a bulky apparatus that, thanks to one of the pathfinders, they dubbed a sarcophagus.

On December 26, Boris Fokin requested then received permission from the relevant department of COMCON to examine the sarcophagus on his own.

As was usual for him, he proceeded in a painstakingly method-ical and cautious manner, spending three days working with the sarcophagus. During that time, his team succeeded in determining how old it was (forty to forty-five thousand years of age), dis-covered that the sarcophagus consumed energy, and even estab-lished a definite connection between the sarcophagus and the ruins situated above it. Even at this early time, someone put for-ward the hypothesis—later confirmed—that the aforementioned ruins weren't ruins at all but rather a component of a vast system designed to absorb and transform all types of renewable energy. This system covered the entire surface of the planet and captured both planetary and cosmic energy: seismic activity, magnetic field fluctuations, weather events, radiation from the central star of the system, cosmic rays, and so on and so forth.

On December 29, Boris Fokin contacted Komov directly and demanded that he send his best embryologist. Naturally, Komov requested an explanation, but Boris Fokin declined to explain, inviting Komov to come see for himself, but again insisting he be accompanied by an embryologist. Once upon a time, in his distant youth, Komov had worked with Fokin, and this had left him with a rather unflattering impression of the man. So he didn't even consider coming to see for himself, but he did send an embryolo-gist, a certain Mark van Blerkom—who, however, wasn't any-where near the best in the field but had merely been the first available (a decision that Komov later had ample opportunity to regret, as Mark van Blerkom turned out to be the bosom buddy of the notorious Isaac P. Bromberg).

On December 30, Mark van Blerkom set out to join Boris Fokin's team, and within a few hours, he sent Komov an aston-ishing (and unencrypted) message. In this message, he claimed that the so-called sarcophagus was actually neither more nor less than an embryo safe of completely fantastical design. The safe contained thirteen fertilized *Homo sapiens* eggs, and what's more, these eggs appeared to be viable, though in a latent state.

We need to give two characters in this story their due—namely, Boris Fokin and COMCON member Gennady Komov. A sixth sense told Boris Fokin that this find shouldn't be trumpeted from the rooftops; Mark van Blerkom's radiogram was the first and last unencrypted radiogram in the subsequent radio exchange between his team and Earth. As a result, this story barely made a ripple in the stream of mass information arriving on our planet—there was only a single terse message, which was never confirmed and therefore attracted almost no attention.

As for Gennady Komov, he not only immediately grasped the crux of the problem materializing before his eyes but somehow also succeeded in visualizing a host of possible consequences of the problem. First of all, he demanded that Fokin and Blerkom confirm the information they had sent (using a special code on his emergency channel), and having received confirmation, he immediately convened a meeting of those COMCON leaders who were also members of the World Council. Among them were such luminaries as Leonid Gorbovsky, August Johann Bader, the young and ardent Kirill Alexandrov, the cautious, always skeptical Mahiro Shinoda, and also the energetic sixty-two-year-old Rudolf Sikorsky.

Komov apprised all those gathered of the relevant facts and asked them point blank: What should they do next? They could, of course, close the sarcophagus and leave everything as it was, limiting themselves to passive observation for the foreseeable future. They could try to jump-start the development of the eggs and see what happens. And finally, in order to avoid the inevitable headaches later on, they could destroy the find.

Of course, Gennady Komov, who by then was already a man of considerable experience, was perfectly aware that neither this emergency meeting nor a dozen subsequent meetings would solve this problem. His intentionally dramatic speech had precisely one goal: to shock the people gathered there and to inspire debate.

It has to be said that he achieved his goal. The only people present who retained apparent composure were Leonid Gorbovsky and Rudolf Sikorsky. Gorbovsky, because he was an intelligent optimist. Sikorsky, on the other hand, because he was by then already the head of COMCON-2. Many words were spoken at this meeting—impetuously heated words and studiedly calm words, quite frivolous words and profound words, words that have long been forgotten and words that have since become part of the lexicon of lectures, presentations, reports, and recommendations. As was to be expected, the only decision they reached was to convene a new, larger meeting the next day, one that would include some other members of the World Council—the experts in social psychology, pedagogy, and the media.

Rudolf Sikorsky stayed silent for the duration of the meeting. He didn't feel knowledgeable enough to speak in favor of this or that solution to the problem. However, his long experience in the field of experimental history, as well as everything he knew about the activities of the Wanderers, led him to the following inescapable conclusion: whatever decision the World Council ultimately made, knowledge of this decision, as well as of all the circumstances of this case, would need to be indefinitely restricted to a set of people endowed with extremely high levels of social responsibility. And that was the gist of the speech he made at the very end of the meeting. "The decision to leave everything as it is and confine ourselves to passive observation is not in fact a decision. There are only two true decisions: to destroy or to jump-start. It doesn't matter when one of these decisions is made—tomorrow or a hundred years hence—but either will be unsatisfactory. If we destroy the sarcophagus, we perform an irreversible action. All of us gathered here today know the price of irreversible actions. If we jump-start the development of the eggs, we let the Wanderers call the shots, even though their ultimate goals are, to put it mildly, unclear to us. I am not prejudging anything and, in fact, don't even feel entitled to vote for either decision. The only thing I will ask—nay, will insist on—is that you grant me permission to immediately take steps to prevent information leaks. If for no reason than to prevent us from drowning in a sea of incompetence . . ."

This little speech made the intended impression, and permission was unanimously granted—especially since everyone understood that they should not be in a hurry, and that it was therefore crucial to create the environment for some calm and serious work.

The expanded meeting was held on December 31. There were eighteen people present, including the chairman of the World Council for social problems, who had been invited by Gorbovsky. Everyone agreed that the sarcophagus had been found accidentally and therefore prematurely. Furthermore, everyone agreed that before making any decisions, they should try to understand—and if not to understand, then at least to imagine—the original intentions of the Wanderers. There were a number of hypotheses proposed, ranging from the familiar to the exotic.

Kirill Alexandrov, known for his anthropomorphic views, suggested that the sarcophagus was a repository of the genetic information of the Wanderers. "All the evidence I've ever heard that the Wanderers aren't humanoid," he declared, "is fundamentally circumstantial." In fact, in his opinion, the Wanderers could very well turn out to be the genetic twins of humans. This conjecture does not contradict any of the available data. Based on this, Alexandrov proposed ceasing all research, putting everything back as it was, and leaving the EN 9173 system.

In the opinion of August Johann Bader, the sarcophagus is—yes!—a repository of genetic information. But it's not the genetic information of the Wanderers—it comes from humans. Forty-five thousand years ago, the Wanderers foresaw the theoretical possibility that the *Homo sapiens* tribes, then small in number, would be at risk for genetic degeneration, and they took this measure to make sure that the human population could be replenished in the future.

The next one to speak was the elderly Park Jin, who delivered another speech under the banner of *let's not think badly of the Wanderers*. He, like Bader, was convinced that we were dealing with human genetic information, but unlike him, he believed that the purpose of this device was more likely to be educational. The sarcophagus is a unique kind of time capsule, and upon opening it, modern earthlings would get the opportunity to personally acquaint themselves with the appearance, anatomy, and physiology of their distant ancestors.

Gennady Komov had a much more expansive take. In his opinion, any civilization that has reached a certain stage of development can't help but seek contact with other intelligent beings. However, contact between humanoid and nonhumanoid civilizations is extremely difficult, if not impossible. Are we perhaps dealing with an attempt to use a fundamentally new method of contact—to create an intermediary being, a humanoid whose genes code for certain significant elements of the nonhumanoid psyche? In that case, we should consider the discovery to be the beginning of a fundamentally new stage in both Earth history and the history of the nonhumanoid Wanderers. In Komov's opinion, the development of the eggs must certainly be jump-started as soon as possible. He, Komov, wasn't much deterred by the obvious prematurity of the discovery. The Wanderers, when calculating the pace of human progress, could easily have been off by a few centuries.

Komov's hypothesis produced a lively discussion, in the course of which doubts were first raised about whether modern pedagogical methods could be successfully used to educate humans whose psychology was significantly different from the average humanoid's.

At this time, the extremely cautious Mahiro Shinoda, an authority on the Wanderers, asked a very reasonable question: Why are you, esteemed Gennady, as well as some of the rest of you gentlemen, so certain that the Wanderers have benevolent intentions toward earthlings? We don't have any evidence that the Wanderers are capable of benevolence toward anyone at all, including humanoids. On the contrary, the (admittedly scarce) available facts attest rather to the idea that the Wanderers are absolutely indifferent to alien intelligence and tend to treat it as a means to an end rather than a partner in contract. Doesn't the esteemed Gennady realize that his hypothesis could just as easily be flipped on its head? Namely, we could just as easily assume that the Wanderers intended these hypothetical intermediary beings to carry out missions that, from our perspective, would be, if anything, undesirable. Why shouldn't we, following the logic of the esteemed Gennady, assume that the sarcophagus is, so to speak, an ideological time bomb, and that the intermediary beings are saboteurs of sorts, meant to be embedded in our civilization? Of course, *saboteur* is an odious word. But we do have a new concept nowadays—the progressor, an earthling whose job it is to accelerate the progress of backward humanoid civilizations. Why not consider the possibility that the hypothetical intermediary beings are Wanderer progressors of sorts? After all, what do we know about the Wanderer point of view on the pace and form of our human progress? . . .

The meeting immediately split into two factions—the optimists and the pessimists. It goes without saying that the point of view of the optimists seemed infinitely more plausible. It was, indeed, hard and maybe even impossible to imagine a supercivilization that wouldn't scorn not only blatant aggression toward lesser intelligences but also tactless experimentation with the same. In the context of our current understanding of the laws of the development of reason, the point of view of the pessimists looked—to put it mildly—contrived, far-fetched, and old fashioned. But on the other hand, there was always a chance, no matter how minuscule, of a mistake. There could be a mistake in the general theory of progress. The scientists interpreting this theory could have made a mistake. And, most important, the Wanderers themselves could have made a mistake. The consequences of these sorts of mistakes for humanity's future on Earth were neither measurable nor controllable.

It was then that Rudolf Sikorsky first had the apocalyptic vision of a creature that was anatomically and physiologically indistinguishable from a human being, and what's more, didn't differ from a human psychologically—neither in its emotions, nor in its reasoning, nor in its worldview. This creature lived and worked in the very thick of humanity, carrying within it an unknown ominous program, and the most terrifying thing was that the creature itself would know nothing about this program and would never know anything about it, even in that indeterminable instant when the program finally turned on, robbed it of its humanity, and led it . . . where? To do what? And even back then, it was crystal clear to Rudolf Sikorsky that no one—especially not him, Rudolf Sikorsky—had the right to reassure himself with the negligible probability and fantastic nature of such a possibility.

At the height of the meeting, Komov was handed another coded message from Fokin. He read it, turned white, and announced in a cracked voice, "Bad news: Fokin and van Blerkom report that all thirteen eggs have undergone their first cell division."

It was a rotten New Year's for all those initiated into the secret. From the early morning of January 1 until the evening of January 3, there was an almost continuous meeting of the spontaneously formed Incubator Committee (the sarcophagus was now being called an incubator). In essence, the committee only discussed one thing: how, taking all the circumstances into account, they should plan the fates of thirteen future new citizens of planet Earth.

The option of destroying the incubator wasn't raised again, although all the members of the committee, including the ones who had initially advocated for jump-starting the development of the eggs, felt ill at ease. They couldn't shake some vague anxiety—it seemed to them that, on December 31, they had been robbed of free will and were now compelled to follow a plan imposed on them from without. Then again, the discussion was fairly constructive in character.

At this early point, they successfully formulated general principles for bringing up the future newborns; selected nannies, attending physicians, teachers, and advisers for them; and outlined the possible directions of the related anthropological, physiological, and psychological research. They located specialists in xenotechnology in general and Wanderer xenotechnology in particular and immediately deployed them to serve on Fokin's team, so that they could perform detailed research on the sarcophagus-incubator, prevent blunders, and, most important, potentially discover some particulars about this machine that would help concretize and clarify the work to be done with the "foundlings." They even came up with public relations campaigns that could be used if one of the proposed hypotheses about the motivations of the Wanderers turned out to be correct . . .

Rudolf Sikorsky did not take part in the discussions. He listened with half an ear and concentrated all his attention on keeping track of every single person who was in the slightest degree involved in the current developments. The list was growing with depressing speed, but he knew that, for now, this was inevitable, and that in one way or another, many people would certainly get mixed up in this strange and dangerous story.

On the evening of January 3, during the final meeting, when people were taking stock and formalizing the spontaneously formed subcommittees, Sikorsky asked to say a few words and announced something like the following.

We've done good work here and we're more or less prepared for all the possible eventualities—at least, as prepared as we can be, given our current levels of awareness and the frankly worthless situation we've found ourselves in against our will and by the will of the Wanderers. We've agreed not to perform any irreversible actions—in fact, all of our decisions can be reduced to that. However! As the head of COMCON-2, the organization responsible for the safety of Earth's entire civilization, I would like to propose a number of requirements that must be fully complied with moving forward.

Number one. All the work the least bit connected with this story should be classified. Information related to this work shouldn't be subject to disclosure under any circumstances. Reason: The well-known Law for Secrets of Identity.

Number two. None of the foundlings should be aware of the circumstances of their births. Reason: The exact same law.

Number three. The foundlings should be immediately separated at birth, and measures should be taken later on to make sure that they not only know nothing about each other but also do not meet each other. Reason: Fairly elementary considerations I don't plan to relate.

Number four. All of them should have careers away from Earth, so that the very facts of their lives and jobs would naturally make it difficult for them to come back to Earth, even for a short time. Reason: The same elementary logic. We're currently forced to consent to taking our cues from the Wanderers, but we should do everything we can to make it possible to step off this beaten path later on—and the sooner, the better.

As you might expect, "Sikorsky's Four Requirements" caused an outburst of indignation. The meeting participants, like all normal people, detested hushing things up—they hated closed topics, secrets, and, frankly, COMCON-2 itself. But Sikorsky had correctly foreseen that the psychologists and sociologists, having vented their spleen, would come to their senses and emphatically come down on his side. You don't mess with the Law for Secrets of Identity. It was very easy to imagine a whole series of extremely unpleasant scenarios that could arise in the future if the first two requirements weren't met. Try to imagine the mental state of a person who finds out that his life began inside an incubator developed forty-five thousand years ago by mysterious monsters for a mysterious purpose, especially if he learns that everyone around him is also aware of this fact. What's more, if he has any imagination at all, he will inevitably arrive at the idea that he, an earthling to the marrow of his bones, who has never known or loved anything but Earth, may perhaps carry within him some terrible threat to mankind. The idea could be so traumatic that even the best specialists may not be able to help . . .

The arguments of the psychologists were buttressed by a sudden and unusually direct speech by Mahiro Shinoda, who bluntly said that we were worrying too much about thirteen unborn brats and not enough about the potential danger they could pose for our ancient Earth. In consequence, all four requirements were adopted by majority vote, and Rudolf Sikorsky was immediately put in charge of coming up with and implementing the necessary arrangements. And the sooner the better.

On January 5, Rudolf Sikorsky received a phone call from a slightly alarmed Leonid Andreievich Gorbovsky. It turned out that half an hour ago, he had a conversation with an old friend—a xenologist from Tagora who had spent the last two years visiting Moscow University. In the course of the conversation, the Tagoran inquired in a seemingly casual way about whether the brief message about an unusual find in the EN 9173 system had been confirmed. Caught off guard by this innocent question, Gorbovsky began to mumble something unintelligible—that he hadn't been a pathfinder in years, that this was outside his sphere of interests, that he wasn't in the loop—and finally, he declared with perfect sincerity and tremendous relief that he hadn't seen this message. The Tagoran immediately changed the subject, but nonetheless, this part of the conversation had left a most unpleasant taste in his mouth.

Rudolf Sikorsky realized that his conversation would have a sequel. And he was right.

On January 7, he got an unexpected visit from a professional counterpart who had recently arrived from Tagora—the eminent Dr. As-Su. The visit was purportedly related to Tagora's official observers on Earth; there was a plan to expand the scope of these observers' activities, and a number of legitimately important details of this plan needed clarification. When they were done with business and little Dr. As-Su began to sip his favorite Earth drink (cold barley coffee with synthetic honey), the two dignitaries began to swap amusing and horrifying historical anecdotes—a pastime they both enjoyed and excelled at.

In particular, Dr. As-Su related how, one and a half Earth centuries ago, as Tagoran builders were laying the foundation for the Third Great Machine, they found an astonishing device in the basalt strata of the Subpolar Continent—in Earth terms, it was an ingeniously constructed hatchery of Tagoran larvae in a latent state. The age of the discovery couldn't be determined with any degree of precision, but it was clear that this hatchery had been installed long before the Great Genetic Revolution—back when every Tagoran went through a larval stage in his or her development.

"Amazing," muttered Sikorsky. "Did your people really have such advanced technology at the time?"

"Of course not!" answered Dr. As-Su. "This was clearly planted by the Wanderers."

"But what was it for?"

"It's too difficult to answer this question. We didn't even try."

"So then what happened with the two hundred little Tagorans?"

"*Hmmm* . . . You ask a strange question. The larvae began to spontaneously develop, and, naturally, we immediately destroyed the device and all of its contents . . . Can you really imagine a civilization that wouldn't do the same in a similar situation?"

"Yes, I can," said Sikorsky.

The next day, January 8, '38, the High Ambassador of United Tagora left for his home planet due to the state of his health. And a few days later, there wasn't a single Tagoran remaining on Earth, nor on any other planet where earthlings lived or worked. And in another month, every earthling working on Tagora was faced with the necessity of returning to Earth. For the next twenty-five years, there was no communication between Earth and Tagora.

THE MYSTERY OF LEV ABALKIN'S IDENTITY (CONTINUED)

They were all born on the same day—October 6, '38—five girls and eight boys, all strong, loud-voiced, perfectly healthy human babies. By the time they were born, everything was ready. They were received and examined by eminent doctors, members of the World Council, and the representatives of the Committee on the Thirteen, then they were washed and swaddled and brought to Earth that very same day on a specially equipped ship. By the end of the evening, in thirteen nurseries scattered across all six continents, attentive nannies were already bustling around the thirteen orphans and posthumous children—none of whom would ever see their parents, and whose only mother from then on would be the entirety of gentle humanity. Cover stories about their origins had already been prepared by Rudolf Sikorsky himself, and, after obtaining special dispensation from the World Council, had been entered into the GWI.

The fate of Lev Vyacheslavovich Abalkin, as well as the fates of his "uterine" brothers and sisters, was predetermined from that point on for many years to come, and for many years it was no different from the fates of hundreds of millions of his ordinary Earth peers.

In the nursery, just like any other newborn, he first lay around, then crawled, then toddled, then ran. He was surrounded by babies just like him, and caring adults fussed over him, the same as in hundreds of thousands other nurseries on the planet.

It's true that he had exceptional luck. On the same day that he was brought to the nursery, Yadviga Mikhailovna Lekanova, one of the world's premier experts in child psychology, started working there as an attending physician. For some strange reason, she decided to descend from the Olympian heights of pure science and return to where she had started decades ago. And when six-year-old Lyova Abalkin, along with his entire cohort, was transferred to Syktyvkar Boarding School 241, that same Yadviga Mikhailovna decided that this was the right time for her to work with school-aged children and transferred to be an attending physician at this school.

Lyova Abalkin grew and developed like a fairly ordinary boy, if one prone, perhaps, to slight melancholy and introversion— however, the divergence of his psychological type from the norm was strictly within acceptable limits, with none of the measured differences close to the maximum. His physical development was similarly satisfactory. He wasn't unlike the others because of either increased fragility or remarkable strength. In short, he was a strong, healthy, fairly ordinary boy, who only stood out among his mostly Slavic classmates due to this straight blue-black hair, which he was very proud of and kept trying to grow out to his shoulders. And that's how it was until November '47.

On November 16, during a routine examination, Yadviga Mikhailovna discovered a small swollen bruise at the crook of Lyova's right elbow. There's nothing surprising about boy with a bruise, so Yadviga Mikhailovna didn't pay any attention to it and would have naturally forgotten about it if, a week from then, on November 23, she hadn't discovered that the bruise hadn't merely failed to disappear but had become strangely transformed. In fact, it could no longer be called a bruise—it looked more like a tattoo, a small yellowish-brown symbol in the form of a stylized letter Ж. Cautious inquiries showed that Lyova Abalkin had no idea how he got it or where it came from. It was completely obvious that until this very moment, he hadn't even realized or noticed that something had appeared at the crook of his right elbow.

After some hesitation, Yadviga Mikhailovna considered it her duty to report this little discovery to Dr. Sikorsky. Dr. Sikorsky took this information down without any apparent interest, but at the end of December, he suddenly called Yadviga Mikhailovna by videophone and inquired about the status of Lev Abalkin's birthmark. No changes, answered a somewhat surprised Yadviga Mikhailovna. If it wouldn't be too much trouble, requested Dr. Sikorsky, please take a discreet picture of the mark and send it to me.

Lev Abalkin was the first of the foundlings to have a symbol appear in the crook of his right elbow. Over the course of the next two months, eight more foundlings developed more or less intricately shaped birthmarks, all of which appeared under identical circumstances: they started out as swollen bruises that had no obvious external cause and were not painful, and in a week, they became yellowish-brown symbols. By the end of '48, all thirteen children bore the "mark of the Wanderers." And then a discovery was made—a truly surprising and unsettling discovery that gave rise to the concept of a detonator.

It's now impossible to say who first introduced this concept. According to Rudolf Sikorsky, this was a very precise—and ominous—characterization of the situation. Back in '39, a year after the birth of foundlings, the xenotechnicians dismantling the incubator came upon a long amberine box containing thirteen round gray disks, each disk bearing a different symbol. In those days, the bowels of the incubator were yielding objects even more enigmatic than this box, and therefore no one paid any special attention to it. The amber case was shipped to the Museum of Extraterrestrial Cultures, was described in the classified "Materials on the Sarcophagus-Incubator" as a component of the life support system, withstood some researcher's feeble attempt to figure out what it was or how it could be used, and then it was finally palmed off on the already overcrowded Special Department for Artifacts of Unknown Purpose, where it languished for a good ten years.

At the beginning of '49, Rudolf Sikorsky's assistant on the foundlings case (call him, say, Ivanov), came into his boss's office and placed a projector set to page 211 of volume 6 of "Materials on the Sarcophagus" in front of him. Excellentz took a look and was dumbfounded. He was looking at a photograph of "life support component 15/156A": thirteen round gray disks nestled in the hollows of an amber case. And he saw the very same thirteen intricate hieroglyphs familiar to him from the crooks of thirteen childish elbows—symbols he had puzzled over in vain and already given up on. A symbol per elbow. A symbol per disk. A disk per elbow.

This couldn't be an accident. This had to mean something. Something very important. Rudolf Sikorsky's first impulse was to immediately demand the so-called component 15/156A from the museum and hide it in his safe. From everyone. From himself. He was scared. He simply got scared. And the worst thing was that he didn't even understand why he was scared.

Ivanov was also scared. They looked at each other and understood each other without words. They were visualizing the same thing: thirteen tanned, rowdy bombs were cheerfully hooting as they climbed trees and swam in rivers, while over here, well within their reach, their thirteen detonators bided their time in ominous silence.

Of course, this was a moment of weakness. After all, nothing frightening had happened. As a matter of fact, there was no reason to conclude that the disks with the symbols were detonators for bombs—activators of hidden programs. It's just that when it came to the foundlings, they were used to assuming the worst. But even if their imaginative panic hadn't misled them—even in this worst possible scenario—nothing frightening had happened yet. They could destroy the detonators anytime they wanted. At any given moment, they could remove them from the museum and send them far, far away—to the edge of the inhabited universe, and if necessary even farther.

Rudolf Sikorsky called the director of the museum and asked him to put exhibit such and such at the disposal of the World Council—that is, to deliver it to his, Rudolf Sikorsky's, office. He was met with a rather surprised, very courteous, but completely unambiguous refusal. It turned out (Sikorsky hadn't the foggiest idea of this before) that museum exhibits—not only ones from the Museum of Extraterrestrial Cultures but from any museum on Earth—could not be taken out of their museum, neither by an individual, nor by the World Council, nor even by the Lord Almighty Himself. If the Lord Almighty Himself needed to work with exhibit such and such, He would need to appear at the museum in person, present the proper authorization, and carry out all of His necessary research right there, within the four walls of the museum—for which, however, He would be very well equipped, as He would have all of their laboratories, equipment, and expertise at His disposal.

This was an unexpected turn of events, but by then, the initial shock had worn off. After all, it was an unambiguously good thing that a bomb that wanted to be reunited with its detonator would, at the very least, need "proper authorization." And, at the end of the day, it was up to Rudolf Sikorsky himself to turn the museum into that same safe, only of rather larger dimensions. And anyway, what the hell? How would the bombs know where the detonators were being kept, or even that they existed at all? No, no, it had only been a moment of weakness. One of few such moments in his life.

The detonators became a subject of intensive study. Appropriately chosen people, after being furnished with recommendations and proper authorization, conducted a series of carefully designed experiments in the museum's extremely well-equipped laboratories. It would have been safe to say that these experiments came to naught, if not for one strange and even, frankly, tragic occurrence.

One of the detonators was used for an experiment on regeneration. The experiment yielded a negative result: unlike many other artifacts of the Wanderers, detonator 12 (Gothic М symbol) did not regenerate itself after being destroyed. And in another two days, a group of twenty-seven schoolchildren from the Templado Boarding School and their teacher got caught in an avalanche in the Northern Andes. Many of the children suffered cuts and bruises, but only one of them died: Edna Lasko, case 12, Gothic М symbol.

Of course, this may have been a coincidence. But as a result, detonator research was first put on hold, then banned by the World Council.

And there was another incident, but much later, in '62, when Rudolf Sikorsky, locally nicknamed Wanderer, was working as a resident on Saraksh.

As a matter of fact, it was due to his absence from Earth that a group of psychologists from the Committee on the Thirteen managed to obtain permission to partially reveal the secret of a foundling's identity to him. The person they chose for this experiment was Korney Jasmaa, number 11, the Elbrus symbol. After being thoroughly prepared, he was told the whole truth about his origins. Only his own. No one else's.

Korney Jasmaa was then graduating from progressor school. All the tests indicated that this was a man with an extremely robust psyche and a very strong will—a person remarkable in every way. The psychologists weren't wrong. Korney Jasmaa received the information with astonishing equanimity—the surrounding world apparently interested him much more than the secrets of his own origins. Although the psychologists cautiously warned him that he might conceal a program that could at a moment's notice cause him to act against the best interests of humanity, this didn't worry him at all. He frankly admitted that even though he understood that he could potentially be dangerous, he didn't believe in this in the least. He was eager to participate in routine self-observation, which, by the way, included a daily examination with an emotion detector, and he himself even proposed undergoing an arbitrarily deep mentoscopy. In other words, the committee could be satisfied: at least one of the foundlings had now become a conscious and strong ally of planet Earth.

When he initially learned of this experiment, Rudolf Sikorsky felt angry, but then he decided that the experiment might ultimately be useful. From the very beginning, he had insisted on the secrets of identity largely to keep Earth safe. If and when the programs were activated, he didn't want the foundlings to have conscious information about themselves and what was happening to them that could be used alongside the subconscious programs. He would have preferred for them to flail, not knowing what they were looking for and therefore inevitably doing absurd and strange things. But, on the other hand, for the sake of having a control case, it would be useful for one (but not more than one!) foundling to have complete information about himself. If the programs in fact exist, they must certainly be capable of withstanding any efforts by the conscious mind. Otherwise the Wanderers wouldn't have bothered with them. But, without a doubt, the behavior of a person who is aware of his program would be dramatically different from the behavior of the others.

However, the psychologists didn't even think to rest on their laurels. Emboldened by their success with Korney Jasmaa, they took advantage of the fact that Rudolf Sikorsky was still stuck on Saraksh and repeated the experiment, this time with Tomas Nilsson (number 02, the Slanting Star symbol), a park ranger on Gorgona. The early indications were quite favorable, and for a few months, Tomas Nilsson continued to do his job without incident, seemingly not at all distraught by the secret of his identity. He was in general a rather phlegmatic man and not prone to emotional displays.

He carefully carried out all of the recommended self-observation procedures and regarded his lot with a certain characteristic grim humor—however, he did flatly refuse the mentoscopy, citing purely personal reasons. And on day 128 from the start of the experiment, Tomas Nilsson died on his Gorgona under circumstances that did not exclude the possibility of suicide.

This was a terrible blow for the committee in general and the psychologists in particular. The elderly Park Jin resigned from the committee, abandoned his institute, his students, and his family, and went into self-imposed exile. And on day 132, a COMCON-2 employee whose duties included a monthly inspection of the amber case, reported in a panic that detonator 02, with the Slanting Star symbol, had disappeared without a trace—there wasn't even a speck of dust left in the groove lined with wiggling fibers of pseudo-epithelium.

By now, the existence of a certain, to put it mildly, semi-mystical connection between the foundlings and their respective detonators was beyond all possible doubt. Nor did anyone on the committee doubt that earthlings would be unable to make sense of this story in the foreseeable future.

JUNE 4, '78

A DISCUSSION OF THE SITUATION

Excellentz told me all this and much more that night, after we left the museum and came back to his office.

By the time he was finished with the story, it was dawn. After he fell silent, he rose heavily, and, without looking at me, went to make coffee. "You may ask questions," he grumbled.

At this point, I was almost entirely in the grip of a single feeling: intense, boundless regret that I had learned all this and was now forced to be involved in it. Of course, if I'd been a normal person with a normal life and a normal job, I'd have taken this story to be one of those bizarre and sinister tales that crop up at the boundary between the known and the unknown, reach us in unrecognizably distorted form, and possess the delightful property that no matter how sinister and terrifying they may be, they are not directly related to our bright, warm planet and won't have a major impact on our daily life—everything has been taken care of, or is being taken care of, or will shortly be taken care of somewhere, somehow, and by someone else.

But alas, I was not a normal person in this sense of the word. Alas, I was one of the people who would have to take care of it. And I realized that I'd have to carry the burden of this secret my whole life. And that along with this secret came responsibility, which I hadn't asked for and, frankly, didn't need. From now on, I'd be obliged to make decisions, and therefore, I'd need to, at a minimum, thoroughly understand all the things that had been understood before me, and probably much more than that. And that meant that I'd be sucked into this secret—a secret that was repugnant like all of our other secrets, and maybe even more repugnant than the rest—and I'd sink even deeper into it, all the way up to my neck. And I felt a kind of childish gratitude to Excellentz for trying to keep me away from this secret until the very last moment. And I also felt an even more childish, almost petulant irritation at him for being unable to keep me away from it after all.

"You don't have any questions?" inquired Excellentz.

I re-collected myself. "So you think the program turned on and he killed Tristan?"

"Let's think logically." Excellentz got out the cups, carefully poured the coffee, and sat down. "Tristan was his attending physician. Once a month, they met somewhere in the jungle so that Tristan could conduct regular prophylactic examinations. This was supposedly to carry out routine monitoring of a progressor's level of mental tension, but it was actually to make sure that Abalkin remained human. Tristan was the only person on all of Saraksh who knew the number of my special channel. On May 30—May 31 at the latest—I should have received three 7s from him, meaning 'All is well.' But on the 28th, the day the examination was scheduled for, he dies. At the same time, Lev Abalkin flees to Earth. Lev Abalkin flees, Lev Abalkin goes into hiding, Lev Abalkin calls me on a special channel that only Tristan knew about . . ." He drank his coffee in one gulp and stayed silent for a bit, making chewing movements with his lips. "I think you've missed the point, Mak. We're no longer dealing with Abalkin—we're dealing with the Wanderers. Lev Abalkin doesn't exist anymore. Forget him. There's only the Wanderers' automaton." He paused again. "Frankly, I can't imagine what could have made Tristan give up the number of my channel—to anyone at all, never mind Lev Abalkin himself. I'm afraid he wasn't merely killed."

"So you think the program is driving him to search for his detonator?"

"I don't have anything else to think."

"But he has no idea that the detonators even exist . . . Or could Tristan have told him this, too?"

"Tristan didn't know anything. And Abalkin doesn't know anything. The program knows!"

"What's happening with Jasmaa? And the rest of them?"

"Everyone's behavior is within normal limits. But then their symbols didn't all develop at the same time. Abalkin's was the first."

This could only mean that Excellentz had already taken the requisite measures with respect to the others, and that, thankfully, I didn't need to know about these measures. They didn't concern me. Yet. I said, "Please don't get me wrong, Excellentz. Don't think that I'm trying to make excuses, or downplaying anything or whitewashing things. But you haven't seen him. And you haven't seen the people he's talked to . . . I get it: Tristan dies, he runs away, he calls you on your channel, he goes into hiding, he finds Glumova, who has access to the detonators . . . It all looks absolutely conclusive. A flawless logical chain. But there are other facts, too! He sees Glumova, and they don't say a word about the museum—only about love and childhood . . . He sees his teacher—and he's hurt his teacher supposedly ruined his life . . . He calls me, and he's upset I purportedly took credit for his work . . . By the way, what did he even see his teacher for? I can make some sense of him calling me—maybe he wanted to see who was tracking him down . . . But why his teacher? And now Puppen and that bizarre, totally absurd request for asylum!"

"It all makes sense, Mak. It all makes sense. The program is one thing and his conscious mind is another. He doesn't understand what's happening to him, you know. The program is demanding something inhuman from him, and his mind is trying to transform this demand into something that makes at least a bit of sense . . . He's flailing, he's doing strange, ridiculous things. That's exactly the kind of thing I expected. . . That's what the secret of identity was always for: to buy us a bit of time . . . And you didn't understand a damn thing about Puppen. There was no request for asylum. The bigheads sensed that he was no longer human and were demonstrating their loyalty to us. That's what happened."

He hadn't convinced me. His logic was almost flawless, but then I had seen and talked to Abalkin, and I had seen and talked to his teacher and Maya Toivovna. Abalkin was flailing, yes. He was doing strange things, yes, but those things weren't ridiculous. He was doing them for a reason, I just couldn't figure out what it was. And then I was sorry for Abalkin—he was pitiful, he couldn't be dangerous . . .

But this was only my intuition, and I knew what intuition was worth. In our business, it wasn't worth much. And then my intuition was based on experience with human beings, and, after all, we were dealing with the Wanderers . . .

"May I have some more coffee?" I asked.

Excellentz got up to brew another pot. "I see that you're skeptical," he said with his back to me. "I'd be skeptical myself if I only had the right. I'm a seasoned rationalist, Mak—I've seen it all, and I've always used reason as my guide, and reason has never let me down. I'm repelled by all these supernatural shenanigans, all these mysterious programs written forty thousand years ago that turn on and off according to some incomprehensible principle, all these mystical extradimensional connections between living beings and thirteen silly lumps stuck in a case . . . The whole thing turns my stomach!"

He brought the coffee and poured it into our cups. "If you and I were ordinary scientists," he continued, "and we were simply studying a certain natural phenomenon, how delighted I'd be to dismiss all this as a series of idiotic coincidences! Tristan died by accident—he's not the first and he won't be the last. Abalkin's childhood girlfriend just happened to have access to the detonators. He dialed the number of my special channel by complete accident as he was trying to call someone else . . . I swear to you, this unlikely chain of unlikely events would have seemed to me more plausible than the idiotic, worthless hypothesis about a satanic program supposedly implanted in human embryos . . . To a scientist, everything is clear: entities should not be multiplied without the utmost necessity. But you and I aren't scientists. At the end of the day, a scientist's mistake is his own business. But we aren't allowed to make mistakes. We're allowed to appear to be ignorant, superstitious mystics. There's only one thing people won't forgive us: underestimating a threat. And if our house suddenly smells of sulfur, we have no right to start philosophizing about molecular fluctuations—we're required to assume that Lucifer himself has turned up nearby, and we have to take appropriate measures, up to and including organizing the production of holy water on an industrial scale. And thank God if it turns out that it was nothing but a molecular fluctuation after all, and everyone on the World Council, not to mention every kid on Earth, gets to laugh at our expense . . ." He testily pushed the cup away. "I can't drink this coffee. And I haven't eaten in four days, either."

"Excellentz," I said, "come now, come on . . . Why does it have to be Lucifer himself? After all, what's the worst we can say about the Wanderers? Look at Operation Dead World . . . They saved the population of an entire planet! Several billion people!"

"You're trying to cheer me up . . ." said Excellentz with a grim chuckle. "Except they didn't save the population of the planet. They saved the planet from its population! Very successfully, too . . . And where the population has gone—that's not for us to know."

"Why the planet?" I asked, taken aback.

"And why the population?"

"Never mind," I said. "That's not the point. Say you're right: program, detonators, Lucifer himself . . . What could he possibly do to us? He's all alone."

"My boy," Excellentz said almost tenderly, "you've barely spent half an hour thinking about this, and I've been beating my brains out over this for forty years. And I'm not the only one. And we haven't thought of anything—that's the worst thing. And we'll never think of anything, because even the smartest and most experienced among us are merely human. We don't know what they want. We don't know what they can do. And we'll never know. Our only hope is that in the course of our frantic, erratic flailing, we will occasionally take steps they didn't foresee. They couldn't have foreseen everything. No one can. And yet every time I make a decision, I catch myself thinking that this must be exactly what they expected from me, that this is exactly what we shouldn't do . . . I've gotten to the point, old ass, where I'm glad that we didn't destroy that damn sarcophagus immediately, as soon as we found it . . . The Tagorans destroyed theirs, and just look at them now! Look at how they've stagnated! This could well be the outcome of the highly rational, highly logical decision they made a century and a half ago . . . Then again, they don't think they've stagnated! They've only stagnated from our human point of view. Whereas from their point of view, they are thriving and flourishing, and I'm sure they think that they owe this state of affairs to their timely radical decision . . . Or, for example, we've decided to prevent the crazed Abalkin from getting at the detonators. What if that's exactly what they expected from us?"

He put his bald head in his hands and vehemently shook it. "We're tired, Mak," he said. "We're all so tired! We're sick of thinking about this. And because we're so tired, we've gotten careless, and more and more often, we find ourselves saying, 'Eh, it'll all work out!' At first, Gorbovsky was in the minority, but nowadays, seventy percent of the Committee accept his hypothesis—the beetle in the anthill . . . Oh, that'd be lovely! How I want to believe it! Some smart fellows, out of pure scientific curiosity, put a beetle in an anthill and are now carefully recording all the nuances of ant psychology, all the intricacies of their social organization. And in the meantime, the ants are frightened, the ants are scurrying around, they're anxious, ready to give up their lives for their mother hill—and little do the poor things know that the beetle will eventually crawl out of the anthill and go on its way, no harm done . . . You hear that, Mak? No harm done! Don't worry, ants! Everything will be OK . . . And what if it's not a beetle in the anthill? What if it's a fox in a chicken coop? Do you know, Mak, what it means to have a fox in a chicken coop?"

And then he lost it. He slammed both his fists on the table and, fixing his wild green eyes on me, started shouting: "Those bastards! Forty years they've taken from me! For forty years, they've made an ant out of me! I can't think about anything else! I get spooked by my own shadow; I don't trust my own stupid head . . . Why are you goggling at me? You'll come to it in forty years yourself, or maybe even sooner, because the pace will pick up! The pace will pick up, and things will happen that we old goats never even dreamed of, and we'll all retire at the same time, because we won't be able to handle it! And then it will all fall on your shoulders! And you won't be able to handle it, either! Because you—"

He fell silent. He was no longer looking at me—he was staring over my head. And he was slowly getting up from the table. I turned around.

In the open doorway, on the threshold, stood Lev Abalkin.

JUNE 4, '78

LEV ABALKIN IN THE FLESH

"Lyova!" Excellentz said in an astonished, touched voice. "Good Lord, buddy! We've been looking all over for you!"

Lev Abalkin made a single move and was suddenly next to the table. Without a doubt, this was a true progressor of the new school, a professional—probably one of the best, at that. It took serious effort for my internal frame rate to keep up with him.

"You are Rudolf Sikorsky, head of COMCON-2," he said in a quiet, remarkably expressionless voice.

"Yes," replied Excellentz with a warm smile. "But why be so formal? Have a seat, Lyova . . ."

"I'm going to say this standing up," said Lev Abalkin.

"Come on, Lyova, why stand on ceremony? Have a seat, please. We're going to have a long conversation, aren't we?"

"No," said Abalkin. He didn't even glance at me. "We are not going to have a long conversation. I don't want to talk to you."

Excellentz was shocked. "What do you mean, you don't want to talk to me?" he inquired. "You, my friend, are still on duty—remember, you're obliged to report . . . We still don't know what happened to Tristan . . . What do you mean, you don't want to talk to me?"

"Am I one of the thirteen?"

"That Bromberg . . ." Excellentz spoke with vexation. "Yes, Lyova. Unfortunately, you're one of the thirteen."

"I'm not allowed to be on Earth? And I must spend my whole life under surveillance?"

"Yes, Lyova. That's right."

Abalkin had superb self-control. His face was completely motionless and his eyes were half closed, as if he were dozing standing up. But I could sense that this was a man almost crazed with rage. "Well, what I came here to say," said Abalkin in the same quiet, expressionless voice, "is that what you did to us was both vile and stupid. You crippled my life and got nothing for it. I'm now on Earth and I don't intend to leave again. I want you to know that I will no longer tolerate your surveillance and will ruthlessly free myself from it."

"Like you freed yourself from Tristan?" asked Excellentz casually.

Abalkin acted as if he hadn't heard that. "I've warned you," he said. "Now you only have yourselves to blame. From now on, I intend to live my life the way I want to, and I'd like you to stay out of it."

"All right. We'll stay out of your way. But tell me, Lev, don't you like your work?"

"From now on I will choose my own work."

"Very good. Excellent. And perhaps in your spare time, you could do a spot of thinking and try to put yourself in our shoes. What would you have done with the foundlings?"

Something like a sarcastic grin flashed across Abalkin's face. "There's nothing to think about," he said. "It's completely obvious. You should have told me everything, made me your conscious ally—"

"And you'd kill yourself in a couple of months? It's frightening to feel like you might be a danger to mankind, you know, Lyova—not everyone could handle it."

"Nonsense. That's just your psychologists' gibberish! I'm an earthling! When I found out that I wasn't allowed to live on Earth, I almost went insane! I've been rushing around like a madman, looking for proof that I'm not an android—that I had a childhood, that I worked with bigheads . . . You were worried about driving me crazy? Well, you almost succeeded!"

"And who told you that you aren't allowed to live on Earth?"

"Isn't it true?" inquired Abalkin. "What, am I allowed to live on Earth?"

"At this point, I don't know . . . Probably. But try to understand, Lyova! On the entire planet of Saraksh, only Tristan knew that you weren't supposed to come back to Earth. And he couldn't have told you about it . . . Or did he tell you that after all?"

Abalkin was silent. His face remained motionless, but it broke out in gray patches that looked like the marks left by an old skin infection—he looked like a Pandeian dervish.

"OK, OK," said Excellentz after waiting a bit. He was pointedly examining his nails. "Say that Tristan did tell you. I don't understand why he'd do that, but say that he did. Why didn't he tell you the rest of it? Why didn't he tell you that you were a foundling? Why didn't he explain the reasons for the prohibition? After all, there were reasons for it—significant reasons, whatever you may think about it."

A spasm slowly passed over Abalkin's gray face, causing it to lose its sharp contours, as though it had sagged—his mouth fell partially open, his eyes opened wide as if in surprise, and for the first time, I heard the sound of his breathing. "I don't want to talk about that," he said loudly and hoarsely.

"That's too bad," said Excellentz. "This is very important to us."

"Whereas all that matters to me," said Abalkin, "is that you leave me alone." His features regained sharpness, he lowered his eyelids, and the gray patches began to slowly fade from his lusterless cheeks.

Then Excellentz spoke in a completely different tone. "Lyova. Of course we'll leave you alone. But I'm begging you—if you feel strange in any way, if you experience any unusual sensations . . . notice any odd thoughts . . . even if you just feel sick . . . I'm begging you, please let us know. It doesn't have to be me. It could be Gorbovsky. Komov. At the end of the day, it could even be Bromberg . . ."

At this point, Abalkin turned around and began to walk away, heading toward the door. Excellentz was almost shouting after him, stretching out a hand toward him: "But do it right away! Right away! While you're still an earthling! I may have wronged you, but the Earth hasn't!"

"I'll let you know, I'll let you know," said Abalkin over his shoulder. "Personally." He went out, carefully closing the door behind him.

Excellentz was quiet for a few seconds, gripping both of his armrests and listening intently. Then he ordered me in an undertone: "Follow him. Don't lose sight of him under any circumstances. Communicate through the wristband. I'll be at the museum."

JUNE 4, '78

OPERATION COMPLETED

Having left the COMCON-2 building, Lev Abalkin strolled down Red Maple Street in an unhurried, leisurely fashion; then he went into a public videophone booth and spoke to someone. The conversation lasted a little more than two minutes, after which Lev Abalkin, still in no hurry, his hands behind his back, turned onto a tree-lined avenue, and sat down on a bench by the pedestal with the Strogov bas-relief.

As far as I could tell, he read everything that had been carved into the pedestal very carefully, then looked around absentmindedly, and for the next twenty minutes remained in the attitude of a man resting after difficult labors: he draped his arms along the back of the bench, threw back his head, crossed his legs, and stretched them out into the middle of the avenue. He attracted a number of squirrels, one of which jumped onto his shoulder and stuck its little face into his ear. He laughed loudly, picked it up, and, tucking his feet beneath the bench, placed the squirrel onto one of his knees. The squirrel stayed put. I think he was talking to it. The sun had just risen, the streets were almost empty, and there was no one but him on the avenue.

Of course, I harbored no illusions that I had managed to remain unobserved. He certainly knew that I wasn't letting him out of my sight, and he had probably already come up with a plan to get rid of me if he needed to. But that wasn't what was on my mind. I was worried about Excellentz. I didn't understand what he was up to.

He had ordered me to find Abalkin. He wanted to meet with Abalkin and talk to him one-on-one. At least that was the case in the beginning, three days ago. Then he became convinced—or rather, convinced himself—that Abalkin was certain to try to get his hands on the detonators. Then he set up an ambush. There was no more talk of tête-à-têtes. Instead, there was an order to take him as soon as he touched the shawl. And there was a gun. Presumably in case we failed to take him. Very good. Now Abalkin comes to him of his own accord. And it's plain to see that that Excellentz has nothing to say to Abalkin. That's no surprise; Excellentz is convinced that the program has been activated, in which case talking to Abalkin is pointless. (I had my own opinion on whether the program was actually active, but that's neither here nor there. First, I had to understand what Excellentz is planning.)

So he lets Abalkin go. Instead of apprehending him right there in his office and handing him over to the doctors and psychologists, he lets him go. There's a threat hanging over the Earth. To prevent it, it's enough to isolate Abalkin. This can be accomplished using very basic means. That would at least put an end to this particular matter. But he lets Abalkin go, and he heads to the museum. This can only mean one thing: he's absolutely certain that Abalkin will, at the earliest possible opportunity, also make an appearance at the museum. To get the detonators. Why else? (You'd think that nothing could be simpler—just stick this amber case in a decommissioned Wraith and blast it through subspace until the end of time . . . Unfortunately, this obviously can't be done—it's an irreversible action.)

Abalkin shows up at the museum (or bursts into the museum after a fight—after all, Grisha Serosovin is waiting there for him) . . . Anyway, he turns up at the museum and meets Excellentz again. Freeze frame. And that's when the real conversation takes place . . .

Excellentz is going to kill him, I thought. Lord have mercy, I thought. He's sitting here, playing with squirrels, and in an hour Excellentz will kill him. It's simple as pie. Excellentz is waiting for him at the museum so he can watch this movie to the end, so he can see and understand for himself how it all happens—how the Wanderers' automaton finds its way, how he finds the amber case (with his eyes? his sense of smell? a sixth sense?), how he opens the case, how he chooses his detonator, what he intends to do with it . . . Only intends to, no more, since at this instant, Excellentz will pull the trigger—taking further risks would be unacceptable . . .

And I said to myself: No, that's not going to happen.

I can't say that I carefully considered all the consequences of my actions. To be honest, I didn't consider them at all. I simply turned onto the avenue and walked straight toward Abalkin.

When I came up to him, he gave me a sidelong glance and turned away. I sat down next to him.

"Lyova," I said. "Get out of here. Immediately."

"I believe that I asked you to leave me alone," he said in the same quiet and expressionless voice.

"They won't leave you alone. Thing have gone too far. No one distrusts you personally. But to us, you're no longer Lyova Abalkin. Lyova Abalkin no longer exists. To us, you are the Wanderers' automaton."

"And to me, you're a pack of crazed, terrified idiots."

"I can't argue with that," I said. "But that's exactly why you should get away from here as far and as fast as possible. Fly to Pandora, Lyova, stay there for a few months—prove to them that there's no program."

"Why?" he said. "Why should I have to prove anything to anyone? That's demeaning, you know."

"Lyova," I said, "if you came across some scared children, would you really find it demeaning to make faces at them and clown around for a bit to calm them down?"

At this point, he looked me in the eye for the first time. He maintained eye contact for a while, almost without blinking, and I saw that he didn't believe a word I said. A crazed, terrified idiot was sitting in front of him and diligently lying, in order to again drive him to the edge of the universe, but this time permanently, this time with no hope of coming back.

"This is pointless," he said. "Stop babbling and leave me alone. I have to go."

He gently shooed the squirrels away and got up. I got up, too. "Lyova," I said, "they'll kill you."

"That's easier said than done," he replied in an offhand manner, and started down the tree-lined avenue.

I walked next to him. I talked the entire time. I was babbling some nonsense—how this wasn't the kind of situation where you could afford to be offended, how it was stupid to risk your life for mere pride, how he ought to try to empathize with the old men; they've been living on pins and needles for forty years . . . He either didn't respond or answered sarcastically. I even him saw him smile a few times—I think my behavior amused him. We got to the end of the avenue, then turned onto Lilac Street. We were walking toward Star Square.

There were already quite a few people on the street. This wasn't part of my plan, but it wouldn't interfere with it, either. After all, people do sometimes faint on the street, and in such cases, someone must take the unconscious person to the nearest doctor . . . I'll take him to the rocketdrome, it's not far, he won't even have time to regain consciousness. They always have two or three Wraiths ready to fly. I will get Glumova to meet us there, and the three of us will land on green Ruzhena, at my old camp. I'll explain everything to her on the way, damn the secret of Lev

Abalkin's identity . . . Aha. I see a convenient glider by the curb. It's empty. Just what I need—

When I regained consciousness, my head was resting on the warm knees of an unfamiliar older woman, and I felt as if I were at the bottom of a well—there were concerned strangers' faces looking down at me, and someone was telling people not to crowd me and give me more air, and someone else was solicitously slipping a foul-smelling vial under my nose, and some judicious voice was declaiming about how there was no cause for undue alarm—after all, people do sometimes faint on the street . . .

My body felt like an overinflated balloon, swaying just over the ground with a hollow ringing. There was no pain. As far as I could tell, I had been the victim of a simple "downturn," although one delivered from a position I'd never seen anyone use before.

"Don't worry, he's already conscious, everything is OK. . ."

"Lie down, please, don't sit up, you just fainted . . ."

"The doctor's coming, your friend has gone to fetch a doctor . . ."

I sat up. Someone was supporting my shoulders. I still felt like there was a ringing inside my body, but my head was perfectly clear. I needed to stand up, but that wasn't in my power yet. Through the picket fence of legs and bodies around me, I could see that the glider was gone. However, Abalkin hadn't managed to finish the job. Had he hit me two centimeters farther to the left, I'd have been lying around unconscious until the evening. But either he missed, or my defensive reflexes kicked in at the last moment . . .

I heard the whistling of wind, then a glider descended next to us and a lanky man jumped over its side, pushing his way through the crowd and inquiring as he went, "What's going on? I'm a doctor! What's wrong?"

Where did I get the energy?! I jumped up toward him and, grabbing his sleeve, pushed him toward the older woman who had just been supporting my head and was still on her knees. "This woman isn't feeling well, please help her . . ."

I could barely get the words out. In the resulting stunned silence, I forced my way through to the glider, heaved my body over its side onto the seat, and started the engine. I caught the astonished screech of protest—"Wait just a minute!"—then in another instant, the sun-drenched Star Square stretched out beneath me.

It was like a recurring dream. As if it were six hours ago. I was running from room to room, from hallway to hallway, weaving between wall displays and glass cases, between statues and scale models that looked like pointless machines, and between machines and instruments that looked like ugly statues, except that this time, everything was flooded with bright sunlight, and I was alone, and my legs were giving way under me, and I wasn't worried about being late, because I was sure that I'd be late.

I was late.

I was already late.

A shot rang out. The quiet, dull shot of a Duke pistol. I tripped over my own feet. This was it. The end. I ran as hard as I could. Up ahead and to the right, a figure in a white lab coat kept flickering between the misshapen objects. It was Grisha Serosovin, nickname Aquarius. He was also too late.

Two more shots rang out, one after the other . . .

Lyova. They will kill you.

That's easier said than done . . .

Grisha and I burst into Maya Toivovna Glumova's workshop at the same time.

Lev Abalkin was lying flat on his back in the middle of the workshop, while Excellentz—giant, hunched, a pistol in his outstretched hand—was carefully inching toward him, and at the same time, Glumova was approaching him from the other side, gripping the edge of the desk with both hands.

Glumova's face was perfectly still and completely devoid of emotion, while her eyes were unnaturally, eerily both focused on the bridge of her nose.

Excellentz's yellow pate and the slightly droopy cheek facing me were beaded with large droplets of sweat.

There was a sharp, sour, unnatural smell of burning gunpowder.

And there was silence.

Lev Abalkin was still alive. The fingers of his right hand were stubbornly and impotently scrabbling along the floor, as if still trying to reach the detonator lying a centimeter away. A disk with a symbol resembling either a stylized letter Ж or the Japanese character *sanju*.

I took a step toward Abalkin and crouched down beside him. (Excellentz croaked some warning in my direction.) Abalkin was staring at the ceiling with glassy eyes. His face was covered in those same gray patches, and his mouth was bloody. I touched him on the shoulder. The bloody mouth moved, and he spoke: "The animals stood by the door . . ."

"Lyova," I called.

"The animals stood by the door," he repeated insistently. "The animals . . ."

And then Maya Toivovna Glumova screamed.

AFTERWORD

BY BORIS STRUGATSKY

It all began a long time ago, in the impossibly distant past, when my young son, surprising himself and everyone around him, suddenly came up with the following counting rhyme:

The animals stood
By the door,
People shot them,
They fell dead to the floor.

He was running around the apartment, shouting out these bizarre, surreal, and strangely unchildlike lines in different ways, and Boris Strugatsky was looking at him and thinking, Damn, what great words! Clever little rascal. It'd make an excellent epigraph for some story! . . . And certain vague images appeared in Boris's head . . . some terrifying, wretched creatures . . . tragically lonely and unwanted . . . ugly, suffering, seeking human help and affection, but instead getting a bullet from terrified, confused people . . .

These vague sensations were successfully conveyed to Arkady, there was a rather incoherent but nevertheless fruitful exchange of emotions and images, and we came up with a sketch, still amorphous and not at all definite. The only things we knew for sure were that the story should be called *The Animals Stood by the Door* and that the "poem by a young boy" would be its epigraph. For the first and the last time, an Arkady and Boris Strugatsky story was inspired by a future epigraph (or rather, by its name, which in this case was the same thing.)

The first draft of the future story appeared in September 1975. It already had a sarcophagus with twelve embryos, and hypotheses regarding this sarcophagus, and twenty-year-old Lev, a student progressor, and Maxim Kammerer, the head of counterintelligence for the Board of Trustees, and many other perfectly serviceable circumstances, situations, and characters. However, there was still no plot, and it was completely unclear how exactly events should unfold.

We continued to discuss *Animals* in October and then in December, but then there was a dramatic change of plan—we started writing a screenplay for Tarkovsky—and we took a long break from working on the new story.

Over the course of 1976, we came back to this story multiple times, and we kept coming up with details, events, new characters, and individual phrases—but no more than that. The plot didn't gel. We simply couldn't figure out how to fit all the things we had come up with together—how to spear all of our shish kebabs on a single skewer. That's why, instead of doing real work, we started developing the plot of a fantastical detective story (in great detail, too) that took place on some island in the ocean and featured a multitude of tragic happenings, secrets, and riddles, as well as numerous deaths—all the remaining characters died en masse in the final scene. We had an extremely detailed description of every incident, the stage was set for work, there was nothing left to do except sit down and write, but instead (and this was already in November 1976), the authors suddenly began working on a storyline that had never even crossed their minds before.

This was the story of our old buddy Maxim, who with his friend the bighead Puppen was walking through a dead city on the unfortunate Planet Hope. The poor *Animals* seemed to have been abandoned and forgotten once and for all. In February 1977, we started and finished a draft of the story about Maxim and Puppen in one breath (that is, in a single sitting)—and we immediately discovered that we had wound up with something strange, something with neither an ending nor even a name. Filled with bewilderment and dissatisfaction with ourselves, we put aside this unexpected and unwanted manuscript and went back to working on screenplays. (It's funny: At the time, we thought we'd been clever to come up with the idea that "genetic structures on Hope had gone berserk," causing a strange and terrible disease that turns a child into an old man in three years. To us, this seemed to be an effective and original invention. And it was only many years later that we learned about premature aging—progeria, a disease well known to modern science—and about the fact that the fantastical phenomena we invented had been described back at the beginning of the twentieth century, when it was dubbed Werner syndrome. It really is impossible to invent anything new; everything you invent has either already existed in the past, or will exist in the future, or currently exists without you knowing about it.)

Back then (during almost all of 1977 and 1978), we were finishing, fine-tuning, and polishing three screenplays at the same time: one based on *Monday Starts on Saturday*, one on *The Dead Mountaineer's Inn*, and one on *Hard to be a God* (the last was the most recent unpromising adaptation for the most recent unpromising director). All of our other work had been abandoned, and it was only in November 1978 that we came back to *Animals* and, characteristically, immediately started writing a first draft. Quantity had apparently finally morphed into quality; it became clear to us how to organize the plot (around the pursuit of the elusive Lev Abalkin) and how to incorporate the already completed piece with Puppen on Planet Hope.

We finished the draft on March 7, 1979, having definitively overcome two obstacles encountered toward the end of the work. First of all, we spent a while unable to decide on the ending itself. The one in which Lev Abalkin died was tragic and effective, but it was also fairly obvious and even trite. The one in which Maxim succeeded at saving Abalkin from death had its virtues but also had its flaws. So we kept hesitating, unable to make a final decision, and thus constantly revising the plot in the process of writing so that we could choose either ending at a moment's notice. When we had exhausted all the possibilities of this maneuvering, we remembered how Ilf and Petrov had decided the fate of Ostap Bender at the end of *The Twelve Chairs*. We prepared two pieces of paper, writing ALIVE on one of them and NOT on the other. The scraps were tossed into Arkady's hat, and, with a steady hand, our mother pulled out the NOT. The fates of the ending and of Lev Abalkin were sealed.

(Memory does play the darndest tricks on us, however. When I wrote the previous paragraph, I was *absolutely* convinced that it was all true. But a month later, looking through our work journal, I suddenly found an entry, dated 10/29/1975, indicating that we did draw pieces of paper, but not to decide whether the ending would be tragic—a "shooter"—or peaceful. We were solving an entirely different problem: how long it takes Lev Abalkin to find out the truth about himself. We considered the following three options:

1. Lev knows nothing and never finds out the truth.
2. Lev knows nothing but gradually finds out the truth.
3. Lev knows everything from the start.

Mama chose (3), a "shooter."

Just look at that! And, in fact, Arkady and Boris ended up writing version 2—another "shooter," it's true. And thank goodness for that, because even a month later, our work journal contains the following entry: "Maybe we should end not with the death but with the run-up to it? Wanderer follows him with his eyes." No, I've always—since before I can remember—doubted the reliability of history in general and memoirs in particular, and it looks like I was right to do so. . . . However, I'll leave the previous paragraph as is. Reflective readers should have this sample of a memoir "goof" at their disposal—one typical of these musings. It might help them evaluate the reliability of the text as a whole.)

Now we come to our second, much more serious obstacle. We knew full well that we were writing something like a detective story—the tale of an investigation, search, and capture. However, detective stories follow their own conventions; in particular, detective stories aren't supposed to leave anything unexplained, and they aren't supposed to have any loose or dangling threads. Our story, on the other hand, was full of dangling threads, and we were supposed to tie them up in some way but really didn't want to. The Strugatskys always had a strong distaste for any sorts of explanations or interpretations within the text, and it blazed up with particular force toward the end of the novel.

1. What happened between Tristan and Abalkin over there on Saraksh?
2. How (and why) did Abalkin wind up at Osinushka?
3. Why did he need to talk to Dr. Goannek?
4. Why did he need to talk to Maya?
5. What did he need from his teacher?
6. Why did he call journalist Kammerer?
7. What did he need from Puppen?
8. How did he manage to get in touch with Dr. Bromberg?
9. Why did he go to the Museum of Extraterrestrial Cultures at the end of the novel?
10. As a matter of fact, what happened at the museum?

And finally, the most fundamental question:

11. Why did he, Abalkin (unless, of course, he really is an automaton of the Wanderers, and according to the authors,

he's certainly not an automaton but an unhappy man with
a mutilated fate), why did he not come to his bosses from
the very beginning and sort out the circumstances of his
case in an easy, nice way? Why did he need to rush around
the planet, jump out from around corners, disappear again,
and then suddenly appear again in the most unlikely places
and with the most unlikely people?

Any self-respecting detective story should, of course, have
carefully and explicitly broken these questions down for the reader
and provided a complete explanation of each one. But we weren't
in fact writing a detective story. We were writing a tragic tale
about the fact that even in a kind, gentle, and just world, the
emergence of a secret police force (of any type, form, or style)
will inevitably lead to innocent people suffering and dying, no
matter how noble the goals of this secret force, and no matter
how honest, decent, and noble the people staffing it may be.
And in the context of this literary goal, the authors found the
idea of explaining minor unexplained plot points both boring and
distasteful.

At first, we planned to write an epilogue especially for this
purpose—one that would cross all the t's and dot all the i's, and
would clarify, explain, predigest, and spoon-feed everything to
the reader. I still have a piece of paper containing the eleven
sacramental questions, with the following postscript below:
"April 30, 1979. Regarding the epilogue—let's consult some qualified people." In fact, I think that the question of the epilogue
had already then been decided, regardless of what any "qualified
people" may have had to say. We already understood that the
story was written in the right way: all the events were presented
from the perspective of the protagonist—Maxim Kammerer—so
the reader knew exactly what the protagonist did at each point in
time, and the reader needed to make the decisions along with him
based on the (by no means complete) information he had available. Given our literary goals, the epilogue became completely

unnecessary. Moreover, experience showed us that "qualified people" either didn't notice the loose threads at all or, if they did, successfully came up with ways to tie them off themselves, each in their own way.

In fact, implicit answers to most of the questions are scattered throughout the novel, and observant readers will be able to discover them without difficulty on their own. For example, any reader should be able to guess that Abalkin materialized in Osinushka entirely by accident (as he was avoiding surveillance—he was seeing spies everywhere), and that he consulted Dr. Goannek in the hopes that an experienced professional doctor could easily distinguish a human being from an android.

Question 1, on the other hand, is fundamentally different. To find an answer to this question, it's not enough to carefully scour the text. Instead, you need to *invent* a certain situation— one that the authors certainly know down to the last detail, but that is only represented in the novel as a consequence tree of the following obvious fact: Abalkin somehow learns (from Tristan, clearly—the mystery is how) that for some reason, he's prohibited from being on Earth and that this prohibition is in some way connected with COMCON-2 (hence Abalkin's flight from Saraksh, his unexpected and impossible call to Excellentz, and all of his strange behavior). I could, of course, use this afterword to relate the key points of this plot-originating situation, but I really don't want to. After all, neither Maxim nor Excellentz knows a thing about what took place between Tristan and Abalkin on Saraksh. They are forced to come up with more or less plausible hypotheses, and to act on these hypotheses. The process of searching and making decisions is at the core of the novel, and I wanted the readers to come up with their *own* hypotheses and make their *own* decisions simultaneously and in parallel with the protagonists, based on nothing more than the information the protagonists have at their disposal. After all, had Excellentz known what actually happened with Tristan on Saraksh, he would have had an entirely different interpretation of Abalkin's behavior, and the novel would have taken a very different course and had a totally different ending—one that wasn't nearly as tragic.

Using this afterword to explain the unexplained would amount to writing the epilogue the authors had already declined to write. Therefore, I won't explain anything here—I prefer to leave the story in its unsullied state, in full accordance with the authors' original intent.

We finished the final draft at the end of April 1979, and this was when—not a moment sooner!—we came up with the new name *Beetle in the Anthill* instead of the old *The Animals Stood by the Door*. The only thing that remained from the original sketch was the epigraph. As I recall, we had to engage in mortal combat with a lunatic of an idiot editor from the Lenizdat publishing house who got it into his head that the true story behind this poem was that the authors had modified (why?!) some long-forgotten marching song used by the Hitler Youth (!!!). Moreover, this actual reason for the editorial activity was only related to me in confidence by "our man in Lenizdat," whereas all we were told openly was that undesirable allusions, connotations, and associations were in some mysterious way connected to the unfortunate "poem by a young boy."

09/09/82—BS: . . . Brandis and I [Yevgeny Pavlovich Brandis was called in as the compiler of the book and the author of the foreword] spent a total of an hour and a half proving to that blockhead that this text didn't have any allusions, connotations, or other aliens, and that, on the contrary, it was full of nothing but Surpassment and Fusion. . . . Tell me, why do they always beat us? I think it's because they are paid to advance, and we're paid to retreat. . . .

The epigraph couldn't be salvaged. We were barely allowed to leave the poem in the text of the novel—but only after seriously disfiguring it. (We would have never agreed to this travesty, but the novel was being included in a collection of works by various authors, which meant that our "petulant obstinacy" was hurting our innocent fellow writers.)